THE DISGRACEFUL MR RAVENHURST

Louise Allen

MILLS & BOON®
Pure reading pleasure™

First published in Great Britain 2009
Harlequin Mills & Boon Limited,
Eton House, 18-24 Paradise Road, Richmond, Surrey TW9 1SR

© Melanie Hilton 2009

ISBN: 978 0 263 20960 0

Set in Times Roman 12 on 15 pt.
08-0209-78100

Printed and bound in Great Britain
by CPI Antony Rowe, Chippenham, Wiltshire

Join favourite author

Louise Allen

as she explores the tangled love-lives of

Those Scandalous Ravenhursts

First, you travelled across war-torn
Europe with
THE DANGEROUS MR RYDER

Then you accompanied Mr Ryder's sister,
THE OUTRAGEOUS LADY FELSHAM,
on her quest for a hero.

You were scandalised by
THE SHOCKING LORD STANDON

Now share dangerous, sensual adventures with
THE DISGRACEFUL MR RAVENHURST

Coming soon

THE NOTORIOUS MR HURST

THE PIRATICAL MISS RAVENHURST

Author Note

In the course of their courtship Ashe Reynard informed Belinda Felsham (THE OUTRAGEOUS LADY FELSHAM) that she should stop match-making for her bluestocking cousin Elinor because what Elinor needed was someone who could match her intelligence.

The problem was, where could Elinor—firmly on the shelf—find such a man? One who would see past the drab gowns and meek studiousness to the warm, loving, adventurous woman inside? Especially when she was convinced she did not want a man at all.

And then there was Theo Ravenhurst, in disgrace and, so his mother kept insisting, off on the Grand Tour. Only I had my suspicions that Theo was not pursuing a blameless course around the cultural sights of Europe but was up to something altogether less conventional. What would happen if these two cousins met? I wondered.

I hope you enjoy finding out and, if you have read the first three **Ravenhurst** novels, meeting again Eva and Sebastian, young Freddie, and the indomitable Lady James.

Coming next will be THE NOTORIOUS MR HURST. Lady Maude Templeton, having escaped marriage to Ravenhurst cousin Gareth Morant (THE SHOCKING LORD STANDON), has already fallen for the entirely inappropriate attractions of theatre owner Eden Hurst. She knows what she wants, and is not used to being thwarted, but this time it looks as though everyone—from Society to the gentleman himself—is set on her not getting her heart's desire.

For AJH for his selfless assistance in researching the food and wine of Burgundy

Louise Allen has been immersing herself in history, real and fictional, for as long as she can remember, and finds landscapes and places evoke powerful images of the past. Louise lives in Bedfordshire, and works as a property manager, but spends as much time as possible with her husband at the cottage they are renovating on the north Norfolk coast, or travelling abroad. Venice, Burgundy and the Greek islands are favourite atmospheric destinations. Please visit Louise's website—www.louiseallenregency.co.uk—for the latest news!

Recent novels by the same author:

A MODEL DEBUTANTE
THE MARRIAGE DEBT
MOONLIGHT AND MISTLETOE
  (in *Christmas Brides*)
THE VISCOUNT'S BETROTHAL
THE BRIDE'S SEDUCTION
NOT QUITE A LADY
A MOST UNCONVENTIONAL COURTSHIP
NO PLACE FOR A LADY
DESERT RAKE
  (in *Hot Desert Nights*)
VIRGIN SLAVE, BARBARIAN KING
THE DANGEROUS MR RYDER*
THE OUTRAGEOUS LADY FELSHAM*
THE SHOCKING LORD STANDON*

Those Scandalous Ravenhursts

RAVENHURST FAMILY TREE

Francis Philip Ravenhurst, 2nd Duke of Allington = Lady Francesca Templeton

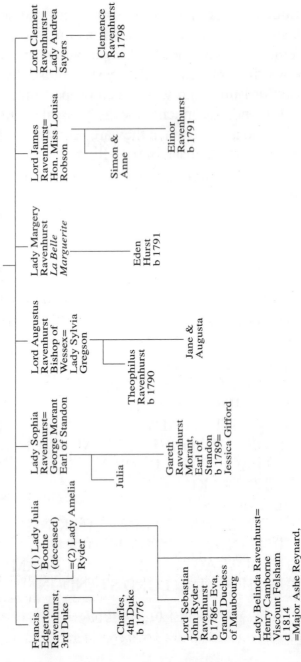

Francis Edgerton Ravenhurst, 3rd Duke

(1) Lady Julia Boothe (deceased)
=(2) Lady Amelia Ryder

Charles, 4th Duke b 1776

Lord Sebastian John Ryder Ravenhurst b 1786= Eva, Grand Duchess of Maubourg

Lady Belinda Ravenhurst= Henry Camborne Viscount Felsham d 1814
=Major Ashe Reynard, Viscount Dereham

Lady Sophia Ravenhurst= George Morant Earl of Standon

Julia

Gareth Ravenhurst Morant, Earl of Standon b 1789= Jessica Gifford

Lord Augustus Ravenhurst Bishop of Wessex= Lady Sylvia Gregson

Theophilus Ravenhurst b 1790

Jane & Augusta

Lady Margery Ravenhurst *La Belle Marguerite*

Eden Hurst b 1791

Lord James Ravenhurst= Hon. Miss Louisa Robson

Simon & Anne

Elinor Ravenhurst b 1791

Lord Clement Ravenhurst= Lady Andrea Sayers

Clemence Ravenhurst b 1798

Chapter One

August 1816—Vezelay, Burgundy

The naked female figure danced in timeless sensual abandon, revelling in the provocation of her blatant sexuality. The face of the hapless man watching her was etched with mingled despair and lust as he reached out for her, blind and deaf to the imploring prayers of the holy man who watched the scene unfold from behind a pillar.

It was hard to see the detail clearly in the shadows, and having to crane her neck upwards did not help, but the scene was unmistakable—and who was at fault, equally plain.

'Honestly! Men!' Exasperated, Elinor stepped backwards, furled parasol, rigid sketch book, sharp elbows and sensible boots, every one of them an offensive weapon.

'Ough!' The gasp from behind her as she made contact with something solid, large and obviously male, was agonised. 'I beg your pardon,' the voice continued on a croak as she swung round, fetching the man an additional thwack with her easel.

'What for?' she demanded, startled out of her customary good manners as she turned to face the doubled-up figure of her victim. 'I struck you, sir. I should apologise, not you.'

As he straightened up to a not inconsiderable height, a shaft of sunlight penetrated the cracked glass of the high window, illuminating a head of dark red hair that put her own tawny locks to shame. 'You were expressing dissatisfaction with the male sex, ma'am; I was apologising on behalf of my brothers for whatever sin we are guilty of this time.' His tone was meek, but she was not deceived—there was strength in the deep voice and a thread of wicked amusement.

Yes, said a voice inside Elinor's head. *Yes. At last.* She shook her head, blinking away the sun dazzle and whatever idiocy her mind was up to, and stepped to one side to see her victim better. He was smiling, a conspiratorial twist of his lips that transformed a strong but not particularly distinguished face into one that was disarmingly attractive. Somehow he had succeeded in charming an answering smile out of her.

She was not, Elinor reminded herself sternly, given to smiling at strange men. It must be part and parcel of hearing things. The voice had gone away now; no doubt it had been some trick of an echo in this cavernous place.

'I was referring to that capital.' Hampered by her armful of belongings she dumped them without ceremony on a nearby pew, keeping hold only of the furled parasol, partly as a pointer, partly because of its merits as a sharp implement. All men, her mother was apt to warn her, were Beasts. It was as well not to take risks with chance-met ones, even if they did appear to be polite English gentlemen. She gestured with the parasol towards the richly carved column top, Number 6B in her annotated sketches. 'It is a Romanesque capital; that is to say—'

'It was carved between 1120 and 1150 and is one of a notable series that makes the basilica of Vezelay an outstanding example of religious art of the period,' he finished for her, sounding like an antiquarian paper on the subject.

'Of course, I should have realised that, if you are visiting the basilica, you must understand architecture,' she apologised, gazing round the wreckage of the once-great church. Outside of service times no one else was going to enter here on a whim. 'Are you a clergyman, sir?'

'Do I look like one?' The stranger appeared mildly affronted by the suggestion.

'Er…no.' And he did not, although why that should be, Elinor had no idea. Many men of the cloth must have red hair. Some must also possess smiles that invited you to smile right back at a shared, and slightly irreverent, joke. And, without doubt, tall and athletic figures graced pulpits up and down the land.

'Thank goodness for that.' She noticed that he offered no explanation of himself in response to her question. 'So…' He tipped back his head, fisting his hands, one of which held his tall hat, on his hips to balance himself. 'What exactly is it about this particular scene that merits your ire, ma'am?'

'It shows, as usual, a man succumbing to his own base animal instincts and lack of self-control and blaming his subsequent moral downfall upon a woman,' she said crisply.

'I must say, your eyesight is excellent if you can deduce all that in this light.'

'I have been studying the capitals for a week now with the aid of an opera glass; one gets one's eye in.' Elinor stared round at the nave, littered with crumbling masonry, broken pews and rubbish. 'I have had to go round at least three times in an attempt to interpret as many as possible when the light is at its best. It is still possible to do that, but unless something is done very soon, I fear they may all fall or be damaged beyond repair or study. See the holes in the roof? The carvings must be exposed to the elements, even in here.'

'You are a scholar, then?' He was squinting upwards, his eyes fixed on the carved figures, frozen in their eternal masque of temptation and yielding. 'Researching the iniquities of the medieval male mind, perhaps?'

'My mother is the scholar, I am merely recording the carvings for her detailed study. She is an authority on the early churches of France and England.' Elinor could have added that the medieval male mind probably differed little from its modern counterpart when it came to moral turpitude, but decided against it. It was not as though she had any experience of turpitude to base the assertion upon.

'Indeed?' The man switched his attention from the carving to her face and this time the smile lit up his eyes as well. They were green, she noticed. An unusual clear green, like water over pebbles, not the indeterminate hazel that looked back at her whenever she spared a glance in a glass to check that her bonnet was at least straight and there were no charcoal smudges on her nose. 'I feel sure I should meet your respected parent. May I call?'

'You are a scholar too?' Elinor began to gather up her things, stuffing pencils, charcoal and paints into the battered leather satchel and swinging it over her shoulder. 'I am joining her now, if you would care to accompany me.'

'Let's just say I have an interest in antiquities.' He removed the easel from her hands, folded its legs up, lashed the straps around it with a competence that suggested he used one himself, and tucked it under his arm. There was a short struggle for possession of the stool, which he won, and for the parasol, which Elinor retained. 'You are staying in Vezelay?'

'Yes, we have been here seven days now. We are making our way down through France, visiting a number of the finer early cathedrals. Mama intends that we will remain at Vezelay for several weeks yet. *Merci, monsieur*.' She smiled and nodded to the verger, who was wielding a broom and stirring up the gritty dust in the porch. 'Sweeping seems pointless, he would be better employed on the roof with a tarpaulin.'

She dropped a coin into the outstretched hand of the beggar by the door and headed diagonally across the open space before the basilica, glancing up at her companion as she did so. 'We have lodgings just down the hill here.'

There was something vaguely familiar about him, although she could not place it. It certainly made him easy to talk to. Normally Miss Ravenhurst would have contented herself with a polite inclination of the head and a murmured *good day* when she came across a male countryman to whom she had not been introduced. It would never have occurred to her to invite one back to their lodgings to meet Mama.

Perhaps it was the red hair, somewhat extinguished now as he clapped his hat back on his head. Being one of the red-headed Ravenhursts, she saw a less spectacular version of it every time she looked in the glass. It was generally considered to be a handicap in a lady, although if hers was less a good match for a chestnut horse and more the flame of well-polished mahogany by firelight as his was, she might have felt more reconciled to it. He seemed to have avoided freckles as well, she noticed with envy, but then, his skin was not as fair as hers was.

'Here we are.' It was only a few minutes' walk down the steep main street, although it always took rather longer to toil back up the slippery cobbles to the basilica. The door was on the latch and she pushed it open, calling, 'Mama? Are you at home? We have a visitor.'

'In here, Elinor.' She followed her mother's voice through into the parlour, leaving her belongings on the hall bench and gesturing to the tall man to put the easel and stool down, too. At the sight of him, Lady James Ravenhurst rose to her feet from behind the table, its chequered cloth strewn with papers and books.

'Mama, this gentleman is a scholar of antiquities who wishes to meet—'

'Theophilus!' Lady James lifted her quizzing glass to her eye and stared, for once clearly out of countenance.

Elinor stared, too. 'Cousin Theo?' Her disgraceful and disgraced cousin Theo? Here? 'I haven't seen you for years.'

'Not since I was twelve, fifteen years ago,' he agreed. 'You must have been about seven. I wondered if it was you, Cousin Elinor.'

'The hair, I suppose,' she said, resigned to it being her most memorable feature. 'I was ten,' she added, ruthlessly honest. It was nice of him to pretend he thought she was only twenty-two now, and not an on-the-shelf spinster of almost twenty-six.

'What are you doing here, Theophilus? I understood from your mama that you were undertaking the Grand Tour.' Lady James gestured impatiently towards the chairs set around the stone hearth. 'Sit.'

'I am, you will agree, Aunt Louisa, somewhat old to be undertaking the Tour with a tutor to bear-lead me.' Theo waited until the two women were seated, then took the remaining chair, crossing one long leg over the other and clasping his hands together. He appeared quite tame and domesticated, although a trifle large. If Elinor had imagined a dangerous rakehell, which she had been informed her cousin was, he would not look like this.

'Mama uses the Tour as code for *sent abroad in disgrace,*' he continued. 'I am earning my living, avoiding English tourists and generally managing to keep my doings from the ears of my sainted papa.'

'Your father, even if Bishop of Wessex, may not be a saint,' his aunt said tartly, 'but you have certainly tried his patience over the years, Theophilus. Where were you when the Corsican Monster returned from exile last year, might I ask?'

'Oh, here in France. I became a Swedish merchant for the duration of the troubles. I found it interfered very little with my business.'

Elinor found she was grappling with unsettling emotions. Of course, she was pleased to see her cousin. Any cousin. The

Ravenhursts were a large and friendly clan. But something—the memory of that unsettling little voice in her head, perhaps?—replaced the calm contentment that was her usual internal state with a cold knot in her stomach. If she did not know better, she would think it disappointment.

'What are you frowning about, Elinor?' her mother enquired. 'Nothing is more productive of lines on the forehead.'

'A slight headache, that is all, Mama.' She had met an intelligent, attractive man—Theo was certainly that, even if he was not exactly handsome—and he turned out not to be an intriguing stranger, but one of the Ravenhurst clan. A relative. So what was there to be disappointed about in that, other than the fact he would treat her like they all did, as Mama's bluestocking assistant? An hour ago she would have said she wanted a man to talk to about as badly as she wanted to be back in London, sitting with the wallflowers in the chaperons' corner through yet another hideous Season.

Whatever Cousin Theo's business was, it appeared to be flourishing. She might not know much about fashion, but she knew quality when she saw it, and his boots, his breeches and the deceptively simple cut of his riding coat all whispered money in the most discreet manner.

'Did you say *business*, Theophilus?' Mama, as usual ignoring her own advice, was frowning at him now. 'You are not in *trade*, I trust?'

'One has to live, Aunt Louisa.' He smiled at her. Elinor noticed her mother's lips purse; he had almost seduced an answering smile out of her. 'My parents, no doubt rightly, feel that at the age of twenty-seven I should be gainfully employed and cut off my allowance some time ago.'

'But *trade*! There are any number of perfectly eligible professions for the grandson of the Duke of Allington.'

'My father has informed me that I enter the church over his dead body. It is also his opinion that I was born to be hanged and therefore a career in the law is ineligible. I find I have a fixed objection to killing people unless absolutely necessary, which eliminates the army and the navy.'

'Politics? The government?' Elinor suggested, smiling as much at her mother's expression as Theo's catalogue of excuses.

'I am also allergic to humbug.'

Lady James ignored this levity. 'What sort of trade?'

'Art and antiquities. I find I have a good eye. I prefer the small and the portable, of course.'

'Why of course?' Careless of deportment, Elinor twisted round on her seat to face him fully.

'It is easier to get an emerald necklace or a small enamelled reliquary past a customs post or over a mountain pass than a twelve-foot canvas or six foot of marble nude on a plinth.' The twinkle in his eyes invited her to share in his amusement at the picture he conjured up.

'You are involved in smuggling?' his aunt asked sharply.

'In the aftermath of the late wars, there is a great deal of what might be loosely described as *art* knocking about the Continent, and not all of it has a clear title. Naturally, if it sparkles, then government officials want it.' Theo shrugged. 'I prefer to keep it and sell it on myself, or act as an agent for a collector.'

'And there is a living to be made from it?' Elinor persisted, ignoring her mother's look that said quite clearly that ladies did not discuss money, smuggling or trade.

'So my banker tells me; he appears moderately impressed by my endeavours.'

'So what are you doing here?' Lady James demanded. 'Scavenging?'

Theo winced, but his tone was still amiable as he replied, 'I believe there is an artefact of interest in the neighbourhood. I am investigating.'

There was more to it than that, Elinor decided with a sudden flash of insight. The smile had gone from his eyes and there was the faintest edge to the deep, lazy voice. The coolness inside her was warming up into something very like curiosity. She felt more alive than she had for months.

'Where are you staying, Cousin Theo?' she asked before her mother insisted upon more details of his quest, details that he was most unlikely to want to tell her. Once Mama got wind of a secret, she would worry it like a terrier with a rat.

'I've lodgings down in St Père.' Elinor had wanted to visit the village at the foot of the Vezelay hill, huddling beneath the towering spire of its elaborate church. She would have enjoyed a stroll along the river in its gentle green valley, but Lady James had dismissed the church as being of a late period and less important to her studies than the hilltop basilica. They could visit it later, she had decreed.

'Rooms over the local dressmaker's shop, in fact. There's a decent enough inn in the village for meals.'

And now he is explaining too much. Why Elinor seemed to be attuned to the undertones in what he said, while her mother appeared not to be, was a mystery to her. Perhaps there was some kind of cousinly connection. She found herself watching him closely and then was disconcerted when he met her gaze and winked.

'Well, you may as well make yourself useful while you are here, Theophilus. Elinor has a great deal to do for me and she can certainly use your assistance.'

'But, Mama,' Elinor interjected, horrified, 'Cousin Theo has his own business to attend to. I can manage perfectly well without troubling him.'

Her cousin regarded her thoughtfully for a long moment, then smiled. 'It would be a pleasure. In what way may I assist?'

'You may escort her to St Père to make some sketches in the church there. I will review your preliminary drawings of the capitals tomorrow, Elinor, and see what needs further detailed work. I doubt St Père will prove of interest, but you may as well eliminate it rather than waste a day.'

'Yes, Mama.'

Theo watched Elinor, puzzled. Where was the assertive young woman from the basilica? It was as though the presence of her mother sucked all the individuality and spark out of his cousin. Sitting there, hands neatly folded in her lap, clad in a slate-grey gown that might have been designed to remove all the colour from her face and disguise whatever figure she might possess, she looked like the model for a picture of a dowdy spinster. He had been flattering her when he made the remark about her age when they last met; she looked every bit the twenty-five she admitted to.

He reviewed his agreement to take her to St Père. Was there any danger? No, not yet. It was probably too early for his client to have become restless over the non-appearance of his goods and, so far as he was aware, none of the opposition had yet appeared on the scene. If they had and he was being watched, escorting his cousin would be a useful smokescreen.

'At what time would you like me to collect you and your maid?' he enquired.

'Maid? There is no need for that,' his aunt rejoined briskly. 'We are in the middle of the French countryside and you are her cousin. Why should Elinor require chaperonage?'

He saw the faintest tightening of Elinor's lips and realised that she was sensitive to the unspoken assumption behind that assertion— that she was not attractive enough to attract undesirable attention.

'I will walk down the hill, Cousin, at whatever time suits you,' she offered. 'There is no need for you to toil all the way up, simply to escort me.'

That was probably true; she seemed to know her way around the large village well enough, and it was a respectable and safe place. But he felt an impulse to treat her with more regard than she obviously expected to receive.

'I will collect you here at ten, if that is not too early. The weather is fine; I have no doubt the inn can provide a luncheon we can eat outside. The interior is not really fit for a lady.'

'Thank you.' Her smile lit up her face and Theo found himself smiling back. Those freckles dancing across her nose really were rather endearing. If only her hair was not scraped back into that hideous snood or whatever it was called. 'You will not mind if I am out all day, Mama?'

'No, I will not need you,' Lady James said, confirming Theo's opinion that she regarded her daughter in the light of an unpaid skivvy. Her other children, his cousins Simon and Anne, had escaped their mother's eccentricities by early and good marriages. His late uncle, Lord James, had been a quiet and unassuming man. Theo's father, the Bishop, had been heard to remark at the funeral that his brother could have been dead for days before anyone noticed the difference.

Elinor was obviously fated to become the typical unwed daughter, dwindling into middle age at her mother's side. Although not many mothers were scholars of international repute as well as selfish old bats, he reflected.

She might be a dowdy young woman, and have a sharp tongue on the subject of male failings, but he found he was pleased to have come across her. Sometimes life was a little lonely—when no one was trying to kill him, rob him or swindle him—and contact with the family was pleasant.

'Is there any news from home?' he enquired.

'When did you last hear? I suppose you know about Sebastian and his Grand Duchess?' He nodded. He had been in Venice at the time, pleasurably negotiating the purchase of a diamond necklace from a beautiful and highly unprincipled contessa. But even on the Rialto the gossip about his cousin Lord Sebastian Ravenhurst's improbable marriage to the Grand Duchess of Maubourg was common currency. He had even glimpsed them together on one of his fleeting and rare visits to London, while their stormy courtship was still a secret.

'And Belinda has married again, to Lord Dereham.'

Now what was there in that to make Elinor's lips twitch? he wondered. 'Yes, I had heard about that, too. I met Gareth and his new wife in Paris and they told me.'

'Your cousins are all settling down in a most satisfactory manner,' his aunt pronounced. 'You should do the same, Theophilus.'

'Should I find a lady willing to share my way of life, then I would be delighted to, Aunt. But so far I have not discovered one.'

'Really? I wonder if perhaps the ladies who were *willing* were among the reasons your parents disapprove of your way of life,' Elinor murmured with shocking frankness, so straight-faced he knew she had her tongue firmly in her cheek. She had a sense of humour, did she, his dowdy cousin?

'They would most certain disapprove if I wanted to marry one of them! Perhaps you will be a good influence upon me,' he countered. 'Having heard a little of your views on male moral decadence, I am sure you can guide me.'

Fortunately his aunt was too busy ringing for the maid to notice this exchange. Theo refused the offer of tea, which he was assured had been brought from England in order to ensure there need be no recourse to inferior foreign supplies, and took his leave. 'Until tomorrow, Cousin.' He smiled a little at the heap of sketching gear and scholarly tomes in the hall; yes, this would prove an undemanding way to pass the time until all hell broke loose.

Chapter Two

Theo was conscious of a familiar presence behind him as he made his way down the steep hill, but the follower at his heels made no move to speak to him until they reached the square at the bottom where the gig was waiting.

'Picking up ladies again?' the other man said, swinging up beside him as Theo guided the horse out and down the St Père road. 'Not your usual style, that one. Dowdy little hen. Still, expect she'll be grateful for the attention. Got some trinkets to sell do you reckon?'

'That *little hen* is my cousin Miss Ravenhurst, so keep your tongue between your teeth and your light fingers off her trinkets,' Theo said mildly.

'Right. Sorry, guv'nor.'

He allowed Jake Hythe, his groom, factotum, valet and right-hand man, a long leash, but he knew that one word was enough to ensure obedience. When you rescue a man from a well-deserved place on the gallows it tended to ensure an uncommon degree of devotion.

'And keep an eye on her, if you see her about,' he added. 'Her mother's mighty careless of her.'

'As if it was your own self,' Hythe assured him. The man had killed before now to protect Theo's back—it was to be hoped for their own sakes that no local bucks attempted any familiarities with

Elinor while he was around. 'There's no sign of *them* at their place on the hill,' he added cryptically, jerking his head back towards Vezelay. 'I reckon you're going to have to get yourself invited to the chateau. How are you going to do that, then?'

There were, perhaps, advantages to having interfering, over-bearing and well-connected aunts. Theo smiled to himself. 'Do you think the Comte de Beaumartin would like my aunt, the daughter-in-law of the Duke of Allington, as a houseguest?' he enquired. 'Because I believe I am going to engineer a meeting.'

'Cunning bastard,' his companion said, in a voice of deepest respect. 'You always thinks of something.'

Elinor was ready and waiting, opening the door the moment Theo laid his hand on the knocker. 'I was watching for you to make sure you didn't knock. Mama is deep in a letter to the Antiquarian Society, disputing claims of the Reverend Anthony's about the development of the ogival arch, and must not be disturbed.'

'Good God,' he said faintly as he took her easel and satchel. 'Ogival arches? Doesn't it drive you insane?'

'Not often.' Elinor shut the door quietly behind them and fell into step beside him, not pretending to misunderstand. 'Compared to being the companion to some old lady with a smelly lap dog in Bath, or being a general dogsbody for my sister and her six *interesting* children, it is a positively desirable existence.

'I get to use my brain and what creative skills I possess. I can read five languages you know, including Ancient Greek. And I have a remarkable degree of freedom. In fact,' she pondered, ducking under a pole with washing on it that protruded into the street, 'I probably wouldn't have this degree of freedom until I was in my forties under any other circumstances. Unless I was a widow, of course. But one has to be married first for that.'

Theo did not reply immediately. Elinor glanced up at him. Today he was dressed in buckskins and boots, a broad-brimmed straw hat on his head. He looked far less English and considerably more formidable for some reason.

It seemed to her that the relaxed, polite and slightly deprecatory young man in the parlour yesterday had been an act. All the Ravenhursts were good actors—there was a family joke that there must have been a scandalous actress in the family tree at some point in the past—perhaps in his line of business that was a useful ability.

'Mama is a very considerable scholar, you know,' she added. 'It is not as though I am spending my time pandering to some pointless pastime. And it is better than sitting at home being a meek wife to some self-important gentleman who thinks women have no role except as mothers and housekeepers.'

'That is not the sort of marriage I imagine our three cousins have lately embarked upon,' Theo observed, fielding a ball aimed inexpertly at him by a small boy. He tossed it back, making sure it was catchable.

'No. Those are real love matches. Marriages of equals, I truly believe.' Elinor shrugged. 'It was extraordinary luck for them, I suppose.'

'Then you do not have much faith in men, Cousin, if you find three happy marriages extraordinary. But I gathered that up at the basilica yesterday.'

'Some of you are perfectly all right,' Elinor said with a smile. 'I suspect men are as much a victim of society as women are; it is just that you seem to have much more fun. Look at you, for example—all over the Continent chasing antiquities and having adventures, I dare say. Just imagine what would happen if I tried it.'

Theo gave a snort of amusement. 'It is a dangerous world out there. Even your valiant parasol would not be much protection.' There were more weapons in her armoury than the sharp ferrule of a sensible sunshade, but Elinor did not judge it prudent to reveal them. Under his unconventional exterior her cousin could well turn out to as easily shocked as most men.

'Here we are.' He led the way to a neat gig drawn up in the shade of a lime tree and helped her to climb up, stowing the easel and the rest of her paraphernalia under the seat. 'Would you like to drive?'

'I've never tried.' No man had ever suggested such a thing and she found herself quite taken aback. But Theo did not appear to be joking; he sat with the reins in his hands, the horse standing quietly, tail flicking against the irritation of the early summer flies.

'I'll show you.'

'Thank you.' Warily she held out her left hand and allowed him to arrange the reins in it. To her relief he kept hold of the whip.

'Now, say *walk on*.'

'In English?'

'It appears to be bilingual.'

Elinor laughed, then stopped abruptly as the animal, obviously hearing the command in Theo's more familiar voice, set off towards the lower road. 'Ah! What do I do?'

'Nothing. Keep contact with its mouth and wait until we need to turn off. Just relax.' He seemed very relaxed himself, for a man who had handed over control of his vehicle to a complete amateur. The horse seemed relaxed too, as did the entire local population of dogs, chickens and small children who might have been expected to rush out and cause the creature to bolt, throwing them both into the ditch and killing them.

Elinor decided it was unfair that she was the only tense one. 'So why, exactly, are you so in disgrace?' she asked.

'Nameless sins,' Theo said with a sinister smile.

'I refuse to believe it. Tell me.'

'Very well. By the time I was sixteen I was disappearing over the school wall every night, bent on a ruinous course of drink, wenching and gaming.'

'And were you ruined?' He did not appear very dissipated—not that she was too certain what a rakehell looked like.

'Morally? Undoubtedly. Financially, not one whit, which was what, I suspect, most infuriated my father. I was buying and selling even then. Buy from one dealer, sell to another. Scavenge around market stalls and pawn shops, clean things up and sell them on to the right person. I found early that I had an aptitude for cards and I was happy to take payment in objects, not coin. By the time I was sent down from university for running a faro school, I was able to support myself financially.'

'I can quite see why that made the Bishop so cross. You should have gone creeping home, all penitence and desperate for him to keep up your allowance and instead you— Ooh! Where is it going?'

'It knows the short cut.' To her alarm Theo left the reins in her hand as the horse turned off the road and began to amble along a track. 'Yes, I came home, announced my independence and I have been living off my wits ever since. I go home occasionally to give Papa the pleasure of delivering a thundering good lecture and for Mama to fuss over the state of my linen and to try to find a nice young lady for me.'

'Without success?'

Theo grinned. 'I run a mile in one direction at the thought of all those simpering misses while their mamas are sending them running in the other direction to escape my polluting influence.'

'Aren't you ever lonely?' She had become so lulled by his relaxed manner and lazily amused smile that the question escaped her before she could catch it.

'Lonely?' The amusement vanished from his eyes, although the smile stayed on his lips. 'Certainly not. Remember all those willing ladies you mentioned yesterday? And what about you? Aren't you lonely?'

'With all those fascinating antiquarian meetings to go to?' Elinor responded lightly. It was no business of hers how Theo lived his life or whether or not he was truly happy. She could not imagine what had come over her to loosen her tongue so.

She was puzzling about it when the reins, which had been sitting so comfortably in her hand, were suddenly jerked forwards violently. Instinctively she tightened her grip and held on, only to find herself falling towards the horse's rump. Then a solid bar slammed into her stomach and she was sitting back in the seat with Theo's left arm still out-flung across her midriff. With his right he dragged on the reins to remove the horse's head from the particularly lush patch of grass it was munching.

'Relaxed is right, total inattention is perhaps taking it a little too far,' he remarked while she jammed her straw hat inelegantly back on the top of her head.

'Indeed. I can see that. Thank you. Walk on.' They proceeded for a few steps. 'You may remove your arm now.'

'What? Sorry.' It had felt warm and hard. He must be both exceptionally fit and very fast to have caught her like that, Elinor reflected. She had no idea how much she weighed, but she knew that, propelled forwards so abruptly, her body would have hit his arm with considerable force. Was the rest of his body as hard?

She caught the thought and felt the blush rise. What was she doing, having such improper thoughts about a man she hardly knew? She flapped her free hand in front of her face. 'My, it is warm, is it not?'

'Unseasonably so, and odd after the shocking summer we have been experiencing.' Theo did not appear to notice anything amiss in her demeanour. 'Turn left down that lane.'

'How?'

Patiently he leaned across and covered her hands with his, looping the reins between her right-hand fingers as well, then using the pressure of his grip to guide the horse. Elinor made herself concentrate on what he was showing her, not how it felt, nor how the sharp scent of citrus cologne cut across the smells of a warm summer day in the countryside.

'Turn again here.' There were houses on either side now, but he left her to manage on her own.

'I did it!' Then, honesty got the better of her. 'But he would have turned anyway, wouldn't he?'

'Probably. You have nice light hands, though. We must try another day on a less familiar road so he will have to be guided by you.'

'Another day?' The church with its towering spire and vast porch was looming before them.

'I expect to be in the area for some days. A week or two, perhaps. Pull up on the far side at that gateway. You can see the ruins of the old church.'

Distracted by the news that there was an older church, one that might perhaps be of interest to her mother, Elinor handed the reins back and jumped down without waiting for Theo.

'Oh, there is hardly anything left.' She leaned on the gate, peering into the jumbled mass of stones, leaning tombstones and brambles.

'You don't want to go in there, do you? It'll wreak havoc with your gown.'

'This thing?' Elinor gave a dismissive twitch to the skirts of her drab brown walking dress. 'But, no, there doesn't seem to be anything to see of any significance. Let's look inside the other one.'

To her amusement, Theo offered her his arm as they walked the few yards to the great porch, big enough to put some of the village hovels into entire. He was an odd mixture of the gallant and the matter of fact, and she found it both pleasant and a trifle disconcerting. Gentlemen did not flirt with Elinor. They treated her with politeness, of course, but she was used to being regarded almost as if she were not there, an adjunct to her formidable mother.

Cousin Bel had made a spirited attempt at pairing her off with

Patrick Layne. But he had been attracted to Bel, not knowing she was having an outrageous and secret *affaire* with Ashe Reynard, Viscount Felsham. The two men fought a duel over Bel in the end and naturally Mr Layne had no thought of turning his attentions to Bel's bluestocking cousin after that.

It was as though being able to read Greek and Latin somehow labelled you as unfit for marriage. Not that she wanted to get married, but it might be nice, just sometimes, to be treated as a lady, not as a shadow, not as a mere companion.

And Theo, while definitely not flirting, *was* treating her like a lady, which was an interesting novelty. He was also acting as though he realised she had a brain in her head and did not blame her for using it—and that was delightful. She turned her head and smiled up at him and he smiled back, a smile that turned into a fleeting frown. Then he was opening the church door for her and she forgot to wonder what had caused that change of expression.

'This is lovely.' The church was full of light, clean, in good repair. Slender columns lifted towards the high roof and the air was full of the scent of incense.

'It is, isn't it? Do you want to sketch? I'll get our things.'

Theo was gone before she could respond, leaving her to wander about the wide side aisles. Light streaming in illuminated an ancient stone statue of a saint in a niche. It might have been old and battered, but it was obviously much loved. A bunch of wild flowers had been placed in a jar on its plinth and many candles had burned out in the stand at the foot of the column.

Elinor found a stool and dragged it across to a position where she had a good view. Footsteps behind her announced Theo's return. 'A good subject. May I use it too?'

'Of course.' She let him set up her easel while she emptied her satchel and found her watercolours. Mainly pencil, she decided. Soft greys with a little white chalk and colour just for the flowers, a splash of poppy red and the deep, singing blue of a wild delphinium.

Beside her Theo was humming under his breath while he flipped open a camp stool and spread a large sketchbook on his knee. There were pencils stuck behind his ear, a long thin brush in his teeth and he looked at the statue through narrowed eyes while his hands unscrewed the top of his water pot. He was definitely an artist, Elinor realised, recognising the concentration and seeing the well-worn tools. She just hoped he would not find her efforts laughable.

It was strange sitting sketching next to someone else. Theo had not done so since his tutor had given him his first drawing lessons and he was surprised to find it so companionable. He rinsed his brush and sat back, biting the end of it while he studied the results of an hour's work. Not bad. A little overworked, if anything. The habit of producing precise drawings to show to possible clients was too engrained now to easily throw off.

His eyes slid sideways to where Elinor was also sitting back, her head on one side as she frowned at the sketchbook propped on her easel. It was turned so he could not see her work; instead he looked at her profile, puzzling over his rediscovered cousin.

She was tall for a woman, slender, as far as one could tell from that badly cut gown. There had been softness, but also firmness against his outstretched arm when he had checked her fall. Her hair, which ought to be her crowning glory, was bundled ruthlessly into a thick net at her nape, presumably to disguise it as much as possible. Doubtless she had grown up being made to feel it was a handicap. His own sisters, Jane and Augusta, had escaped the family hair, and left him in no doubt about what a tragedy it would have been if they had not.

Her hands, unprotected by gloves, were long fingered, strong and ink-stained, her walk a stride that easily kept up with his. He suspected she was unused to gentlemen paying her much attention and found that rather endearing. But why on earth did she dress as though determined to appear a frump? The hair he could understand, even though he deplored it. But why sludge brown and slate-grey gowns that seemed to have been badly altered from ones made for a larger woman?

She tipped her head on one side, her lower lip caught in her teeth, then leaned forwards and touched her brush to the paper once more. 'There. Finished.'

'May I see?' Jane or Augusta would have blushed and dimpled, pretending to be too modest to let a gentleman look at their work, while all the time waiting for praise. Elinor merely leaned forwards and turned her easel so he could look. 'That's incredible.'

'It is?' She was rather pleased with it herself, but she did not expect such praise.

'You handle the drawing with such freedom. And the way you have so simply touched in the flowers with colour lifts the entire composition. I am envious of your talent.'

'Thank you.' She could not think of what else to say. She was unused to being praised and thought her work merely competent. 'Recently I have been experimenting with a looser style. I must admit to being influenced by Mr Turner. He is very controversial, of course. It does not do for the sketches of record for Mama, of course, but I am enjoying experimenting. May I see what you have done?'

Wordlessly Theo handed her his sketchbook. The drawing was precise, focused, full of tiny detail she had not noticed. It should have been cold, yet he had changed the position of the flowers so they wreathed the ancient figure with a tender beauty.

'But that is lovely. You saw things that I never knew were there.'

'I am used to having to be very precise.' He shrugged and she realised she was embarrassing him.

'I can see that. No, I mean the way you have used the flowers to echo the curve of the mantle and highlight the sweetness of her smile.' She handed the book back. 'I shall look more carefully in future for the emotion in what I am drawing.'

Now she had really done it. Men did not enjoy being accused of emotion, she knew that. Theo was packing away his things somewhat briskly, but he looked up and his eyes smiled. 'Perhaps we can learn from each other.'

I expect to be in the area for some days. A week or two perhaps, he had said. They could go sketching together again.

'I am sure we can, if you have the time.'

'I hope so. My plans are uncertain.' Theo folded her easel and his own stool. 'Shall we explore some more?'

They wandered through the church, peering into corners, admiring carvings. 'Is your mother interested in domestic architecture as well?' Theo asked.

'Yes, although she has not made such a study of it. Why do you ask?' Elinor moved a moth-eaten hanging to one side and sneezed as she disturbed a cloud of dust.

'There is a very fine and ancient chateau in the village of St Martin, beyond St Père. I have…business with the count. Perhaps she would care to visit with me when I call. I would not be surprised if he did not invite us all to stay.'

'Really?' Elinor had clambered up on to a rush-seated chair to study the stained glass more closely. 'Staying in a chateau sounds fascinating, but why should he ask us?'

'Count Leon spent much of his life in England with his father during the French wars. They were refugees. I am sure he would welcome English visitors.'

'You must mention it to Mama,'—who would not have the slightest qualms about moving into a chateau full of complete strangers if it interested her, Elinor knew full well. 'Have you—?'

The ancient rush work sagged beneath her feet, then began to give way. 'Theo!'

'Here, I've got you.' He swung her down easily and set her on her feet.

'Thank you—you have saved me again.' Elinor began to brush down her skirts. 'I have been scrambling over the wreckage in the basilica for hours without so much as a turned ankle and today I am positively accident prone.'

'Cousin—why do you wear such frightful gowns?' Theo said it as though it was a pressing thought that had escaped unbidden.

She could still feel the press of his hands at her waist where he had caught her. Shock and indignation made her voice shake, just a little 'I…I do not!' How *could* he?

Chapter Three

'Yes, you do,' Theo persisted, seemingly forced to speak. He did not appear to be deriving much satisfaction from insulting her dress sense. 'Look at this thing, and the one you wore yesterday. They might have been designed to make you look a fright.'

'Well, really!' A fright indeed! 'They are *suitable*.'

'For what?' he demanded irritably. 'Prison visiting?' Although what *he* had to be irritable about she had no idea. She was the one being insulted.

'Suitable for the sort of life I lead. They are practical. I alter them from old ones of Mama's.'

'A well-tailored gown in a colour that suits you would be equally practical. Green or garnet red or amber.'

'What business have you to be lecturing me about clothes?' Elinor demanded hotly. Theo looked equally heated. Two redheads quarrelling, she thought with a sudden flash of amusement that cut through the chagrin. She was not ready to forgive him, though. He might think her a dowd—he had no need to say so.

'If you were my sister, I would—'

'I am not your sister, I am thankful to say.'

'You are my cousin, and it irritates me to see you dressing so badly, just as it would irritate me to see a fine gemstone badly set.'

'A fine gemstone?' she said rather blankly. Theo was comparing her to a *gemstone*? Some of the indignation ebbed away to be replaced with resignation. He was quite right, her gowns were drab beyond description—even tactful Bel had told her so.

'As it happens, I have a couple of walking dresses that Bel bullied me into having made. I will wear one of those if we call at the chateau; I would not wish to embarrass you in front of your friends.' She was willing to concede he had a point, although she could not imbue much warmth into her agreement.

'That was not what concerned me—I am sorry if I gave you the impression that it was.' He regarded her frowningly for a moment, then smiled, spreading his hands in a gesture of apology. 'I truly am sorry. I spoke as I would to an old friend, out of bafflement that a handsome woman would diminish her looks so. But you rightly tell me to mind my own business; a chance-met cousin has no right to speak in such a way. I did not intend to hurt your feelings.'

And he had not, she realised, disregarding the blatant flattery of him calling her *handsome*. If she was honest with herself, she recognised in his outburst the same exasperation that sometimes led her to blurt out frank, or downright tactless, comments. She could remember demanding outright of a drooping Bel if she and Ashe were lovers. In comparison with that, a blunt remark about clothes was nothing.

'I know you did not. Let us go and have our luncheon,' she suggested. 'I am starving.'

Theo ducked his head in acknowledgement of her gesture. 'I will take the gig and our painting gear round to my lodgings first. It is on the way.'

A gangling youth came to take the reins as they led the horse up to a substantial village house. Theo lifted down the pile of easels and stools and opened the door while Elinor waited. From the exchange of words, it seemed his landlady was at home and after a minute she came out, a piece of sewing draped over her arm, a needle and thread trailing from the bodice of her crisp white apron.

'*Bonjour, madame.*' Elinor inclined her head and was rewarded by a flashing smile and an equally punctilious acknowledgement. Theo's landlady was a handsome woman in her late thirties. Her abundant brown hair was coiled on top of her head and her simple gown showed off a fine figure. It could not, Elinor reflected wryly, be much of a hardship for him to lodge there. She was also, if the cut of her own gown and the fine pleating around the hem of the sewing she was holding were anything to judge by, a fine sempstress.

'The inn is over here.' Theo took Elinor's arm and guided her towards the bridge. 'We can sit under that tree if you like.'

The food was good. Plain country fare, and all the better for it in Elinor's opinion, which she expressed as she passed the coarse game pâté across the table to Theo. 'Do you keep house for Aunt Louisa?' he asked, cutting them both bread.

'Me? Goodness, no! I am quite hopelessly undomesticated. I do not have any of the proper accomplishments for a young lady.' She glanced down at the lumpily-hemmed skirts of her offending gown and added, 'As you have already noticed.'

'Why should you, if your inclination is not in that direction?' Theo took a long swallow of ale. 'I have no inclination for any of the things I ought—I know nothing of estate management, my knowledge of politics is limited to keeping a wary eye on the international situation, it must be years since I went to a play...'

'But I am a lady and for me not to have accomplishments is disgraceful, whether I want them or not. You are a man and may do as you please.'

'True. A gratifying circumstance I must remind myself of next time Aunt Louisa is informing me that I am a scapegrace or Papa is practising one of his better hellfire sermons on me. Do you ride?'

'Papa taught me when I was little, but I could never keep my seat on a side saddle. When I reached the age when I could not possibly continue to ride astride, I had to stop.' Elinor sighed with regret. 'Perhaps I will persevere with trying to drive instead.'

'I knew a lady who rides astride,' Theo remarked. 'She has designed a most ingenious divided garment that looks like a pleated skirt when she is standing or walking. It was necessary to have the waistline made unfashionably low, of course, near the natural line. But it would be more suitable for your activities in the ruins, I imagine. It certainly appeared to give her considerable freedom.'

There was a faint air of masculine nostalgia about Theo as he spoke. Elinor bit the inside of her lip to repress a smile—or, worse, an indiscreet question. She would hazard a guess that the lady in question enjoyed more freedoms than simply unconventional dressing and that her cousin had enjoyed them with her.

'That sounds extremely sensible,' she observed, visited by an idea. 'Do you think your landlady could make me such a garment if you were to draw it for her?'

'But of course. From what I have seen on her worktable and her stocks of fabrics, she makes clothes for most of the ladies in the area, including those at the Chateau de Beaumartin, I imagine.' Theo set down his glass and sat up straighter, reaching into his pocket for the big notebook he seemed to take everywhere. 'Let me see what I can recall.'

What he recalled proved beyond doubt that he had a far more intimate knowledge of the garment in question than he should have. Elinor preserved a straight face as diagram followed diagram until she could resist no longer. 'How clever of you to deduce all of that from the external appearance only, especially, as you say, the garment is designed to conceal its secrets.'

'Ah.' Theo put down his pencil. 'Indeed. And I have now revealed a situation that I should most definitely not discuss with my sisters, let alone you, Cousin. How it is that I do not seem able to guard my tongue around you, I do not know.'

'Was she one of the willing ladies I most reprehensibly referred to yesterday?' Elinor enquired, not in the slightest bit shocked, only slightly, and inexplicably, wistful. Her newly rediscovered cousin was nothing if not a very masculine man. Doubtless he had to beat the ladies off with sticks.

'Yes, I am afraid so. Rather a dangerous lady, and willing, very much on her own terms.'

'Good for her,' Elinor retorted robustly. It sounded rather a desirable state, being dangerous and dealing with men on one's own terms. 'May I have those?'

She reached for the little pile of sketches, but Theo held them out of reach. 'On one condition only.' She frowned at him. 'That I choose the colour.'

'Certainly not! I cannot go and discuss having gowns made with a man in attendance, it would be quite shocking.'

'Gowns plural, is it?' He grinned at her, still holding the papers at arm's length. 'I am your cousin, for goodness' sake, Elinor, and she is my landlady. All I want to do is help you pick colours.'

'Dictate them, more like,' she grumbled, trying to maintain a state of indignation when truthfully she found she was rather enjoying this. It had been a long time since she had allowed herself to think about clothes as anything but utilitarian necessities. 'Very well. And, yes, gowns plural if it will save me from being nagged by you.'

'I am forgiven for my plain speaking, then?' He moved the sketches a little closer to her outstretched hand.

'About my clothes or your mistress?' Elinor leaned forwards and tweaked them from his fingers.

'Your clothes. And she was never my mistress—a term that implies some kind of arrangement. I am too careful of my life to entangle myself with that dangerous creature.'

'Tell me about her.' Elinor folded the sketches safely away in her pocket and regarded him hopefully.

'No! Good God, woman, Aunt Louisa would have my hide if she had the faintest idea what we are talking about. I don't know what has come over me.'

'We are becoming friends, I think,' she suggested. 'I find you very easy to talk to, perhaps because we are cousins. And I am not the sort of female you are used to.'

'That,' Theo observed with some feeling, 'is very true. Would you like anything else to eat? No? Then let us go and consult Madame Dubois.'

After five minutes with Madame, Theo was amused to observe that Elinor stopped casting him embarrassed glances and dragged him firmly into the discussion, even when he judged it time to retreat and began to edge towards the door.

'Come back,' she ordered, sounding alarmingly like her mother for a moment. 'My French is not up to this, I do not have the vocabulary for clothes.'

'What makes you think I have?' he countered. She slanted him a look that said she knew all to well that he had plenty of experience with French *modistes* and turned back to wrestling with the French for *waistline*.

Between them they managed well enough and Madame grasped the principles of the radical divided skirt very quickly. 'You could start a fashion, *mademoiselle*,' she remarked, spreading out the sketches and studying them. 'Your English tailors say we French cannot produce riding habits to their standard—let us see!'

They agreed on the riding skirt with a jacket and a habit-shirt to go beneath it, a morning dress and a half-dress gown. 'Now, this is the fun part.' Theo began to poke about in the bales of cloth and had his hand slapped firmly away by Madame.

'Zut! Let *mademoiselle* choose.'

'No, I trust Monsieur Ravenhurst's judgement,' Elinor said bravely, apparently only half-convinced of the wisdom of that assertion.

'That for the riding habit.' Decisive, he pulled out a roll of moss-green twill. 'And that, or that, for the morning dress.' Elinor submitted to having a sprigged amber muslin and a garnet-red stripe held up against her. Madame favoured the amber, he the red. Elinor wrinkled her nose, apparently unhappy about pattern at all.

'No, look.' Theo, carried away, began to drape the cloth around her. 'See? Pinched in here to show your waist off, and here, cut on the bias across the bosom—' He broke off, finding himself with both arms around Elinor, his nose not eight inches from where her cleavage would be if it was not swathed in fabric.

'It is *my* bosom,' she pointed out mildly. He felt heat sweep through him, dropped the fabric and stepped back abruptly. She caught the falling cloth, plainly amused at his discomfiture. 'I like this garnet stripe, I think, and I agree with Monsieur Ravenhurst's suggestions about the cut.' She tilted her head provocatively, disconcerting him by her agreement.

'*Alors.*' Madame appeared to have become resigned to her mad English clients, or perhaps she was simply used to him and inclined to be indulgent. 'The evening gown. Amber silk I have. A nice piece.'

'Violet,' Theo said, pointing. 'That one.'

'With my hair?' Elinor asked in alarm. He grinned at her. There would be no hiding in corners in a gown of that shimmering amethyst.

'Definitely.' She was not going to prevail this time. And he felt as though he had found a ruby on a rubbish tip and had delivered it to a master jeweller for cleaning and resetting. It was really rather gratifying.

A price and a startlingly short delivery time having been agreed, Elinor found herself outside with Theo, feeling somewhat as though she had been caught up in a whirlwind and deposited upside down just where she had been originally standing. 'I came out to look at a church,' she observed faintly, 'and now I've driven a gig, had my clothes insulted, eaten at an inn and bought three outfits.'

'You may express your gratitude when you see the effect.' Theo placed her hand in the crook of his elbow and began to stroll. 'A walk along the river bank before we go back?'

'I did not say I was grateful!' Elinor retrieved her hand, but fell into step beside him.

'Admit that was more fun than drawing capitals all day.' He turned off the road and began to walk upstream.

'It was *different*,' she conceded. 'Oh, look, a kingfisher.' They followed the flight of the jewelled bird as it fished, moving from one perch to another. The water was clear with long weed streaming like silk ribbons over the mosaic of pebbles and here and there a weir broke the smooth surface into foam and eddies.

There did not seem to be any need to speak. Sometimes Theo would reach out and touch her arm and point and she would follow the line of the long brown finger up to where a buzzard soared overhead or down to a yellow butterfly, unnoticed almost at her feet.

She picked a tiny bunch of wild flowers—one sprig of cow parsley, one long-stemmed buttercup, a spray of a blue creeping thing she had never seen before—and tucked them into his button hole. He retaliated by capturing her straw hat, which she had been swinging by its ribbons, unheeding of the effect on her complexion, and filling it with dog roses, won at the expense of badly pricked fingers.

The path began to meander away from the riverside. Then Theo pointed through a tangle of bushes to where a shelving stretch of close-cropped grass ran down to the water. 'Rest there a while, then walk back?' he suggested.

Elinor nodded. 'I could wander along here all afternoon in a trance, but I suppose we had best go no further.' It was the most curious sort of holiday, this day out of time with the almost-stranger she could recall from her childhood. Restful, companionable and yet with an edge of something that made her not *uncomfortable* exactly…

'You'll have to duck.' He was holding up a bramble. Elinor stopped pondering just how she was feeling and crouched down under a hawthorn bush, crept under the bramble and straightened up. 'Careful—too late, stand still.'

Something was grasping her very firmly by the net full of hair at her nape. Impatient, she shook her head and felt the whole thing pull free. 'Bother!' She swung round, her hair spilling out over her shoulders, only to find Theo disentangling the net from a blackthorn twig. 'Thank you.' Elinor held out a hand.

'Torn beyond repair, I fear.' Theo scrunched it up in his hand and tossed it into the river where it bobbed, forlorn, for a while, then sank, soggily.

'Liar!' Elinor marched up until she was toe to toe with him. 'It was fine. It is just like my gowns.'

Theo dropped to the ground, disconcerting her as she stood there trying to rant at him. 'I wanted to see your hair. Would you like a drink?'

'Yes, I would, but I'm not drinking river water—look, cows. And you did not have to throw my hairnet away.'

Theo was fishing in the satchel she had thought contained only sketching equipment, emerging with a bottle, a corkscrew and two horn beakers. 'I did. What would you have said if I'd asked you to let your hair down?'

'No, of course.' Exasperated Elinor sat down too, hugging her knees. Hair was in her eyes and she blew at it.

'I rest my case. Here, try this. It really ought to be cooler, but never mind.'

'Do you always get what you want?' Elinor took the beaker resentfully. The first mouthful of wine slid down, fruity and thirst quenching. She took another, her irritation ebbing away. It seemed impossible to be cross with Theo for very long.

'I try to.' He was lying back, his beaker balanced on his chest, hat tipped over his eyes. 'There's a leather lace in my bag some-where if you want to plait it.'

'And a comb, no doubt.' Elinor began to rummage. 'Honestly! And men complain about all the things women keep in their reticules. You could survive for a week in the wilds on what you have in here.'

'That's the idea.' Theo sounded as though he was dropping off to sleep.

Notebook and pencils were the least of it. There was rye bread folded in greased paper, a water bottle, a red spotted handkerchief, a fearsome clasp knife, some coiled wire she suspected was for rabbit snares, the comb, a tangle of leather laces, some loose coins… 'Ouch!'

'That'll be the paper of pins. Have you found what you need?'

'Thank you, yes.' Sucking a pricked finger, Elinor bundled every-thing back into the satchel and began to comb out her hair. Thanks to the careless way she had stuffed it into the net that morning it was full of tangles now and the task took a good ten minutes.

Finally she had it smooth. Her arms ached. Plaiting it seemed like too much trouble. She reached for the beaker of wine, found it empty and refilled it. As though she had called to him, Theo picked the beaker off his chest, sat up and pushed the hat back out of his eyes. 'Finished?'

'I have to plait it yet.' The late afternoon sun was warm and the burgundy, unaccustomed at this hour, ran heavy in her veins. Sleep seemed tempting; Elinor straightened her spine and tipped the un-finished half of her wine out on the grass.

'I'll do that.' Theo was behind her before she could protest, the weight of her hair lifting to lie heavy in his hands. 'Give me the comb.'

He seemed to know what he was doing. Elinor reached up and passed the comb back over her shoulder, then wrapped her arms around her drawn-up knees and rested her forehead on them. It was curiously soothing, the sweep of the comb through her hair from crown to almost her waist. Soothing to sit there in the warmth with the birds chattering and the river splashing and her own pulse beating…

Chapter Four

'Time to go.'

'Mmpff?' Elinor woke up with a start to find the shadows lengthening over the meadows and Theo on his feet, stretching hugely. 'I've been asleep?'

'For about half an hour. Me too.'

As she moved her head, the weight of her plait swung across her shoulders and curls tickled her cheeks. 'What have you done to my hair?' Reaching up, she found he had braided it, not from the nape, but elaborately all the way down from the crown, leaving wisps and curls around her forehead and cheeks.

'Plaited it. Isn't it right? I did it like I would a horse's tail.' Elinor eyed him, unsure whether this was the truth or whether she had just been given some other woman's hairstyle.

'Thank you,' she said at last, settling for brief courtesy and wishing she had a mirror to check it in. She ran a cautious hand over her head, half-expecting to find he had woven in buttercups while he was at it.

Theo was moving about now, stooping to pick up the wine bottle and the beakers, fastening the satchel. He moved beautifully, Elinor realised, the image of his body elongated in that luxurious stretch proving hard to dislodge from her mind. Long legs, long back tapering from broad shoulders to narrow hips—all those markers of perfect classical proportion it was acceptable for a lady to admire, provided they were depicted in chaste white marble.

She seemed to have spent the past few months surrounded by men acknowledged to be the best looking in society—some of them her cousins, one Bel's new husband—and she could honestly say she had felt not the faintest stirring of interest in anything other than their conversation. Why she was noticing now that Theo's boots clung to his muscular calves in quite that way was a mystery. It was not as though he was good looking.

Elinor got to her feet, brushed off her skirts and catalogued all the ways in which he was not good looking. His nose, though large and masculine, was undistinguished. His jaw line was strong, but his chin had the suspicion of a dimple which somewhat diminished its authority. His eyebrows were much darker than his hair and he showed no tendency to raise one in an elegant manner. His mouth was wide and mobile and he seemed more prone to cheerful grins than smoothly sophisticated smiles. Yes, she could quite see why Cousin Theo would not fit in to London society.

He was ducking under the treacherous brambles again, holding them up for her with one hand, the other outstretched. Elinor took it, crouched lower and was safely through. Somehow her hand remained in his as they turned back along the path towards St Père and somehow it felt remarkably normal to have those warm fingers wrapped companionably around hers.

'I will come at ten tomorrow and see if Aunt Louisa would like to call on the Count.'

'It is her writing day tomorrow, it may not be convenient. She will probably wish to make it the day after.' And tomorrow would be a free day for Elinor, unless she was required to redraw her basilica sketches. If Theo was not going to make his call...

'It is, however, the day on which I am calling on him, so I am afraid your dear mama will just have to fit in with someone else's convenience for once.' She blinked, startled by the thread of steel in Theo's tone. 'I will come in with you when we get back, if you would prefer not to pass on that message.'

'No, no, please do not trouble yourself. I will make sure she understands that any other day would not be possible.' His chin, elusive dimple or not, suddenly looked really rather determined. Elinor shrank from the thought of finding herself in the middle of a confrontation between her mother and Theo.

'Does she bully you?'

'No. Not at all.' He made no response to that. Elinor walked in silence, well aware that her mother did not bully her for the simple reason she never had any occasion to stand up to her. Given that she was on the shelf, and the alternative ways of life were so unappealing, she simply went along with whatever Mama wanted. What would happen if she ever did find herself in opposition?

'We are nearly back; you had best put on your bonnet again.' Theo fished another lace from his satchel and gathered her prickly roses into a bunch so she could tie on the flat straw hat again.

'That,' he remarked, flipping the brim, 'suits you. We will save it from the bonfire.'

'What bonfire?'

'The one for your gowns and any other garment you possess that is sludge coloured.'

'You are just as much a bully as Mama,' Elinor remarked, climbing into the gig and waving away his offer of the reins.

'Am I?' Theo's mouth twisted into a wry smile. 'Say *no* to me, then, and see what happens.'

'Very well. I will not burn my old gowns.'

'What will you do with them?'

'Give them to my maid, who will probably sell them.'

'An excellent solution. See, no opposition at all.'

'You are all sweet reasonableness, in fact.'

'Of course.' The horse toiled up the hill to the square below the long steep street to the basilica while Elinor tried, and failed, to come up with a retort that was not thoroughly unladylike. Theo guided it towards the hitching post in the shade.

'No, I can walk from here, honestly.' He looked doubtful, then clicked his fingers at a burly man lounging against the tree trunk.

'Hey, you. Carry this lady's things up the hill for her.' The man caught the coin tossed in his direction neatly, then came to lift the sketching paraphernalia from the gig, shouldering the easel and waiting for Theo to hand Elinor down.

'Tomorrow at ten, then? Thank you for my day.'

'And for the new gowns?'

'I reserve judgement on those until I see what they look like.' She laughed back at his smile and set off up the hill, her porter at her heels.

Theo caught Hythe's eye and nodded almost imperceptibly before the man set off in Elinor's wake. He tipped his hat over his eyes, leaving just enough room to see under the brim, and leaned back against the backboard, apparently asleep. It was a useful trick, and had served him well in the past.

That had been an unexpected day. Unexpected, different and quietly pleasant. It had left him with the desire to set a match to the entire contents of his aunt's study, though. Poor Cousin Elinor. No—he had started out feeling sorry for her, but that, he acknowledged, was not the right emotion.

She was intelligent, amusing, artistically talented and really rather lovely, if she could ever be brought to see it. On the other hand, her very unconsciousness of her looks was part of her charm.

Or was it just him? Certainly no other gentleman had shown her overt attention in the past or she would not have been so completely relaxed in his company. It seemed she vanished at will behind a mask that disguised her as *spinster bluestocking* and both she, and all the men she came in contact with, accepted that.

When he thought of the liberties he could have taken with her—probably *would* have taken with someone of more sophistication—he shuddered. The feel of her, her waist trim between his palms as he lifted her down from that chair in the church. Her hair, glossy under his hands as she let him handle it. Her total relaxation as she slept on the riverbank beside him. And her warm, long-fingered hand trusting in his as they walked back.

Through his narrow viewpoint Hythe came into sight, striding down the hill. 'That the same cousin, guv'nor?' he asked when he was up on the seat and Theo was lifting the reins.

'The same. Why?'

'Thought her a bit of a drab piece yesterday. Different today, bit of a sparkle about her.'

'She needed some fresh air,' Theo said. Fresh air, a change of scene and someone to appreciate her. Perhaps Count Leon would take a fancy to her; that would distract him nicely.

Was there any danger, taking his aunt and cousin into that chateau? No, surely not. Even if it were the count who had robbed him of the ch—the *object*. Even to himself he did not name it. It seemed hard to believe that he was the culprit, the man who had struck Theo down and murdered the old count, his father. If he was innocent, then the danger would come when whoever did have it attempted to sell it back to the count. Theo could send the women packing as soon as that happened.

His hand went to the small of his back where the pistol was wedged into his belt and then down to check the knives slipped into his carefully made boots. Things were safe enough now. His mouth settled into a thin smile that did not reach his eyes.

* * *

'Good afternoon, Elinor.' Lady James hardly glanced up from her work table as Elinor came in, a rustic jug with the wild roses in her hands. She looked around for a free flat surface, then gave up and stood them in the hearth.

'Good afternoon, Mama. Did you have a good day?'

'Passable. Those sketches of yours are acceptable, I do not require any of them redone. What was the church at St Père like?'

'Of as late a date as you supposed,' Elinor said indifferently. At least she did not have to spend any more time squinting into shadows in the basilica. 'There are the ruins of the old church next to it, but nothing of any interest remains.'

'You were a long time.'

'Cousin Theo and I went for a walk. I found the exercise invigorating after so much time spent drawing.'

'Very true. A rational way to spend the day, then.' Lady James added a word to the page, then looked up, apparently satisfied with the sentence she had just completed. 'What have you done to your hair?'

'Oh.' Elinor put up a hand, startled to find the softness against her cheek. 'My hair net caught on a twig and was torn. I had no hair pins, so braiding it seemed the best thing to do.' In for a penny... 'I ordered some new gowns while I was in the village. Cousin Theo's landlady is a dressmaker.'

'Nothing extravagant, I trust. There is plenty of wear in that gown for a start.' Clothing, especially fashionable clothing, was not just an unnecessary expense, but a drug for young women's minds, in Lady James's opinion.

'They are well within my allowance, Mama—a positive bargain, in fact—and they are practical garments.' She had lost her mother's attention again. Elinor half-stood, then sat down again. Normally at this point she would retreat and leave Mama in peace, but today, after

the experience of spending hours with someone who actually understood the concept of a reciprocal conversation, she felt less patient.

'Mama, Cousin Theo tells me that there is a most interesting
chateau in St Martin, a village beyond St Père. He has an introduction to the count and thought you may like to accompany him
tomorrow and see the building.'

'Hmm?' Lady James laid down her pen and frowned. 'Yes, if
that is the Chateau de Beaumartin, I have heard of it. I believe it
has an unusual early chapel, a remnant of an earlier castle.
Tomorrow is not convenient, however.'

'It is the day Cousin Theo will be visiting. That and no other, he
says, so I am afraid we will have to be a little flexible if we are not
to miss the opportunity.'

'Flexible? He obviously has no concept of the importance of
routine and disciplined application for a scholar. Very well. I never
thought to see the day when I would have to accommodate the
whims of a scapegrace nephew.'

'I believe he is calling on business, not for pleasure, Mama. And
he is a most accomplished artist,' she added, feeling the need to
defend Theo in some way. He would be amused to hear her, she
suspected. Somehow he seemed too relaxed and self-confident to
worry about what one eccentric aunt thought of him. 'He will be
here at ten, Mama.'

'Indeed? Well, if we are to spend tomorrow out, then we have
work to do. Those proofs will not wait any longer, not if I am to
entrust them to what passes for the French postal system these days.
It pains me to find anything good to say about the Corsican
Monster, but apparently he made the mails run on time.'

'Yes, Mama, I will just go and wash my hands.' It did not seem
possible to say that she would rather spend the remainder of the afternoon while the light held in working up some of the rapid sketches
she had made during the day. The one of Theo drawing, for example,

or lying stretched out on the river bank with his hat tipped over his nose, or the tiny scribbled notes she had made to remind her of the way that blue creeping flower had hugged the ground.

Never mind, she told herself, opening the door to her little room on the second floor. They would still be there in her pocket sketchbook, and her memory for everything that had happened today was sharp. All except for those soft, vague minutes while Theo had been plaiting her hair and she had fallen asleep. That was like the half-waking moments experienced at dawn, and likely to prove just as elusive.

She splashed her face and washed her hands in the cold water from the washstand jug without glancing in the mirror. She rarely did so, except to check for ink smudges or to make sure the parting down the middle of her hair was straight. Now, as she reached for her apron, she hesitated and tipped the swinging glass to reflect her face. And stared.

Her nose was, rather unfortunately, becoming tanned. Her cheeks were pink and her hair… She looked at least two years younger. Which was probably because she was smiling—not a reaction that looking in the mirror usually provoked. Or *was* it that?

Elinor assumed a serious expression. She still looked—what? Almost pretty? It must be the softness of those ridiculous tendrils of hair escaping around her forehead and temples. Looking pretty was of no practical use to a bookish spinster. On the other hand, it was rather gratifying to discover that her despised red hair could have that effect. And the unladylike tan at least disguised the freckles somewhat.

What would have happened five years ago during her disastrous come-out if she had dressed her hair like this instead of trying to hide it? Nothing, probably. She was still the younger daughter, destined to remain at home as Mama's support. And she had always been studious, which immediately put men off. It took a long time, and numerous snubs, before she realised she was supposed to pretend she was less intelligent than they were, even when their conversation was banal beyond belief. But she never could bring herself to pretend. It was no loss; she would be bored to tears as a society wife.

The apron she wore when she was working was still in her hand, the cuff-protectors folded neatly in the pocket. She looked down at the sludge-coloured gown and tossed the apron on to the bed. The gown was going, it might as well go covered in ink spots.

Elinor ran down the twisting stairs, humming. Even the waiting proofs of *A comparison between early and late eleventh-century column construction in English churches* did not seem so daunting after all.

'Pink roses?' Lady James levelled her eyeglass at the crown of Elinor's villager hat, decorated with some of yesterday's roses. 'And ruby-red ribbons? Whatever are you thinking of?'

'The ribbons match my walking dress, Mama. And I think the roses look charming with it. The dress is one of those Cousin Belinda persuaded me to buy, if you recall. I thought I should make an effort for our call.'

'Hmm. Where has that young man got to?' As the clocks had not yet struck ten, this seemed a little harsh.

'He is just coming, Mama.' Reprehensibly Elinor had her elbows on the ledge of the open casement and was leaning out to watch the street. 'Good morning, Cousin Theo. You are very fine this morning.'

'And you, too.' He swept off his tall hat and made a leg, causing a passing group of young women to giggle and stare. Biscuit-coloured pantaloons, immaculate linen, a yellow silk waistcoat and a dark blue coat outshone anything to be seen on the streets of Vezelay on a workaday Wednesday morning. 'Has the bonfire occurred?'

Jeanie, their Scottish maid who had travelled with them from London and who was proving very adaptable to life in France, came down the stairs, opened the door with a quick bob to Theo, then vanished down the street with a large bundle under her arm.

'Unnecessary, as I told you.' Elinor whispered, conscious of her mother behind her gathering up reticule and parasol. 'Jeanie's on her way to the used-clothes dealer right now.'

'Do you intend to converse with your cousin through the window like a scullery maid, Elinor, or are we going?'

'We are going if you are ready, Mama.'

'I am. Good morning, Theophilus. Now, then, who exactly are these friends of yours?'

'Good morning, Aunt. Not friends, I have never met the family. I did business with the count's late father earlier this year, just before his death. There are…complications with the matter that I need to discuss with the son.'

Lady James unfurled her parasol, took Theo's arm and swept off down the hill, leaving Elinor to shut the door and hurry after them. 'Count Leon is about my age and lived almost entirely in England since just before the Terror.'

'His father obviously had the sense to get out in time.'

'The foresight, certainly. He moved his money to English banks and his portable valuables he placed in hiding in France. The estates and the family chateaux were seized, of course. Most of the furnishings and paintings were dispersed.'

'And your business with the late count?'

'Mama!' Elinor murmured, cringing at the bluntness of the enquiry. Theo was hardly likely to answer that.

'Why, helping him retrieve the missing items,' he answered readily. 'I had some success, especially with the pictures. They are easier to identify than pieces of furniture.'

'Ah, so you have located some more items,' Lady James said, apparently happy now she had pinned down Theo's precise business.

He did not answer. Which means, Elinor thought, studying the back of his neck as though that singularly unresponsive and well-barbered part of his anatomy could give her some clue, Mama is not correct and his business with Count Leon is something else entirely. How intriguing.

Waiting at the bottom of the hill was a closed carriage. Theo's own? Or had he hired it especially? Determined not to be as openly inquisitive as her mother, Elinor allowed herself to be handed in and set to studying the interior.

Dark blue, well-padded upholstery. Carpet underfoot. Neat netting strung across the roof, cunningly constructed pockets in the doors and pistol holders on either side. Theo's own, she was certain. Her cousin was a man who enjoyed luxury and valued practicality, she deduced, her gaze on the swinging gold tassels of his Hessian boots and her memory conjuring up the contents of his sketching satchel. But what sort of life encompassed carriages of this quality and the need for rabbit snares?

She lifted her eyes to find him watching her, one dark brow raised. She had been wrong to think he would not do that, she thought. Today, far from the comfortable cousin of yesterday, he was a society gentleman and a rather impressive one at that.

'I was admiring the appointments of your carriage,' she said calmly, in response to the raised brow. 'Although I cannot see the container for the game you snare.'

He gave a snort of laughter, the gentleman turning back into Cousin Theo again. 'You guessed it was mine?'

'I am coming to know the style,' she said, and was rewarded by a smile and an inclination of the head. He looked rather pleased at the compliment.

'Whatever are you talking about, Elinor?' Lady James did not wait for a response, but swept on. 'How far is it, Theophilus?'

'Another five miles, Aunt. I do not suppose I can prevail upon you to call me Theo?'

'Certainly not. I do not approve of shortening names. Most vulgar.'

Under cover of brushing his hair back he rolled his eyes at Elinor, almost provoking her to giggles. She frowned repressively and set herself the task of talking her mother into a good humour before they arrived. 'Do tell me about this chapel, Mama. I am sure I will not appreciate it without your guidance.' This time Theo crossed his eyes, making her cough desperately and be thankful that the interior of the carriage was dim enough for Mama not to notice.

He was back to being the perfect gentleman again by the time they rolled past the outlying farmhouse, through the gatehouse and into the courtyard of the chateau. 'I sent ahead yesterday to apprise them of our visit; we should be expected.'

As he spoke the great double doors at the top of the steps swung open and a young man stepped out, two women dressed in mourning black just behind him. Elinor did not like to stare and with the fuss attendant on having the steps let down, retrieving her mother's reticule from the carriage and following her up the steps, it was not until she was within arm's length of the count that she saw his face.

It was only the tightly tied garnet ribbons under her chin that stopped her jaw dropping: the Comte Leon de Beaumartin was quite the most beautiful man she had ever seen.

Chapter Five

The pain in his right hand recalled Theo to the fact that he needed to be making introductions, not reacting to the look in Elinor's eyes when she saw the Count. He relaxed his grip on his cane and removed his hat. His cousin was once more demurely composed; he doubted anyone else had noticed her widening eyes. The count had been looking between them as though to assess their relationship. Now a polite social smile replaced the assessment.

'Monsieur le Comte?'

'Monsieur Ravenhurst. I am delighted to meet you at last. My father, unfortunately, told me so little about you.'

I'll wager he did, Theo thought grimly. 'Aunt Louisa, may I introduce Comte Leon de Beaumartin? *Monsieur,* Lady James Ravenhurst, my cousin Miss Ravenhurst.'

The count switched his attention to the ladies, and more particularly to Elinor. Theo was close enough to see his pupils widen. *And, of course he has to kiss her hand.* Lady James received an elegant bow, Elinor the full flourish ending with a kiss a fraction above her gloved hand. *Why the hell does she have to look so damnably pretty this morning? And she doesn't even realise.*

'Lady James, Miss Ravenhurst. Allow me to introduce my mother, the Countess Christine, and Mademoiselle Julie de Falaise.' Theo bowed, the countess and Lady James bowed, the younger ladies curtsied. It was all extremely proper. Now all he had to do was engineer an invitation to stay for the three of them and he would be able to search the chateau from garrets to cellars for his property. It was what he needed to do, yet suddenly his appetite for it was waning. Surely that beating he got when the *object* was taken hadn't shaken his nerve?

'We will take coffee,' the countess pronounced, leading the way across a stone-flagged hallway.

'My aunt is a notable scholar of ancient buildings,' Theo interjected smoothly, pulling himself together and following the ladies. 'As I explained when I wrote, the purpose of our visit is largely that I had hoped you would be willing to show her your famous chapel, ma'am.'

The countess stopped, turned to Lady James and positively beamed. 'But it is our family pride and joy, *madame,* I would be delighted to show it to you.' Her English, like her son's, was fluent, although accented. Hers was a heavier accent; the count's, Theo thought darkly, was precisely the sort that sent impressionable English ladies into a flutter. Elinor, of course, was made of sterner stuff. Or so he would have said half an hour ago.

'Excellent. Kindly lead the way.' Aunt Louisa thrust her parasol into the hands of the waiting footman, produced a notebook from her capacious reticule and stood waiting.

'Before coffee?' The question seemed rhetorical, the countess recognising single-minded obsession when she saw it. 'This way, then.'

Theo followed them as they went through a small doorway and began to climb a spiral staircase. 'If you don't mind?' he said over his shoulder to the count. 'I would be most interested.' And taking advantage of every legitimate opportunity to study the layout of the chateau was essential. He had no intention of creeping about in the small hours with a dark lantern any more than he had to.

He did not stop to see what the other man's response might be, but ducked through the doorway in the wake of Mademoiselle Julie's slight figure. There was silence behind him for a second, then the sharp snap of booted feet on the stone floor. Count Leon was coming to keep an eye on him, or was it Elinor?

The turret stair wound up, passing small doors as it went. At one point Aunt Louisa gave an exclamation and pointed to a change in the stonework. 'Interesting!' Then, when they had reached what Theo estimated must be the third floor above the ground, the countess opened a door and led them through into a dark, narrow passageway, through another door and into a tiny chamber blazing with coloured light.

Even Theo, who had some idea what to expect, was startled by the rose window filled with red and blue glass that occupied almost the entire end wall. On either side ranged columns with richly carved heads. 'They are so like those at Vezelay!' Elinor exclaimed, darting across to study one. 'But in such good condition, and low down, so we can see them.'

Lady James, for once in her life, appeared speechless. 'I must study this,' she pronounced finally. 'In detail.'

Theo strolled across to Elinor's side and stooped to whisper, 'Do what you can to engineer an invitation to stay. For all of us.' She looked up, startled, then nodded. 'I would appreciate it.'

The count was standing in the middle of the room, unmoved by Lady James's ecstasies, his eyes on Theo. 'Are you really interested in this, Ravenhurst?' he enquired, his voice puzzled. Theo chose to treat the question as a joke, smiled warmly and continued to study the walls of the chapel. No cupboards, no niches, no apparent changes in the stonework to indicate a blocked-up hiding place. But then, he had not expected to find it here. It would take an atheist, or someone with a careless approach to their faith, to hide that thing in the family chapel.

There was another door on the far side from where they had entered. He strolled across, passing the count. 'Shall we leave the ladies? There is something I would appreciate discussing with you. Through here, perhaps? I would prefer not to have to spin round another tower.'

Silently Leon led the way, opening the door on to a broad corridor. Theo followed as slowly as he dared, looking about until they reached a panelled door and passed through into what was obviously the study.

Theo suspected it had been the old count's and hardly changed by his son in the month since he had succeeded. He took a chair on one side of a vast desk, noticing he was not offered refreshment.

'To what do we owe the pleasure of this visit? Your letter was somewhat lacking in detail beyond your aunt's interest in architecture,' Leon remarked, dropping into the chair with its carved arms and high back. Darkly saturnine, he looked like the wicked prince in a fairytale as he frowned across the wide expanse of desk.

'You will know I assisted your father in recovering some of the family artefacts lost during the Revolution?' The other man nodded. 'There was an item I wished to purchase from him, something that had remained in hiding throughout the family's exile from France.'

Theo watched the count's face for any betraying sign that he knew that Theo had in fact purchased that item and had lost it, in violent circumstances, a week after the transaction. He rubbed the back of his neck as he waited. The bruising and the torn muscles had healed, but the pain of having been taken completely off his guard still lingered. He had had not so much as a glimpse of the person who had struck him down. Was he facing him now?

'If you speak of the object I assume you are, it has vanished.' Leon's frown deepened, his well-modelled lips thinning. 'My father was murdered the day after he arrived in Paris, having removed it from this chateau in circumstances of extreme secrecy.

No sum of money equivalent to even a tenth of its worth was found on him, nor in the Paris house, nor with our bankers.' He shook his head, his face grim. 'I still find it hard to believe he could ever have sold it—it was an heirloom. And yet it is gone.'

'Indeed? I can assure you he intended to.' Either the man was a damn good actor or he did not know that Theo was the purchaser. 'What use is an heirloom so shocking that you could never openly admit you had it? An heirloom that none of the ladies of the house must ever catch a glimpse of? Your father intended to sell it because he needed the money. I wish to buy it as the agent of an English collector who will pay handsomely.'

Who had, in fact, paid very handsomely indeed and was expecting the arrival of his purchase days ago. No one else knew about the sale except three rival treasure seekers, one of whom had been sharing his bed. He had not believed Ana, or the English couple, had realised why he was in Paris, his security had been so tight.

'Perhaps he *had* already sold it,' he ventured, probing. 'Was there no receipt?' Theo had certainly exchanged them with the count. His had been taken along with the item as he had lain unconscious on the inn floor.

'There was no receipt in my father's papers or on his person.'

'How did your father die?'

'A blow to the head. We hushed it up as the result of a fall. He was found across the hearth, the back of his skull against the iron fire basket. It *may* have been an accident,' Leon conceded as though it caused him pain to do so. 'But I want the Beaumartin Chalice back.' He regarded Theo through narrowed eyes. 'You think I killed him, don't you?'

That was precisely what Theo thought. That the count had quarrelled with his father, had taken back the Chalice and was now pretending it had gone to cover his actions.

'Indeed, that had seemed the most logical explanation to me.

That you quarrelled with your father when you discovered that he had sold the Chalice, that there was a terrible accident.' It seemed odd to be naming the thing out loud after months of secrecy, code words and whispers.

They sat looking at each other in silence, contemplating Theo's cool suggestion. It was the count whose eyes dropped first. 'I disagreed with him about this. Violently. But we exchanged words only, before he left Beaumartin. I did not kill him, even by accident.'

'Of course,' Theo said, injecting warmth into his voice. Now he spoke to the man he was inclined to trust him. Leon had been raised in England—did that mean he shared the same code of honour as Theo? Perhaps.

'Why do you want it back—other than the fact you cannot trace the money that was paid for it if it was sold and not stolen?'

'Do you imagine I want that thing out there, bearing our name? It has taken years for the rumours about the family to die down.'

'It is a work of art and was no doubt destined for a very private collector.'

'It is an obscenity,' Leon snapped.

'Indeed. And a valuable one. Too valuable to melt down and break up.'

'When I get it back, it will go back into safe keeping, in the most secure bank vault I can find. My father, and his before him, kept it hidden here, in this chateau. After his death I checked—it had gone.'

It is not going into any bank, not if I can help it, Theo thought grimly. His client had paid Theo for the Chalice. It was now his, however much the count might deny it. His lordship would not even accept the return of his money. He wanted that Chalice, and what he wanted, he got.

It was an impasse. He thought the Court believed Theo did not have it, had not bought it in the first place and was here now attempting to locate it. Count Leon was convincing, too, when he said that it was missing and that he had not harmed his own father, but Theo had not been in this business so long without learning to trust no one. It could be an elaborate bluff to remove all suspicion from the family and keep the money.

And if the man did have it, he had no belief in Leon's announcement that he would put it in a vault. Leon was a traditionalist—it would stay here, in hiding, as it had been for hundreds of years. He was still going to check. 'Shall we rejoin the ladies?'

'Of course. Your cousin is most striking. Are you all redheads in your family?'

Theo bit back a demand that the count refrain from discussing Elinor if he did not want to find his elegant nose rearranged, and shook his head. 'Some are brown-headed, some dark. But in most branches of the family there are redheads.'

'With tempers to match?' The count led the way down a broad staircase into the front hall. The place was a rabbit warren.

'We learn early to control them that much better, *monsieur*.' *But don't chance testing mine…*

The ladies were sitting in a room that was pure eighteenth century—white and gilt and mirrors in startling contrast to the medieval parts of the building. Wide glazed doors opened on to a terrace with lawns sloping away down towards the river. Elinor turned as they came in. 'Cousin Theo, it is so delightful, the Countess has invited us to stay next week. There is to be a house party.'

'Delightful indeed,' he said enthusiastically. 'I, for one, accept with much pleasure.' The countess had her face under control in an instant. The younger woman had less experience; Theo, plainly, had not been included in the invitation. But no one could say so now. He smiled sunnily at the count. 'Delightful.'

There was an awkward moment while Mademoiselle Julie plastered a smile on her face, the count looked like thunder and the countess recovered herself. 'It will be quite an English party,' she declared. 'Sir Ian and Lady Tracey are joining us. You may know them? I met them in Paris, soon after my poor husband's death. They were such a support until dear Leon could reach me.'

The Traceys? Here? So they *do not have it either. Have they followed me or will I come as a nasty surprise to them?* If he did not have it, and Leon did not have it and the Traceys did not, then that left only one person in the game. He would let the houseparty run its course, satisfy himself that the Chalice had not come home and that this was not some complex manoeuvre on the part of the English collectors, and then he would find Ana. And wring her very lovely neck.

'I have met them,' he conceded. The last time had been just before he had bribed their coachman to take the wrong road south to Paris from the coast and then, when they were well lost, to engineer a broken axle. He was sure Sir Ian was going to be just as pleased to encounter him again as he was to see them. 'It will be most interesting to become reacquainted.'

Elinor was watching him, her head tipped a little to one side. She knew there was something going on beneath this polite surface chatter, something beyond the odd fact that he had asked her help in securing an invitation to stay in a chateau where he already had an entrée of sorts.

'Is anyone else coming?' she asked now, gazing directly at the count. If it did not seem too bizarre a phrase to use in connection with Elinor, she was positively batting her eyelashes at him.

'Some relatives of ours,' he answered, strolling over and taking the place next to her on the sofa. 'This is a large house, we can accommodate a lot of people.' He shot Theo an unreadable look as he said it, then turned to smile at Elinor. Behind their back Mademoiselle Julie bit her lip and began to make brittle conversation with Lady James. *The paid companion? A poor relation? Whichever it is, she does not like the count paying attention to another woman. And neither do I. Not that one.* Which was strange. He supposed it was because he was used to keeping an eye out for his sisters. But Elinor was not his sister.

Aunt Louisa was drawing on her gloves. 'Until Monday afternoon, then. I shall look forward to it. Come, Elinor, there is much to do.'

'Packing?' Mademoiselle Julie ventured.

'Packing? No, I have my work on the basilica to complete.' The poor girl looked daunted, but she did not return the conspiratorial smile that Elinor directed at her.

'Well, that is most satisfactory,' Lady James pronounced, settled back in the carriage. 'Four days should see a considerable advance in my researches. The chapel will provide a most valuable addition to chapter four.' She took up her notebook and began to scribble, frowning as the carriage lurched over a rut.

'You timed that announcement very neatly, Elinor.' Theo was not smiling, however. He looked almost grim, she decided, puzzled. She had done what he had asked, hadn't she? And the prospect of a house party at the chateau was something to be looked forward to, surely?

'Thank you. I decided the only option to ensure they could not exclude you was to gush like that. Why did you assume they would not invite you? You knew the late count, after all.'

'His son does not like me.' It appeared to be mutual.

'Really? I did notice a certain tension, but I assumed it was business matters.' Tension was an understatement. The count had looked like the demon king and Theo positively dangerous. 'He is very charming, and incredibly good looking.'

Her cousin regarded her through narrowed eyes for a long moment, but all he said was, 'Who is Mademoiselle Julie?'

'I am not entirely certain. A distant connection of the countess, I think. She seems to act as her companion.'

Theo lapsed into silence and Elinor recalled something she had noticed on their arrival at the chateau and had no opportunity to mention. 'The driver of this coach is the man you hired to carry my things up the hill yesterday.'

'Yes.'

'He was waiting for you.'

'Yes.'

'And he is already in your employ?' He nodded. Elinor opened her mouth to demand to know why Theo's employee was hanging around the town pretending to be a stray loafer looking for casual work and then closed it again. *Not in front of Mama*. He nodded again in recognition of her tact, the glimmer of a smile touching his mouth. It was the first genuine sign of pleasure she had seen from him since they arrived at Beaumartin.

'You could stop now and have a fitting for your new gowns,' Theo suggested as the carriage rolled into St Père. It was far too early for even the most industrious sempstress working alone to have anything ready for a first fitting. He knew it and she knew it. Only Lady James, loftily above such trivia as gowns would not think it strange. Perhaps Theo was going to confide in her at last.

'What a good idea.' Elinor sounded suspiciously bright and breezy, even to her own ears. 'Will you drive me back to Vezelay later in the gig?'

'Yes, of course. Aunt Louisa, that will be all right, will it not?'

'What? Oh, yes, whatever will waste least time on fripperies.' Lady James went back to frowning over her notebook.

Theo stood watching the carriage vanish round the bend, leaving a cloud of dust and two yapping dogs in its wake, then fished a key out of his pocket and opened the door into the dressmaker's shop.

'Madame is not even here, is she? So, are you going to tell me what all the mystery is about?'

'There is no mystery.' Theo ignored her sceptical expression. 'Just a confidential business matter. However, I need to talk to you about the count. It had not occurred to me that he may not be a suitable person for you to associate with. You should keep your distance from him throughout the stay. I could wish I had not involved you now.'

'Why ever not?' Elinor demanded, perplexed. 'He is quite charming…'

Theo shrugged. 'If you like that sort of all-over-you hand kissing.'

'And extremely good looking.' He merely snorted. 'And delightful to talk to.'

'The accent, I suppose. Really Cousin, I am surprised you, of all people, would fall for such facile attributes.'

'*Facile?* Well, and if he is, what is the harm, pray? I am sure he will be a delightful host.' Theo was frowning. 'And unless you give me a good reason why he is not a *suitable person*, I have every intention of associating with him as much as I please. I am going to be his guest—to oblige you—after all.' She glared at his unresponsive face, then remembered another grievance. 'And what do you mean, *you of all people*?'

'I thought you were past the simpering débutante stage—'

'Too old, you mean? A spinster?' Elinor enquired, her voice dangerously quiet. 'I should not enjoy conversing with an attractive and charming man? In effect, I would be making a fool of myself and would appear to be angling for his attention?'

'Damn it!' Theo's hands were on his hips, his expression a mixture of frustration and anger.

'And do not swear at me, if you please,' Elinor said, with the deplorable intention of infuriating him further. 'I am certain Count Leon would not do so, however annoyed he might be,' she added sanctimoniously, throwing oil on the flames.

'But he would do this,' Theo snapped, taking her by the shoulders and kissing her, his mouth hard, hot and angry on hers.

Chapter Six

As first kisses went, it was a lamentable disappointment.

Elinor bit Theo's tongue which was, to her alarm, between her lips, stamped on his instep and fisted her right hand in his hair, giving it a violent tug. 'And if Count Leon did assault me in that manner, that is what I would do!' she spat, wrenching herself free to stride to the door and throw it open.

She was out on to the quiet street before he could reach her. The door banged back against the frame and she took three strides away from it, shaking with humiliated shock. Two small children playing on a doorstep with a puppy looked up at the noise, a woman leaning out of a window to shake a rug stopped flapping it for a moment to stare and the rider on the raking bay horse walking down the middle of the street reined in as the animal tossed its head and snorted.

'*Excusez-moi,*' Elinor apologised, struggling to find her French, blinking against the light. The bright sun was the reason her eyes were blurry with unshed tears, of course. That, or anger.

'It is nothing.' The rider spoke with a heavy accent. It took Elinor a moment to realise that she had been identified as English, which was disconcerting, and that the speaker was a woman, not French, and was riding astride. Riding astride, moreover, in a skirt just like the one Theo had sketched.

She was not paying Elinor any further attention. *'Teó, mi amor.'* She smiled over Elinor's head. *Spanish?* It was not one of Elinor's languages, but she could work it out from Latin.

'Ana.' He sounded less than delighted to see her, but Elinor could not bring herself to turn round and look at him. Not yet. Possibly being addressed as *my love* by one woman, in front of another who has just bitten and kicked you when you kissed her, was enough to strain any man's temper. Well, hers was most uncertain also, just at this moment. 'What the devil are you doing here?'

'Following you, Teó, all the way from Picardie. You did not make it easy. You have sold the object back to the new count?'

'I have not got it, and if I had, it is not, as you very well know, mine to sell.' They were talking in riddles, but this must have something to do with Theo's secretive behaviour and his wish to stay at the Chateau de Beaumartin. Elinor kept her eyes on the woman. 'You are telling me *you* do not have it?'

'But, no, I do not! You thought I had? This is enchanting.' She laughed, a throaty chuckle. Elinor's fingers curled into her palms. 'So someone has taken it from you, my poor Teó. By force, one assumes? Were you hurt, *mi amor*?'

'My skull is thick and has recovered. I thank you for your concern.' His cold voice sounded anything but grateful.

'Do, please, introduce me, Theo,' Elinor asked, flicking a glance over her shoulder and managing to sound as though they had all just met in Green Park.

'Yes, please do.' The other woman smiled, plainly relishing the awkwardness of the situation. Elinor moved slightly so the sun was no longer behind the horse and she could see her more plainly. Tall, whip-cord slim, with honey-gold hair coiled elegantly under a broad-brimmed hat. And older than she, older than Theo. Thirty-five? More? She found she was shocked, which was ridiculous.

Men took lovers and wives ten years their junior—why should women not have younger lovers?

'Marquesa, may I introduce my cousin, Miss Ravenhurst. Elinor, this is the Marquesa Ana de Cordovilla.'

'Marquesa.' Although it seemed bizarre in the middle of a dusty French village street, Elinor produced a curtsy fit for the wife of an English marquis, which she assumed was correct. The Marquesa inclined her head graciously.

'Charming. A family party, in effect.'

'You have just missed my mother, Lady James Ravenhurst,' Elinor said politely. She was damned if she was going to be goaded into discourtesy, although she rather thought that by introducing her as his cousin, Theo had surprised the Marquesa. Doubtless she had thought she was embarrassing him in front of a new lover. 'We are staying in Vezelay.' After a moment she added, 'With our household.' The fact that the household consisted of one maid was neither here nor there. This woman appeared, shockingly, to be travelling quite alone.

The comment did not provoke her into any form of explanation; she was obviously far too self-assured for that. 'And where are you staying, Teó?'

'Why, in Vezelay, with my aunt,' he lied easily. 'In fact, we must be getting back as Elinor's dressmaker does not seem to be at home.' He took Elinor's arm. For a moment she tensed, unsettled by his touch, which sent strange ripples of sensation down her arm. She wanted to free herself, then thought better of it. 'And you, Ana?'

'Why, at Beaumartin, of course.'

'You have been invited, too?' Elinor said, then caught herself up before she could blurt out anything more.

'Not yet.' The Marquesa produced that throaty chuckle again. 'But I will be. I have letters of introduction. So, we will meet again.' She looked down at Elinor. 'And you will be another relative

of Lord Sebastian Ravenhurst, of course. Such an *interesting* man.'
She touched her spurs to her horse's flanks. *'Hasta luego.'*

'Well!' Momentarily distracted from her own preoccupations,
Elinor watched the horse and rider vanish round the bend. 'Do you
think she and Sebastian—'

'Probably. He had a…lively life before he met Eva. She never
mentioned him when we were—I mean, she has never mentioned
him before.'

'She is a good ten years older than you.' Elinor tried to sort out
her emotions—anger over that kiss, curiosity about the Marquesa,
her need to find out exactly what Theo was up to. She could hardly
remonstrate over the kiss, not in the middle of the village street,
but somehow that woman was tangled up with the way she felt
about it: shaken, angry and very confused.

'So?' He raised one eyebrow.

'It's disgusting!'

'Nonsense.' He appeared amused by her reaction, not shamed
as she had expected. 'What a little prude you are, Elinor.'

'I am not.' Did he also think her a prude because she would not
let him kiss her like that? If that was prudish, then the cap fitted
indeed. He was strolling towards the stable and she followed. 'But
you said she was dangerous, did you not? And she appears to have
been Sebastian's lover once, and she is mixed up with whatever is
going on between you and the Count.' He pulled out the gig and
began to harness the horse, his movements practised and economi-
cal. The stable smells of straw and hay and warm horse were oddly
soothing. 'You cannot tell me you loved her?' she asked.

'*Love* is not why one has affairs, Elinor.'

'So it was just sex, then?'

'Elinor!'

'You cannot accuse me of being a prude and then come all over
mealy-mouthed yourself.'

He gave a snort of amusement. 'Let us just say that it was an exciting experience. You have heard about female spiders who eat their mates? One does not remain the lady's lover for long, not if one has any sense.' He backed the horse into the shafts, fastened the traces and led it out. 'Come on. We need to talk.'

'Indeed we do. About all sorts of things,' she added crossly to the broad shoulders in front of her. It was not until she was sitting next to Theo that it occurred to Elinor that she should be having the vapours and refusing to have anything more to do with him.

She wondered if she had been to blame for him kissing her. Had he sensed the way she had looked at him, fooling herself into believing it was simply aesthetic appreciation of his long, fit body? Surely not? Surely they had just been friends and now... Now they weren't. Obviously she was completely lacking in sensibility, because all she wanted to do was understand. Understand why he had kissed her, why it had been so horrid and disappointing and why, despite that, she felt so disturbingly, pleasantly, confused inside.

Damn, damn, double—no, make that triple damn. Theo let the horse find its own way. Beside him Elinor was almost radiating emotion. The trouble was, he was not certain he could read it. She must be furious with him about that kiss. Upset as well—she was a virgin, he reminded himself, rubbing salt in the wounds. But he was not ready to discuss that kiss yet—not until he worked out why he had done it. On the other hand, that left very little else to safely talk about. The fact that he had lost his temper and kissed her was like having an elephant in the gig with them—it somewhat dominated both their thoughts.

There was a flush on Elinor's cheeks and her lower lip looked swollen. *Hell, did I do that?* Probably. He had kissed her with temper, not gentleness, for God knows what reason other than that to see her responding to the count was more than he could stand.

And it was not, he admitted to himself with painful honesty, simply because he did not trust de Beaumartin. His bluestocking Cousin Elinor was getting under his skin in a way he did not recognise and was very sure he did not like. It was not lust, exactly. He knew what that felt like perfectly well. This was different.

He shot her another glance, less obviously this time. She was sitting, apparently composed, but with a faint frown line between her brows. Then it came to him, like a blow to the solar plexus: that had probably been her first kiss.

It was not that she had retired to sit on the shelf and be a comfort to her mother because after three lively Seasons she had failed to secure an offer. No, Elinor had never come out, not in the way his sisters had, with parties and all the expectation that they would secure husbands. The whole extended Ravenhurst clan appeared to accept from the start the fact that 'poor dear Elinor' with her red hair and her freckles, her alarming scholarship and intelligence and her inability to pretend she was a brainless butterfly, was destined for spinsterhood amidst the dusty splendour of her mother's library. Had any man so much as flirted with her before?

'I should not have kissed you,' he said abruptly as they came into the square that sat on the saddle of land a third of the way up the Vezelay hill.

'No,' she said quietly. Out of the corner of his eye he could see that her hands were knotted in her lap, but her face was composed. Was she so used to swallowing insult and neglect then?

'Not like that,' Theo pushed on in the face of her lack of response. 'I was angry with him, and frustrated by not being able to see my way through this problem I have concerning him.' He reined in. From the far side of the square Hythe got up from the wine shop under the lime trees and begin to walk across. 'That is not an excuse, you understand.'

'No,' she agreed again, her voice colourless as she began to gather up her skirts in one hand so she could climb down.

On an impulse Theo shook the reins and the horse moved forwards. He waved Hythe away and they continued across the square and down the hill on the other side. The road turned as it went, so they were out of view of the houses almost immediately, passing between small trees and bushes, the farmland opening out in front of them. Theo turned the gig into a wide, flat opening that must once have been a small quarry, reined in and wrapped the reins around the whip in its stand.

They were in a small green amphitheatre, quite alone. A skylark was singing overhead. Beside him Elinor sat silent; at least she was not scrambling down in alarm to escape him.

'Had you ever been kissed before?' Theo asked abruptly, a way of asking tactfully escaping him.

'No, I have not. And if that is a sample of what to expect, I am not sorry.' The tartness in her voice made him smile, despite his guilty conscience. Elinor was not about to succumb to maidenly hysterics. He rather wished she would, he could deal with those.

'It was an extraordinarily inept performance on my part,' he apologised. 'I would like to believe I usually do better than that.' She was silent, but he could almost hear her mind working. 'Shall we get down and talk? You aren't in a hurry to get back, are you?' *That might have been better put, you idiot.*

'This is a lovely spot.' Elinor jumped down without waiting for him—or commenting that she was quite naturally anxious to get out of his company and into her mother's protection as soon as possible—and went to sit on a grassy bank spangled with daisies. She wrapped her arms round her knees defensively and watched him as he walked across to stand before her. 'I *think* I understand. You really wanted to box my ears, didn't you Theo?'

'Yes, I wanted to box your ears. But I also wanted to kiss you.' He dug deep for complete honesty. 'I wanted to do both because I did not want *him* kissing you. Does that make any sense?'

'Dog in the manger?' Elinor suggested, untying her bonnet and dropping it on the grass beside her. She tipped back her head and watched him, her expression open and candid and curious. She seemed strangely relieved by that explanation.

'In a way. It was territorial, certainly. I'm afraid men do tend to react that way when women are involved. If you were my sister I could stand over you and frighten off any man showing an interest. But—'

'I am not your sister and so other…instincts come into play?' She was interested, he realised, intellectually interested in how he and de Beaumartin were interacting. 'And I was not meekly doing what you wanted, so you did the male equivalent of stamping your foot.' And now she was laughing at him; he could see it in her eyes despite the puzzlement on her face.

'How very unflattering, the strong light you hold up to my primitive thought processes,' Theo said wryly. He shouldn't be feeling better, but he was. Her very lack of feminine wiles was refreshing.

'So, we have come here so you can apologise, or so you can show me what a proper kiss is like?' Elinor enquired, taking him aback.

'Would you like me to?' he asked, looking down at her, his hat in his hands.

'I thought you would never ask,' she said with such startling frankness that he burst out laughing. 'I am dying of curiosity now. And stop laughing—I am sure you can't do it properly if you are laughing.'

'Oh, yes, I can.' He set his tall hat on the grass and dropped down to sit beside her, stripping off his gloves. 'But laughing while kissing is an advanced lesson.'

The pupils of her eyes were wide and dark as she watched him, but she did not seem apprehensive. Theo cupped her shoulders with his hands, feeling the fine bones through the cloth, conscious, as he had not been in his anger, of her warmth and the faint, innocent, scent of soap. He wanted to kiss her very much, he realised, pulling her towards him as he bent his head and found her lips, careful, aware that they would be tender.

Elinor came against him with no resistance, her hands clasping his elbows as if to steady herself. He let their own weight carry them down until she was lying on the turf, eyes closed, mouth still pliant under his. The curves of her body were distracting, sending his own body messages he had no intention of listening to. Theo moved, careful not to let her become aware of his instant state of arousal, and concentrated on making love to her mouth.

If Elinor had thought about kisses before, she had imagined sensation purely on the lips. A pressure, warmth, possibly distasteful moistness. This, the thing Theo was doing to her, involved her whole body and every sense, even though he was touching only her mouth and her shoulders.

Distantly she could still hear the birds, almost drowned by the hammering of her heart. Her nostrils were filled with the scents of crushed grass and warm man. Theo smelt of clean linen, of leather, faintly, and not unpleasantly, of hot man and subtly of something she could only guess must be his own, indefinable scent.

His mouth was certainly moist. She had not expected to find that exciting, nor had she expected the heat and the way his lips moved gently over hers, caressing them. Then she felt his tongue running along the seam of her lips, pressing, and understood that he wanted her to open to him. Why? He was not angry with her as he had been before, when she had perceived the invasion of his tongue as an assault, not a caress.

Now the intrusion made her gasp with the sensual shock, the sound swallowed up as his tongue probed, found her own, caressed the sensitive flesh. Then he was sucking, nibbling, at her lower lip and the gasps became moans and she found her body was arching, shockingly, against the weight of his chest as he hung, poised, over her.

And then he had released her, was lying beside her, his weight on one elbow while he stroked the hair back from her flushed face. 'Now that, Nell,' he said with a smile that was oddly tender, 'was a *proper* kiss.'

Elinor shut her eyes hastily, unable to meet his. Not yet. From behind closed lids she tried to come to terms with her body, which, alarmingly, was not returning to normal now he had stopped. Her breasts ached, there was heat in her belly and lower. She felt restless and agitated and—

What did he call me? She opened her eyes on to the bright sunlight and pushed herself up on to her elbows. Theo's eyes were dark and heavy-lidded and suddenly she did not want to speculate about what he might be feeling.

She had asked him to kiss her out of curiosity, pure and simple, because she was never going to get the chance to be kissed again and he was, after all, just her friend and the only man she could possibly ask such a thing of. And now… Now she realised she had started something that she could not stop, for herself at least. You could not put that sort of knowledge back in the bottle and forget you did not know what a man's mouth felt like on yours, how his body felt, so intimately close. How he tasted, smelt. How *this* man felt. And there, at the back of her mind, was the nagging doubt that it had not been simply curiosity, that she had wanted him to kiss her because…

'That was very interesting.' Elinor sat up abruptly. It was essential she gave him no clue how this had affected her. If he thought she was a little idiot for naïvely asking him to kiss her, so much the better. 'I can quite see why young ladies are not supposed to do it.' She made herself look at him again and was surprised to find that he was still Theo, large and friendly and smiling at her, the dimple appearing in his chin. If she leaned forwards, she could just reach it with her lips. *No! No, this wasn't the same. He had not changed, but she had.*

'Thank you,' she added, sounding stilted to her own ears. Knowing how she felt, guessing how she must look, Elinor had a sudden recollection of a number of occasions when she had seen Cousin Bel looking just like that. *Goodness, that must have been when she was meeting Ashe!* Hastily she shut down her imagination and concentrated on smoothing her skirts.

'It was my pleasure, I'm glad you enjoyed it,' Theo said, as though she had just thanked him for carrying her easel. 'I did,' he added, making her blush.

'I said it was *interesting*,' Elinor said, speaking sharply in her anxiety least he think she would want him to do it again. 'I certainly will not allow Count Leon to do any such thing,' she added.

'I should hope not. Save all your kisses for me,' Theo teased. At least, she supposed he was teasing—they would not do this again, of course. His expression became suddenly serious. 'You now know so much about why I am here that it is probably more dangerous, for both of us, not to tell you the whole.'

Elinor caught her breath. *At last he is going to confide.* And whatever it was, however dreadful, at least it would be something she could deal with intellectually, not some emotional puzzle she could not understand.

Chapter Seven

'I told you that I make my living buying and selling antiquities.' She murmured assent, forcing her scattered wits to focus on this and not on what had just happened. 'I often work for collectors, on commission. Sometimes for a specific object, sometimes simply to keep my eyes open for whatever it is that interests them—early Italian paintings, small Roman ceramics and so forth. In the case of the late Count de Beaumartin, it was to track down the dispersed furnishings and paintings from his Paris house and the chateau.

'I had some success and gained his confidence. He hinted that he had an object of great worth he wished to sell, but it was for a specialised market. Finally I managed to tease out of him that it was a piece of seventeenth-century metalwork of a highly erotic nature. I need not go into detail—'

'For goodness' sake, Theo, you may as well. I am not going to faint away.' It was completely unladylike, but now, with her body still singing from his kiss, she was more than a little curious about what a *highly erotic* item might look like.

'Very well, don't blame me if you are shocked. Two hundred years ago the then count was highly dissolute, positively depraved in fact. He, and like-minded friends, formed a club of sorts to indulge these tastes.'

'Like the Hellfire Club,' Elinor interrupted. 'Sir Francis Dashwood. Don't look like that,' she added as Theo stared at her. 'Mama does not censor my reading and there are books on every sort of subject in the library. I think we have something on him because of the architectural interest of the temple and catacombs at West Wycombe that Dashwood built.'

'This was very much worse than Dashwood's play-acting at monks and nuns with his friends,' Theo said grimly. He did not sound even faintly titillated by the tale he was unfolding. 'Dashwood employed prostitutes, but de Beaumartin took the women he wanted by force, and the more innocent they were, the better. He died mysteriously and the rumours were that outraged local peasants, tired of their daughters being debauched, rose up and murdered him.'

Elinor felt a sudden chill. This was not amusing any more—they were talking about a seriously unpleasant man. 'A revolting person—but surely that is not why you are warning me about the present count?'

'No. The family has spent a century and a half trying to live down the association of their name with depravity. But rumours still persist, amongst them the tale that objects of great value and artistic merit were created for the fellowship to use in their rituals. The finest of them was a chalice and that was what the late count offered to sell me. He needed the money and it is not an object that could ever be shown publicly.'

'But you have seen it?'

'Yes. I saw it, drew it and went back to England to discuss it with a certain connoisseur—let us call him Lord X—who collects objects of that nature. He owns some of Dashwood's paraphernalia as well, but this far surpasses them in quality.'

'May I see the drawings?' she asked, interested in the craftsmanship more than anything else. She knew nothing about early seventeenth-century goldsmiths' work.

'Certainly not! I returned, with a very substantial amount of money and the authority to negotiate with the count. I purchased the Chalice from him at their Paris house, we exchanged receipts, I left for the coast. An hour from Dover I stopped at an inn to eat and change horses and I was attacked, knocked unconscious and the Chalice and the count's receipt stolen.'

'You have no idea by whom?' Elinor found she was leaning forwards, her fingers clasped tightly together, completely caught up in the tale.

'I thought at first it was Count Leon. He is very unhappy about the scandalous object being out of their family control. However, when I heard that his father had been found dead the next day, his head split open on the hearth, I did wonder. Would he go to such lengths to avert even the hint of scandal? But sons have killed fathers before now and it may have been an accident in the course of a quarrel.'

'So you have come back to find it?'

'I have told him I want to buy it, not revealing that I already have. He says he does not have it, that it has been stolen, but I do not know that I believe him. There were others I suspected, but they are all converging on Beaumartin. Why should they do that if they have the Chalice?'

Elinor gave an unladylike whistle. 'No wonder the atmosphere was tense. From the way you spoke to the Marquesa, is she one of the suspects?'

'She is in the same business as I am. Whether she was ever married to the Marqués de Cordovilla, or even if that gentleman existed, I have no idea. We met, acted upon a certain mutual attraction, and I can only guess she found my notebooks. So she is a possibility. She certainly has the cold-blooded determination for theft, to hit me over the head and possibly even to murder. And there are the two English collectors, man and wife, Sir Ian and Lady

Tracey, who appear to have become aware of the Chalice from a leak at Lord X's end of things. I had thought I had disposed of them neatly with a harmless trick. I would not suspect them of the violence, to be honest, but they owe me a grudge, and I cannot afford to dismiss anyone.'

'And they are attending the house party, too. Goodness.' They were silent. Elinor digesting what she had just heard while Theo picked daisies and began to pull the petals off, his expression one of brooding thought. Doubtless he had gone over and over the conundrum, all to no avail. 'I can understand why you started to become alarmed that you had involved Mama and me. Never mind, I am sure I can be a great help,' she reassured him.

'You will be no such thing,' he said hotly. 'You will be a perfect English miss.' Elinor snorted. When had she ever been one of those? 'You will pretend this is a normal houseparty and—'

'Steer clear of my host who may be a parricide, my fellow guests who may also be murderers, one of whom was your lover and the other two who are your deadly rivals?'

'Exactly.' He ran his hands through his hair. 'No. Put like that, it is clearly impossible. We must write and decline, say you have been taken ill or something. I will find some other way of searching the place.'

'I do not agree; anyway, I would have to be at death's door, otherwise Mama will simply leave me with Jeanie. She is not a clinging parent.'

'I had noticed.' Theo turned to look at Elinor, the frown even more pronounced. His indignation on her behalf gave her a twinge of pleasure. It felt strange to have a friend who defended you. 'I try to imagine my mother abandoning one of my sisters if she was ill in a foreign town, and failing.'

'Mama has even less sensibility than I.' It was too late to start feeling hurt about it. Mama, if challenged, would simply look puzzled and explain patiently that it was simple common sense and that hovering about her daughter when she felt unwell was not going to assist her recovery. One should call the doctor and get on with one's work. That was the rational approach.

The trouble was, the rational approach was beginning to feel a very cold thing to Elinor. Was that the result of one kiss? Surely not? Perhaps it was that Theo was making her see her mother, and her own situation, through his eyes. It was not a very comfortable picture.

'I want to go to Beaumartin,' she said, meeting his eyes squarely and putting all the conviction she could muster into the statement. 'Mama can be in no danger—I doubt very much if she would notice a full-scale orgy taking place when she is working—and I am forewarned. I will just keep out of the way and let you get on with your search.'

There was a long pause while he thought about it. Elinor concentrated on looking as much like a meek and biddable young lady as was possible under the circumstances. 'I am forewarned,' she repeated as the silence lengthened. 'And I know who to avoid.'

'Very well,' Theo surrendered with a frown. 'It is going to be thoroughly awkward if we pull out now. But, Elinor—you stick to Aunt Louisa and concentrate on drinking tea and drawing interesting architectural features. Absolutely nothing else. You promise?'

'I quite understand.' Elinor nodded earnestly. *And that is not a promise.*

'Then we had better be getting back. Even Aunt Louisa is going to notice that you could have tried on an entire wardrobe of clothes in this time.'

Theo got to his feet and stood looking down at her. She was aware of a moment of hesitation before he held out his hand to draw her to her feet. Against the light his body was reduced to a powerful male silhouette. Elinor placed her hand in his, conscious of the strength of the long fingers as they clasped hers, and was pulled

easily to stand in front of him. The temptation to sway towards him
and see what could happen was powerful. No, her curiosity, if that
was what it was, had got her into enough trouble already, and
Theo, she was sure, was regretting that kiss, even if she could not
bring herself to. She applied some self-control instead and stepped
briskly towards the gig.

'You did not tell me about your man, the one who carried my
things and drove the carriage.'

The big watchful figure was waiting still when they came back
into the square. 'All you need to know about Hythe,' Theo said as
he reined in, 'is that if anything happens and you can't find me,
you may trust him with your life.'

He tossed the reins to the man. 'I am going to walk Miss
Ravenhurst back. Wait for me.'

The next day they saw nothing of Theo and Elinor could only guess
what he was up to. She and Lady James worked hard at the draft
chapters on the basilica, visited three very ancient local antiquaries
and the prior and got up to date with their letter writing. With Lady
James engrossed in more academic correspondence, writing to her
siblings was left to Elinor. As she wrote, trying to make an interesting narrative of their researches and the visit to the chateau, she
wondered if everything that had passed with Theo had been a dream.

Then a little shiver ran down her spine and that pooling heat deep
in her belly reminded her that, yes, she had been kissed and held
in those strong arms. And if truth be told, she wished very much
it would happen again. She sat back, biting the end of her pen and
thought ruefully that the legend about Pandora and her box was
something she should have attended to.

On Friday morning a local lad brought a note from Madame
Dubois telling her that her clothes were ready for the first fitting.

'Is there a horse and gig to be hired in the town?' she asked the boy. 'A very quiet horse?'

'*Mais oui, mademoiselle.*' He nodded earnestly. 'Jean le Grand down in the square has a livery stable, he will have something for *mademoiselle*. He is not busy just now, I know, for I help him. Shall I run down and ask him to make one ready?'

He was hoping for a tip from both ends, Elinor guessed, smiling at the slightly grubby face upturned to hers. 'I will come down now. You run ahead and talk to Monsieur le Grand for me. A quiet horse, remember!' she called after him as he took to his heels.

'Mama, I am going down to the dressmaker. I expect I will be back later this afternoon—there are all the gowns to try on.' And she might meet Theo and have luncheon at the inn. Or walk by the river again. And try to pretend that kiss never happened.

'You are walking?' Lady James looked up from her work.

'No, driving, Mama.'

'Good.' The rigidly coiffed grey head bent over the table again. *She hasn't even remembered I cannot drive,* Elinor thought, snatching up her hat. She hesitated over her bulging satchel, wondering if she should take just her reticule, then lifted it and slung it over her shoulder. There might be an opportunity for some sketching.

The lad, whose name, he informed her, was Pierre, had been as good as his word and the stable owner was standing in the square, holding the head of a placid-looking grey mare harnessed to an equally elderly gig. 'As quiet as you could wish, *mademoiselle*,' he assured Elinor, helping her up. 'She will give you no trouble.'

'Thank you.' She leaned down and handed the lad a coin and he doffed his cap, informing her that he, above all the other boys, was at her service for any errand. The reins felt stiff and awkward in her hand, and she did not risk trying to hold the whip as well. 'Walk on!'

The mare pricked her ears and set of at a reassuringly steady pace. Elinor took a deep breath and tried to look as though this was not the first time she had ever driven a carriage all by herself.

By the time they had reached St Père her back was aching and her arms were weary, but the little mare had been as good as gold and she felt sure she could drive back after a rest. 'Good girl!'

Stretching, she led the mare into the lean-to stable and found the gig and Theo's horse. He was here. With a smile of anticipation she tied up the mare, pulled some hay into the manger in front of her and lugged over a water bucket before lifting down the satchel and going to the shop.

The door was ajar, so she tapped and pushed it open. Garments in fabrics she recognised lay on the work table, white basting stitches all over them and the hems raw. A tape measure and a big pincushion were on top and the stool was overturned.

'Madame?' No answer. Puzzled, Elinor righted the stool and wondered if she should sit down and wait here, or go outside and watch for the dressmaker.

There was a thump from overhead, the sound of something heavy landing on the boards, a man's voice muffled and then abruptly cut off. She could make none of it out clearly, but it sounded like violence. *Theo?*

She might be making a complete fool of herself, but she was not going to risk ignoring it. Elinor delved in her satchel and came out with two objects that she eyed with some misgiving. She untied her bonnet and set it on the table and kicked off her shoes. There was another thud from upstairs. Cautious on the old boards, the pulse pounding in her throat, she began to climb the winding stair in the far corner.

It emerged on to a dark landing, lit only by a small window at the far end. The door leading to the room over the shop was ajar. She hesitated, wondering if she was imagining things. Then a voice that she realised after a moment was Theo's said, 'How many times must I tell you? I haven't got the damned thing, and I haven't got the money either.' It sounded odd, as though he was speaking with no air in his lungs.

'His lordship isn't going to like that,' said another voice, also speaking English, closer to the door and much clearer. It was a man and he sounded profoundly unimpressed by what he was hearing. 'His lordship is going to be very unhappy indeed.'

'I gathered tha—' Theo's voice was cut off in a grunt. The sound of the blow made Elinor flinch. The silence that followed was broken only by Theo's gasping breaths. 'I am trying to find out who took—' This time she heard a body hit the floor and the sound of retching. Her stomach churned. *Theo.*

'If anyone did take it.'

There had to be two of them, the one who was hitting and the one who was talking. And Theo was not going to stand around to be hit without fighting back, so at least one of them must have a firearm. Elinor swallowed hard and edged the door open, then slid through the gap.

One man was standing with his back to her, a shotgun in his hands, blocking her view into the room. He was about Theo's height and build with strands of greasy black hair slicked over a bald head. His companion she could just glimpse, a great bruiser of a man, his attention on something at his feet. She had to duck down to see Theo lying on the floor, his body curled up protectively as the man drew back his booted foot to kick. There was a great deal of blood on the boards, on Theo's shirt, on what she could see of his hands raised in front of his face.

Anger washed through her, driving away her fear and the shock of the violence. Elinor gripped the object in her right hand and pressed it firmly into the small of the bald man's back, right into his spine. 'Tell him to stop. Now.' She could feel her voice shake and steadied her diaphragm as though she were singing to try to stop it.

'What!' The man half-swung round and she jabbed harder, nauseated by the stink of sweat, blood and violence emanating from him.

'Stand still. This is a pistol, it is loaded and I am holding it at half-cock. My thumb is not very strong; I suggest you do not make me lose my grip.'

'It's only some gentry mort,' the other man said, his attention distracted from Theo for a moment. 'Where would she get a pop from? Just a bluff—you get her, Bill, and we'll have some fun with her. That'll make him talk.' Theo moved convulsively and was kicked in the head.

'It is no bluff, and neither is this.' Trying not to think about what was happening to Theo, Elinor lifted her left hand and pushed the point of the old kitchen knife she kept in her satchel for sharpening pencils against the man's throat. 'Put down the gun carefully and tell your bully boy to step away from him.'

'That's a chive right enough, Bill,' the big man conceded.

'I know it is, you jolterhead. It's my throat the silly girl is sticking it into.' The bald man bent his knees slowly and Elinor followed him down as he laid the gun on the floor. She put out a foot and kicked it across to Theo, praying he was conscious.

'Theo!' He stirred and looked up, his face a mask of blood. 'The shotgun.' He pushed himself up with one arm and reached for it with the other and then all hell broke loose.

The man in front of her turned so fast that she lost her footing. The pistol in her hand went off, the explosion deafening her, and spun away into a corner of the room. Elinor felt herself falling and struck out with the knife, found flesh without knowing what she had hit, then was knocked away with a backhanded blow to her jaw.

The big man was roaring, the words meaning nothing, then there was sudden, shocking, silence. 'If she is hurt, you are dead,' Theo said in a voice she hardly recognised and Elinor opened her eyes to see him leaning against the wall, the shotgun in his hands and the two men huddled together in the opposite corner. 'Nell?'

'I'm fine,' she said firmly, managing to stand up, dizzy with her ringing ears. It was true, you did see stars…

'Come round here, don't get between me and them. My satchel is on the bed—take out some of those leather laces. You two, turn around.' He waited until they obeyed him before he moved, and as he began to walk towards them Elinor realised why: he could hardly stand. 'Kneel down, hands behind you.'

They went down on their knees and she approached cautiously from the side, looped the leather around first one and then the other, pulling it as tight as she could, making herself concentrate on the knots.

'Guv'nor?'

The voice from below had her spinning round in alarm, but Theo called out, 'Jake!' as feet pounded up the stairs.

'Oh hell.' Hythe burst through the door and stopped at the sight of Theo, then saw Elinor, 'Saving your presence, ma'am. Who are these two?'

'His lordship's men. I have not been able to convince them that I have neither the object nor the money.'

'Yeah, they look a bit thick. What'll we do with them, then? Nice deep river out there.'

'Go and get the carriage. You can drive them over to our friend in Avallon—I'm sure he'll keep them snug for a week or two.'

'Yeah.' A broad grin spread over Hythe's face. 'I'll do that thing—the carriage is outside, I haven't taken the team out of harness yet. You all right, guv'nor?'

'Fine. You know what head wounds are like for blood. Nothing we can't take care of.'

Elinor wrestled the shotgun out of his hands and gave it to Hythe, then followed the man down the stairs, pistol in hand, until she was sure he had the two helpless in the back of the carriage. 'One of them's bleeding, I got him in the arm.'

'He'll live, miss.'

'It is Mr Ravenhurst's carpet I am worried about,' she retorted, earning herself a broad grin and a wave of the hand as he whipped the horses up.

When she got back upstairs Theo was still leaning back against the wall, apparently keeping himself upright by sheer willpower. 'Lie down this instant!' Something inside her seemed to clutch at her heart, something primitive and fundamental. Something to do with the fact that here was her…her friend and he was hurt and he was brave and he was very, very male and she wanted…

'Come here.' He waited until they were toe to toe, then focused painfully on her. One eye was cut across the brow and almost closed, the other caked in blood. 'Are you all right, Nell?'

'Perfectly. It was a glancing blow, he caught me off balance. Now you—' he was not going to be sensible, so she had to be. *Think, Elinor. Bandages, a doctor, should I give him brandy? No, that is bad for head injuries…*

'Oh God, Elinor. They could have ra— killed you.' *Thank God.* He had her in his arms and was kissing her with a sort of desperation before she could get any of her sensible words out. The desperation of his kiss echoed the way she felt, the wave of emotion that had run through her when she had seen him on the floor, battered, in pain and yet defiant. It was shocking that they should be clasped in each other's arms like this, but nothing else could express what she felt.

Hazily Elinor was aware that they were holding each other up, and then they were not and she was tumbling on to the bed to end up sprawled on Theo's chest.

'Theo!' Then she found his mouth and was kissing him back. It was clumsy, instinctive and the smell of blood and sweat was making her dizzy, but the heat of his mouth under hers and the thud of his heart against her breast told her that they were both alive, both so thankful to be alive. *Mine,* that echo in her mind said. *Mine...*

Chapter Eight

Theo's head fell back on to the pillows and Elinor stared down at him, realising how battered he was, realising she should be tending his wounds, not behaving in an utterly wanton manner with a man who was barely conscious. Just because she felt like this about him did not mean he wanted her throwing herself at his injured, battered body.

'God, Nell, where the hell did you get that pistol? I thought you were bluffing when I heard you.'

'Mama and I carry one each. Mama says one can never rely on having a man to hand when one needs one, so we must be self-reliant.' *Mama had obviously never met this man in a crisis!*

'I can hear her saying it.' He closed his eyes. 'Have you ever fired it?'

'No.' Elinor swallowed. 'But I would have done if they hadn't stopped hitting you.' She slid off his body and got, somehow, to her feet. 'Now, you stay there—' he gave an amused snort, apparently at the thought of doing anything else '—while I find some water and bandages.'

Where was Madame Dubois? Elinor called out her name as she opened the door at the back of the shop and found herself in a kitchen. There was no response. She filled a basin with cold water and carried it back. Over one end of the work table was a clean sheet, apparently used for covering sewing in progress. Elinor put it over her shoulder, hooked her finger through the handle of the cutting shears and went back upstairs.

Theo was sitting on the edge of the bed. He had pulled the shirt off over his head and was dabbing with the stained cloth at the cut over his eye. His torso was streaked with blood and covered in reddening marks that were obviously about to become bruises.

'Are you hurt below the waist anywhere?' she asked briskly to cover the fact that she wanted to put down the basin and weep. She never cried. *Never.* 'He didn't kick you in the kidneys or anything?' Could she touch him? Dare she? She wanted to, so much. But that was self-indulgence. It would do him no good, it would satisfy only that jumbled mass of emotions she did not properly understand. He was her *friend* and he was hurt. That was enough.

'No, I was rescued by a dragon before he got to those.' Theo looked up and dropped the shirt. 'Thank you, Nell. That was so brave.'

Now she *was* going to cry. Elinor bit her lip until she recovered her composure. 'I could hardly leave you, could I?' she demanded. 'And why are you calling me Nell?' She knelt down and began to cut up the sheet. 'Let me see your eyes.'

Somehow he kept from flinching as she washed and dabbed. 'Nell suits you. Elinor wears dust-coloured gowns and bundles her hair into a net and has her nose stuck in a book all day. Nell lets her hair out and walks by the river and has fun.'

He had only started calling her Nell after he had kissed her. She did not point that out; she didn't know what it meant. She made him bend his head so she could search through the thick red hair for any cuts on his scalp, running her fingertips carefully through the springing mass, trying not to think about how sensual it felt. There were some vicious lumps, but the skin was not broken.

Obedient to the pressure of her hands, he bent further and she found herself staring down at the nape of his neck, the tendons supporting the skull, the recent scar that must be the result of the last attack when he had lost the Chalice. Her fingers hovered over it, a fraction of an inch from the skin, then she snatched them back, her breathing quickening.

Theo reached for a piece of cloth, wet it and began to clean the blood off his chest. 'Less dramatic than it looks,' he said lightly. 'Most of that blood's from the cut over my eye. I'll be fine in a minute.'

'Yes, of course you will,' she agreed to keep him quiet, dipping another piece and beginning to work on his back. She had heard those muffled blows that must have landed solidly in his stomach. 'There, no cuts on your back.'

Theo straightened cautiously and she put one hand on the bands of muscle just above the waistband of his breeches and pressed. He drew a sharp breath as though she had stuck in a knife.

'I thought so. Fine, indeed! Lie down.'

'I *am* fine.' She shifted her hand to his chest and pushed. He resisted and she saw his lips tighten as the abused muscles were forced to work to counter her lesser strength.

'Liar.' He met her eyes and shook his head. 'Theo, if you do not lie down and rest, I am going to fetch Mama. I mean it—I cannot think of any other threat you might pay attention to.'

It worked; he lay down and smiled at her, turning her insides to jelly. 'That's the trouble with an intelligent woman—you know how to terrify a man.' There was a moment's silence while they looked at each other. Was he going to say anything about that kiss just now?

No, of course not. She was an *intelligent woman*, a *dragon* who just happened to have become over-emotional for a moment. Theo would dismiss those crowded moments, when he had kissed her with fervour and she had returned the embrace with just as much passion, as due to shock, relief, thankfulness they were both safe.

She acknowledged the truth of all of those emotions. But there had been something more, something she sensed but did not understand.

'Take your breeches off and get into bed.'

'Not with you in the room! And don't try to threaten me with Aunt Louisa again—I'm even less likely to undress in front of her. You go and ask Madame for some coffee. Where is she?'

'I don't know. She sent me a note to say she was ready for my fitting, that's why I'm here. You don't think they hurt her?'

Theo tried to sit up and she pushed him down again ruthlessly. 'I'll go and look—and you get into bed.'

It took ten minutes, but eventually Elinor found the dressmaker in the woodshed, tied and gagged, furious but unharmed. She freed her and helped her back to the kitchen, explaining that Theo had been attacked by two men who thought he was carrying a considerable sum of money.

'*Cochons!*' Madame spat out. '*Monsieur* is unhurt?'

'No. He is somewhat battered, I am afraid; fortunately, his man arrived and is taking the miscreants to the authorities.' Elinor skated as lightly as she could past her own part in all this. 'May I make us some coffee?'

'I will make it. You go and make sure he is all right and I will bring it up. Then we fit your gowns.'

'But, *madame*, after the experience you have had—'

'You think I allow these creatures to interfere with my business? Huh!'

Sunday morning found Elinor filing papers and her mother collating notes. Elinor suspected that the absence of a Protestant church for miles was no hardship for her mother, whose views on religion were somewhat relaxed. She enjoyed listening to a good sermon, largely to engage afterwards in vigorous debate with the clergyman, but otherwise seemed inclined to call upon the support of Greek gods in an emergency. Elinor had become used to quietly reading her prayer book to herself if no Anglican congregation was within reach and then treating Sunday as if it were any other day.

But they rarely had callers on a Sunday. Even fewer who caused Jeanie to scream and drop the tray of dishes she'd been balancing on one hand as she opened the door.

After Friday's drama, Elinor was prepared for anything. She had the paperknife in her hand as she ran out into the hallway to find Jeanie scrabbling amidst the potsherds and Theo, his face sporting dramatically black, blue and purple bruising, attempting to reassure her.

'Cousin Theo, good morning.' Somehow she got her breathing under control. It was doubtful the girl heard anything other than irritation in her tone. 'Jeanie, fetch a brush and a bucket and clear this up and stop crying, then bring coffee to the front parlour. Mama is in the back room, I am sure she would like a cup, too.'

She led the way, smiling brightly until Theo closed the door. 'What in Heaven's name are you doing?' she scolded. It was easier to rant at him like a fishwife than to do what she wanted, which was to kiss those bruises better—or turn and flee. She was not sure which. 'You should be in bed. I told Mama you had fallen down some stairs; she assumes you must have been drunk at the time. I did not disabuse her of that opinion.'

'You didn't come to look after me,' he said with an unconvincing attempt to sound pathetic. 'So I had to get up.'

'*Madame* has been looking after you very well, I make no doubt. It would have been highly improper of me to visit you in your bedchamber.'

Theo attempted to raise one brow quizzically, winced and grimaced. He did not have to say it. What they had been doing last Friday in that very room was beyond improper. No wonder he seemed so uncomfortable. How could he look on her as his friend if this kept happening? 'Why are you brandishing that knife?'

Elinor realised she was gesticulating with the paperknife and put it down. 'Jeanie screamed. For all I knew it could have been more of Lord X's henchmen. I do wish you would tell me who he is.'

'So when you get back to England you can go and tell him off? I think not.'

As that was exactly what she had been brooding darkly about doing before he arrived, there was really no answer to that. She studied the man in front of her critically. Leaving aside his face, which completely justified Jeanie's screams, he was moving more easily than she could have believed possible. Her hands tingled with the desire to run them over his chest again. It had felt so good. So hard and smooth and deeply disturbing. Did that make her wanton? Or merely a very inexperienced virgin in intimate contact with an attractive man for the first time? The latter no doubt, as it was certainly the least interesting option.

'He deserves horsewhipping,' she said, 'but I will leave that to you. Theo—how are you?' She felt her voice wobble and controlled it. 'Truthfully?'

'Truthfully?' Neither of them had taken a seat. Now he walked forwards until he was standing in front of her, took her right hand and laid it against his midriff. Elinor caught her breath and made herself stay passive as one fingertip slid between the buttons and touched flesh. Reprehensibly she left it there. 'Sore. You want me to be even more frank? I was humiliated that I had to be rescued by a woman—'

'He had a shotgun! What could you possibly have done against that?'

'Let me finish,' he said mildly. 'My first reaction, when I got over being thankful we were both alive and more or less in one piece, was to feel humiliated. My next was to be angry with myself for that thought—I would not have been shamed to have been rescued by Hythe, just profoundly grateful. That was what I was hanging on to, the hope he would be back soon from the blacksmith's.

'Hythe would have barrelled into that room, yelling his head off, fists flying. Someone would probably have got killed. You used courage and cunning and we're all alive. I'm just very thankful that you are on my side. You *are* on my side, aren't you, Nell?' he added, his voice dropping into an intimate, husky whisper.

Elinor looked down. He had taken her hand in his, her fingers feeling very small within the strong grip. She swallowed. What did he mean? What did he want? What did she want, come to that? She had been perfectly content until Theo had come into her life and now everything was a jumble: her mind, her emotions, her body.

'Of course I am. I am your friend. We Ravenhursts stick together, don't we?' *The safe answer. Pretend there is no ambiguity, pretend I understand what is happening here.*

'Your sense of family duty is strong.' He lifted his hand, apparently studying the tips of her rather inky fingers.

'Not particularly,' she admitted. 'Only for the relatives I like.' The silence seemed to stretch on. 'Why are you here, Theo?'

'Because this morning, when my head finally stopped aching, it occurred to me that if Lord X has sent any more—minions, was it?'

'Henchmen,' Elinor supplied.

'What *do* you read? Sensation novels? I'm shocked. Henchmen, then. You are staying here quite openly using our own name and I should be taking better care of you.'

'I don't think he would have. Sent any more, I mean.' She freed her hand and went to perch on the edge of the big chestnut wood table. His close proximity was too confusing. 'Two would seem adequate and they'd have to find you and report back. If I were he, I would not be concerned about not hearing from them. Not yet.' Theo nodded and leaned against the window frame, his eyes on the street outside.

'You don't think—?' she began, then broke off, shaking her

head. 'I did wonder if he had had it stolen himself, but there would be no advantage, would there? He might have had the count murdered to get back the money, but you were bringing him the Chalice.'

'You are talking about a highly respected member of the peerage.' Theo sounded amused by her speculation.

'The man's a pornographer.'

'A collector of erotic art,' Theo corrected her. 'When it costs that much money, it is art, believe me.'

'Anyway, by tomorrow we'll all be safely inside the chateau.'

'Oh, yes, all the suspects in a murder case tucked up within nice thick walls with the portcullis down. Your idea of *safe*, Nell, is unique.'

The door opened on Jeanie with the tray, Lady James at her heels. 'Theophilus, I am appalled. What your poor mother would say if she could see you now I shudder to think. Let that be a lesson to you to foreswear strong drink.'

'Good morning.' Theo took the onslaught with admirable calm. 'Thank you for your concern, Aunt Louisa. I am not in any great pain now.'

'Huh! You should be suffering from a hangover, if nothing else. Why are you here, other than to alarm Jeanie and cause her to break the china?'

'To offer you my escort to morning service, naturally, Aunt.'

'I do not chose to attend the Roman rite, I thank you, Theophilus. However, it shows more sensitive feeling in you to have offered than I would have expected.'

'I also brought a copy of a plan of the chateau, which I thought might be of interest to study before we arrive.' He removed a package from his satchel and handed it to Elinor. 'How accurate it is I do not know, it appears to date from the middle of the last century. I found it in a bookseller's in Avallon.'

'I will make a copy.' Elinor spread it open on the table. 'I am sure Mama would like to have one to make notes on.' If they had several copies she and Theo could mark each chamber and passage as they searched it—once she had persuaded him to let her help, that was. It showed the chateau from cellars to roof, floor by floor, each part numbered in a crabbed hand. Down the edge, in the same hand, ran the key.

Theo came to stand close beside her while she ran her forefinger down the list, squinting to try to decipher the writing. 'Looking for a chamber marked *orgies*?' he murmured.

'There might be some clue,' she whispered back, refusing to rise to his satirical tone. 'The group must have called themselves something, and this is an old plan. With a key apparently written by a drunken spider,' she added, depressed.

'I will leave it with you,' Theo said. 'Until tomorrow, Aunt.'

One did not have first cousins who included a duke and an earl, an uncle who was a bishop and numerous titled relations by marriage, without having stayed in many fine and historic mansions. But this was the first time Elinor had ever found herself in a castle complete with battlements and turrets, and, according to the plan, dungeons as well.

She rested her elbows on the sill of the window in her allotted bedchamber and looked out. Below her the hillside sloped down through parkland, into fields and ended at the river, out of sight behind its fringe of trees. The shadows were lengthening now, the long summer dusk making the valley mysterious and tranquil.

On either side of her window the wings of the chateau stretched away. It seemed to have grown over the centuries without any coherent plan, each count adding and adapting to suit his needs. She and her mother were in rooms that dated from the seventeenth century, with fine panelling and great chestnut beams overhead. From the window she could see the medieval part with its turrets to her right and the incongruous eighteenth-century wing to her left, overlooking the formal gardens.

Lady James had a room next door and Theo was opposite. Where the marquesa was lodged, she had no idea. Doubtless she had secured a chamber close to Theo, Elinor thought, fighting a losing battle trying not to think about Theo's relationship with the woman.

It was none of her business and she shouldn't be thinking about such things in any case—the love life of an adult male was a highly unsuitable subject for speculation by an unmarried lady. But this was Theo, and he had kissed her, and now her overactive imagination was visualising him kissing the marquesa. Only she, of course, knew exactly what she was about and he would enjoy it very much indeed and—

'And nothing.' Elinor pushed herself upright and stalked into the room. He had kissed her for a number of reasons, none of which had anything to do with why a respectable young lady should wish to be kissed by a man. And Theo was her friend and should not be the focus for her romantic daydreams. If *romantic* was quite the word to describe the odd, shivery, yearning feeling that kept washing over her when she thought about touching Theo. Or Theo touching her. And it was more than touching, more than the vague and disturbing things that haunted her dreams. She wanted to be close to him with her mind as well as her body.

The only thoughts she should be having about her cousin were schemes to involve herself in his quest to find the Beaumartin Chalice, and that was likely to be difficult enough to banish all other considerations from her mind. Elinor smoothed down the skirts of her new evening dress and went next door to see if her mother was ready to go down.

The door diagonally across from hers opened at the same time. Of course, the marquesa had managed to secure a chamber next to Theo's. Why was she not surprised?

'Ma'am.' Elinor curtsied, realising as she did so that her punctilious behaviour was a way of subtly pointing out the other woman's seniority.

'My dear Miss Ravenhurst—Elinor, is it not?—call me Ana. We are going to be friends.'

'I am sure we are.' Elinor managed a warm smile of utter insincerity. 'I look forward to discovering what interests we have in common.'

The other woman's brows drew together sharply, then she laughed. 'Interests in common besides Teó? Indeed, yes. And I look forward to meeting your esteemed mother.' She swept off down the corridor, a tall, slender lesson in elegance, her mass of golden brown hair coiled at her nape, her severe gown emphasising her figure with every step.

'Ouch,' Elinor muttered as she opened her mother's chamber door. She had hoped to be subtle and had been neatly countered by the other woman's alarming frankness. She saw Elinor as a rival for Theo—a pitiable one, no doubt—and she was quite prepared to make that clear.

'I have just met the Marquesa de Cordovilla, another of the guests,' she remarked, wondering whether to say anything about the woman. The marquesa would go through a polite drawing room like a shark through a school of fish. Her mother might be amused. On the other hand, like a ship of war, she might simply train her powerful guns on the other woman and fire a broadside.

'Indeed? What is there in that to amuse you?' Lady James settled a handsome toque on her grey curls and nodded decisively at her reflection in the mirror. When she chose to dress up, she did it with a vengeance and usually with an ulterior motive.

'She is somewhat unconventional. And she does not like me.'

'Indeed? Why is that? It appears extreme on a fleeting encounter.'

'I met her in St Père when I was with Theo. I believe she is…attracted to him and thinks I am a rival.'

Elinor expected her mother to give a snort of amusement, probably encompassing both disbelief that any titled lady might desire her nephew and that anyone should see Elinor as competition. Instead she fixed her daughter with a disconcertingly direct look. 'One of Theophilus's past lovers?' she enquired.

'Mama!'

'Do not be namby-pamby, girl. He's a man; a lady of your age is not ignorant of these matters, she simply pretends not to see them. What is the woman doing here? Or was she invited to distract Julie from Theophilus and keep her attention on the count, for whom I assume she is intended?'

She had thought her mother too absorbed in the chateau's antiquarian curiosities to have done more than notice its inhabitants in passing; this degree of cynical insight was fascinating. She had not thought it worth commenting on the possibility that the marquesa saw Elinor as any kind of rival. That, of course, was too ridiculous. But the marquesa would soon see that for herself once she realised that Theo saw her merely as his friend and relative.

'I believe the marquesa came to visit the chateau in passing because of her interest in art and antiques and was invited to join the party. She is in much the same business as Theo, I understand.'

'The company promises to be reasonably congenial,' Lady James commented, picking up her fan and reticule and getting to her feet. 'Is that one of your new gowns, Elinor?'

'Yes, Mama. I think madame has done excellent work with it.'

'Hmm. Where are your pearls?'

'I did not bring them, Mama. I thought it unlikely I would need jewellery on our journey.'

'Jeanie!' The maid emerged from the dressing room with her mistress's stole over her arm. 'Fetch out my jewellery case again.' She removed the key on its long chain from her reticule and opened the box. 'The amethyst and diamond set, I think.'

'I thought you did not believe in unmarried girls wearing diamonds or coloured gem stones, Mama.' The ornaments glittered and sparked as Lady James lifted them out and laid them on the dressing table.

'I do not. But you are past the age where one need worry about that, Elinor. The earrings and necklace, I think—this is merely a family dinner.'

'Yes, Mama.' Elinor hooked the drops into her ears, feeling the unfamiliar cold caress as they swung against her neck. Jeanie fastened the necklace, rosettes of amethysts interspersed with diamonds, and stood back to admire the effect.

'You look very fine, Miss Elinor.'

'Yes, I do.' Startled into agreement, Elinor looked into the mirror. Theo had been quite right about the colour of the silk: it made the pale skin of her neck and shoulders gleam. The softness of her hair-style continued to work its magic on her face and the sophistica-tion of the jewels gave her a confidence she had never felt before.

'It would have been better if you had kept your hat on and had not burned your nose,' her mother added, flattening her mood somewhat. 'Still, you do not appear a complete hoyden.'

Exchanging a wry smile with Jeanie, Elinor followed her mother to the door. Burned nose or not, she felt suddenly more confident of holding her own with the marquesa.

Chapter Nine

'Mademoiselle Ravenhurst, *enchanté*.' Count Leon bowed over her hand, and this time he actually kissed it. Elinor bit the inside of her cheek to stop herself ginning. That she, of all people, should be having her hand kissed was too ridiculous. Still, it would not be long, once he had discovered she had no talent for social chit-chat nor a tendency to sit gazing at him admiringly whatever he said, before he was treating her as simply her mother's companion. It was to be hoped that, in the meantime, Theo did not become territorial again.

'Lady James.' He bowed. 'May I introduce you to our other guests? The Marquesa de Cordovilla, an authority on art.' The marquesa bowed, Lady James inclined her head. Elinor struggled with the precedence in her head: the daughter of an earl, daughter-in-law of a duke versus the widow of a Spanish marquis. Yes, Mama had it right.

'Sir Ian and Lady Tracey. English connoisseurs of the fine arts.' Elinor curtsied, her mother nodded and smiled, the Traceys made their bows. He was an athletic-looking man in his late thirties, she was tall for a woman, slim and dark with an alertness that intrigued Elinor. Could these two really be conniving adventurers? Her antipathy towards the marquesa inclined Elinor to suspect her, but it could be dangerous to overlook other possibilities.

The countess took over the introductions, presenting an elderly cousin, whose name Elinor did not catch, Monsieur Castelnau, the countess's widowed brother-in-law, and two girls, five or six years Elinor's junior, who were introduced as nieces. 'Laure and Antoinette. I am sure you young ladies will have much to talk about,' the countess said firmly, leading Elinor over to where they sat side by side on a sofa opposite Julie.

Mademoiselle de Falaise appeared as pleased to find herself sitting next to Elinor as Elinor was, and rather less adept at hiding the emotion. Elinor smiled brightly and did her best with small talk in French. There was no sign of Theo.

The large room was arranged with sofas grouped facing each other. Out of the corner of her eye Elinor could see her mother was talking to Sir Ian while Lady Tracey was chatting animatedly with Monsieur Castelnau. The count could be heard discussing Venetian painting with the marquesa while his mother watched them. In her corner the elderly relative appeared happily engaged with her tatting.

'Yes, I have been out for several years,' Elinor answered Laure's question. Or was it Antoinette? They appeared indistinguishable: both blonde, both blue eyed, both animated. 'Did you both remain in France during the Revolution?'

It appeared they had spent the years of the Terror in Scotland with relatives, but had learned very little English. Elinor told herself it was good for her to practise her French and soldiered on. Beside her she was conscious of Julie, her eyes on the count, while his attention was fixed on the marquesa.

Then the door opened, drawing every eye in the room, and Theo walked in. *'Madame.'* He went straight to the countess. 'My apologies for my tardiness; I have to confess I became completely lost and had to be rescued by one of your footmen. What a fascinating building this is.' He turned and regarded the rest of the company.

'I must apologise also to the ladies for my somewhat battered appearance—I fell down the stairs two days ago.'

Elinor was conscious of a subtle shifting of attention in the room. Both the young ladies beside her sat up and smiled brightly at the sight of another man, even one who was black and blue. Julie stared at the count, a small smile on her lips. The marquesa turned her head languidly and directed a smile of unmistakable intimacy at Theo and the count got to his feet, bowed to Theo and made his way over to stand beside Elinor.

Sir Ian rose slowly. 'Your sense of direction deserting you again Ravenhurst? The directions you so kindly gave to my coachman on the last occasion our paths crossed led us sadly astray.'

'I am sorry to hear that.' Theo strolled across and bowed to Lady Tracey. 'My apologies, ma'am, although the instructions I gave him were clear enough—what did he have to say for himself?'

'As he vanished into the countryside five minutes after our axle broke, I have no idea.' To Elinor's surprise, neither of the Traceys appeared as angry as one might have expected. Almost there was a sense that they had been beaten fair and square at a game. *How very English*, she thought with amusement. Perhaps her instincts were correct and they were not the villains of the piece.

Theo, apparently happily unconcerned by the fact that eight of the nine women in the room were watching him, drifted across the vast Aubusson carpet, took a seat next to the elderly cousin and began to compliment her on her tatting in loud, clear French.

The youngest ladies pouted, Lady Tracey went back to her conversation, Julie directed a look of spiteful amusement at Elinor and the marquesa smiled a sphinx-like smile that made Elinor uneasy. Irritated with her company, she got to her feet and went to sit next to Sir Ian. 'I did not realise you knew my cousin,' she began, crossing her fingers at the untruth.

'Oh, yes, we are rivals of old,' he said readily. 'Having been outwitted once recently, I am hoping that I can even the score eventually.'

Elinor asked him about his particular field of collecting and realised with surprise ten minutes later that they had been having a perfectly sensible and intelligent conversation without him once patronising her.

Theo was still deep in the intricacies of tatting, his elderly companion having had the amusing idea of teaching him how it was done. The sight of a large flame-headed man in impeccable evening dress with his big hands wielding a shuttle and a mass of fine white thread gradually drew the attention of everyone.

Eventually the marquesa got up and went over. 'Teó, show us what a tangle you are making.'

Theo looked up and smiled. 'How could I make a tangle,' he said in French, 'when I have such a skilled teacher?' He opened his hands and there, hanging from the shuttle, was an inch of fine lacy tatting. Amidst general applause he handed the shuttle back to the old lady.

'Oh, Monsieur Ravenhurst, will you give me your tatting?' It was Laure, blue eyes wide.

'But, no, it is unworthy to trim your handkerchief, *mademoiselle*. Here, take my seat and allow *madame* to show you how to do it yourself.'

'Wicked,' Elinor murmured as he stood by her side to admire the sight of a petulant young lady trying to look pretty whilst getting in a tangle.

'Aren't I just?' he murmured back. 'How are you getting on with Tracey?'

'I can't believe it is he.' Theo raised a brow. 'He is too sporting about your ruse.'

'And he treats you like a human being with sensible opinions,' Theo countered. Apparently his attention for the last half-hour had not been entirely on learning tatting. 'Don't be flattered into dismissing him, Nell.'

Irritated that he did not accept her judgement, Elinor turned away, only to encounter the marquesa's interested stare. Impulsively she turned back, laid her hand on Theo's sleeve and looked up into his eyes. 'I am sure you are right,' she said softly, holding the green gaze for a long moment.

Unholy amusement flickered in the depths of his eyes. 'Just be guided by me, Nell,' he said, adding under his breath. 'Now go and make friends with her.'

'Who?'

'Lady Tracey. Not Ana, not unless you have all your wits about you.' Under her gloved hand his arm was steady and warm. She bit her lip and saw his pupils widen. Inside, something reacted to that look. Something primitive and female. 'You look very lovely in that gown and with those jewels.'

'Thank you.' She was not sure what devil possessed her, but she turned—slowly, with a lingering smile over her shoulder—and went across to take the seat next to Ana. What was the matter with her? She never flirted. If anyone had asked, she would have said she had no idea how to. And here she was exchanging lingering glances and fleeting touches with...with her friend Theo, that was who.

'Marquesa. May I sit here?'

'But of course.' Ana fanned herself, gentle, sweeping movements. 'Why are you here, Miss Elinor?'

'Miss Ravenhurst,' Elinor corrected with a smile. 'I am the eldest unmarried daughter.'

'Of course you are. The oldest *and* unmarried. I am so sorry...for my mistake.'

I walked right into that one, Elinor thought grimly. 'Why am I here? This is an unoccupied seat and I wished to sit down.'

'Here at the chateau, with Teó.' There was a slight snap in the richly accented voice. Obviously young ladies were supposed to wilt before her barbs.

'I am here with my mother. Meeting Theo was completely un-expected. But I am so pleased we did.'

'Por qué?'

'I am sorry, I read five languages, but Spanish is not one of them. Let me guess— was that *why*?' She did not wait for Ana's sharp nod. 'Theo was able to introduce us to the count and it will be so useful for Mama's researches to study the chapel here.'

'So that is why you are here? To study architecture?'

'Oh, yes,' Elinor said, allowing her gaze to linger on Theo's beautifully tailored back. 'To study…form.'

Fortunately, given the hiss of indrawn breath from the woman at her side, dinner was announced before she could add any further kindling to the fire. This really was an amusing diversion, pretend-ing they were rivals for Theo's affections. She seemed to be con-vincing the marquesa; doubtless the family talent for acting was coming to her rescue.

The rest of the evening provided less challenging entertain-ment. Dinner was excellent and both Sir Ian and Monsieur Castelnau, her partners on either side, proved to be lively con-versationalists. Coffee in the salon with the ladies afterwards was duller.

Ana announced that she had the migraine and retired, looking more like a cat setting out on an evening's prowl than someone suffering from a headache. The younger women chattered amongst them-selves, Julie brooded and the countess made brittle conversation with Lady Tracey, Lady James and Elinor until the men joined them.

Watching the door, Elinor saw Theo's eyes as he scanned the room, then frowned. *So, he is looking for* her *is he?* Unaccountably irritated, Elinor got to her feet. She did not want to pay games. 'Do excuse me, *madame*, Mama. I think I will retire now. Goodnight.'

* * *

An hour later Elinor sat up straight and stretched, yawning. A copy of the plan of the chateau was spread on the table before her, coloured now to show the ages of the different parts. She could see clearly which areas remained from the time of the wicked count and his orgies.

But was that any help? She pushed the chair away from the table and began to walk up and down. It would be logical to assume that the original hiding place for the valuable artefacts was close to where the orgies had been held, but that did not mean that later de Beaumartins had not hidden the things elsewhere. Or that part of the chateau may have been demolished to make way for the eighteenth-century additions. Had she wasted her time? Perhaps, although Mama might find it useful.

From the corridor outside she heard the sound of footsteps, doors shutting. Everyone, it seemed, was going to bed. Elinor stood up to close the lid of her paint box and swirl the brushes in the water pot, then stood, dripping brushes poised in mid-air. Now was probably as good a time as any to corner Theo and persuade him to let her help in his search. She would give it half an hour to let everyone else settle down. Elinor reached out to trim a guttering candle and settled down to study the plan again.

Theo padded around his room, studying its furniture and pictures with automatic professional interest while his mind sifted through the impressions of the day. Either the Traceys were very, very good at dissembling, or they were exactly what they seemed: keen amateurs with the money and leisure to indulge their interests and the temperament to regard rivalry as an amusing sport.

Ana would not be here, surely, if she already had the Chalice? On the other hand, she had all the instincts of a cat and nothing would appeal to her more than to see him threshing around looking for the thing when she knew she had it safe. He arrived in front of an ornate baroque mirror and realised that he was still stark naked, distracted when he had finished washing by the sight of an interesting Italian Primitive hanging by the door.

The mirror was one of the items he had tracked down for the late count. Now he stood in front of it and studied himself critically. The swelling on his face had subsided, but the cuts and bruises did nothing to enhance his looks. Not that his face was something he ever paid much attention to. His body was another matter—he relied on that to function well and to keep him out of trouble. He sucked in his stomach muscles and winced, then flexed his shoulders, critically studying the way the muscles moved, identifying each twinge of discomfort. That was better, less pain there now and the bastards had not got round to kicking him in the kidneys.

The heavy silk dressing gown lay across the end of the bed and he pulled it on, enjoying the slither of cool silk over warm skin. He would sleep for an hour, perhaps two, then dress again and begin the systematic search of the castle that would take him several nights to complete. If Leon was bluffing and had the Chalice, he would find it.

He left the candles burning, lay back on the heaped pillows and closed his eyes. Outside his door a board creaked. He had noticed it that evening, registering it as something to be avoided on his nocturnal wanderings. Now he opened one eye a fraction and slid his right hand up under the pillows beside his head until he could grip the butt of the pistol.

The door opened. Even in the dim light the figure was unmistakeable. He did not relax his grip on the weapon. 'Teó? Are you asleep?'

The champagne silk négligé was familiar, he could remember buying it for her. It was an elegant confection and not one that could conceal as much as a stiletto. He removed his hand from under the pillow and sat up warily. 'What do you want, Ana?'

'Such a warm welcome.' She sat on the end of the bed, her back against the post, and arranged herself languidly. It was no surprise to find a warm foot caressing his instep. Nor was he surprised at the way his groin tightened or by the heavy ache of arousal. She was a beautiful woman and he knew very precisely what she was capable of in bed. What was new was the complete indifference of his mind to the promise of her body.

'Poor Teó, were you so injured in your—fall, did you say?—that you cannot please a woman?'

'No, it was not a fall and I have no desire to have my back raked by your talons, Ana. Tonight or any night.'

She showed no sign of displeasure at his rebuff, nor did the caressing foot stop its sensual slide over his calf. The heavy silk slithered off his knee, exposing the length of his leg, and her eyes narrowed as her foot moved higher. 'Your patron is unhappy not to receive the Chalice, then?'

'Yes. He is not a patient man.' He concentrated on regulating his breathing and not flinging off the bed away from her. It was what she wanted, a reaction from him, any sign she was hurting him. Men did not refuse Ana de Cordovilla, she rejected them.

'And if you cannot retrieve it?'

'Then I will have to repay him.'

'Can you afford to?'

'Yes.' It would clean him out; he would probably have to sell some of his own carefully selected investment collection and the carriage as well if he was to retain the resources to travel, earn again.

'You are a richer man than I realised. But better not to have to. Better by far to deliver the Chalice and to earn your fee, which must be substantial. Big enough to share, perhaps?'

'Is that an offer of help?' Her toes had reached his groin, slipping under the edge of the robe, the lovely taut line of her leg fully extended. Theo closed his hand around her ankle and lifted her foot away. He had no intention of gratifying her with the evidence of the effect she was having on his body. If she was angling after a cut of the fee, then she did not have the Chalice. Or was it simply a bluff to distract him while she negotiated with the count for some other pieces?

'Why not?' Ana curled her legs under her, a still golden figure in the candlelight. 'We are a formidable team. I will begin by seducing Sir Ian—perhaps he knows something.'

'We were never a team, Ana, and, no, I do not require your help. And leave the man alone, he loves his wife, they do not need your meddling.'

'Love?' A flicker of anger passed over her face. 'Foolishness. What is the use of love? You are too sentimental, Teó.' Before he could move she had uncurled herself from the end of the bed and was in his arms, her mouth hot and hungry on his, her long fingers curling around him in a blatant caress. It was so very different from the last pair of lips that had pressed themselves to his.

He made himself lie still until she lifted her head, staring down haughtily at his unresponsive face. 'Embracing chastity, Teó?' Her hand moved, sliding expertly down his aroused flesh. 'Difficult, is it not? Or perhaps you are saving yourself for your virginal spinster cousin. I am sure she would appreciate your…interest.'

Theo lay still until he heard the door close behind her, his eyes on the underside of the bed canopy. He reached down and flicked the skirts of his robe back across his legs, despising himself for reacting to Ana in any way, uncomfortably aware that her jibe about Nell had focused that tense ache on her image.

My virginal spinster cousin. He had polished the gem stone a little and now she sparkled, but it was not simply her looks that had attracted him. He knew it was her humour and her stoicism and her intelligence and that gleam in her eyes when she looked at him and the trust of her hand in his and her mouth under—

'Theo?' Nell was inside the room, the door closing behind her, and he had not even heard her opening it. He was hallucinating—he had fallen asleep and was dreaming.

Chapter Ten

'What the hell are you doing in here?' Theo sat bolt upright, appalled. Inappropriate thoughts about a young lady were one thing, finding her in his bedchamber, quite another.

'Shh! I knew you were awake, I saw the marquesa leaving.' She perched on the end of the bed on the rumpled patch of cover where Ana had coiled her long body and regarded him critically. 'Are you sure that it is a good thing, becoming intimate with her again?' She blushed. 'I mean, of course…trusting her?'

'I—' Theo snapped his mouth shut. He'd been within an inch of explaining that he had rebuffed Ana's advances, being defensive as though there was something between Nell and himself, something beyond friendship. 'What the devil were you about, watching my door? Is there a queue out there?'

Disconcertingly Nell snorted with laughter. 'I am sure Laure and Antoinette would be there if they dared. I was watching because I wanted to talk to you about searching the chateau.'

'This is not the place, nor the time. Have you any idea what would happen if you were discovered in here?'

'It would be all right, you are my cousin,' she began, for the first time sounding doubtful. He saw her eyes flicker to the robe he was wearing and to his bare feet and ankles. All he had to do was to reach out, push her down on to the bed and use his strength and his sensual expertise and she would be his. She was too innocent not to yield, he thought, disgusted at himself, fighting to make sense of his impulses. What was the matter with him? He had just repulsed a sensual and experienced lover and here he was contemplating seducing an innocent.

Self-recrimination made him snap, 'I am a *man*, you idiot girl. Do you want to end up married to me? Because I am damned sure I don't want to find myself in that situation.' What, he asked himself savagely, finding reasons to push her away, would he do with a wife?

He realised he could not interpret the expression in her eyes. Shock at how indiscreet she was being? Alarm at finding herself in a man's bedchamber? She slipped off the bed and went to the door. Theo felt the breath he had been holding sigh out of his lungs, then she turned the key in the lock and padded back and sat down. 'Now no one can walk in and surprise us,' she said prosaically. 'You are quite safe.'

Which was more than she was. 'You look about seventeen,' he said crossly. It was not what he had intended to say: *Get back to your room this minute* being the highest on the list. She was valiant, his Nell. But she was regarding him candidly from those wide hazel eyes, clad from head to toe in a plain cotton nightgown of utter respectability with her hair in a heavy plait over one shoulder. A greater contrast to Ana it would be hard to imagine. And yet he was aroused. Painfully, embarrassingly and inconveniently aroused in both body and mind by a virgin bluestocking with no experience except a few kisses.

'I do not think that was a compliment,' she observed severely. 'Theo, listen, I have been studying the plan. It will take ages for one person to search alone, but if we do it together—'

'And if we are found?'

'We will think of something. Two brains are better than one.' He shook his head, feeling control beginning to slip away from him in the face of her certainty. 'Well, in that case I will search by myself, which is not a rational way to proceed.'

Silence. Theo regarded Nell, wondering what would happen if he took her by the shoulders and shook her. He rather thought he could not trust himself to touch her. But he believed her threat to explore by herself. And somewhere in all of this mystery was the person who had knocked him unconscious and taken the Chalice.

'Very well. If you are still awake at two, then get dressed and we will search.' Once upon a time, before he met his cousin Elinor, he had thought himself in control of his life. At least if she was with him he would know what she was up to. 'We will start in Leon's study.'

'I agree,' she said, nodding approval of the plan as though they were equal partners in this. 'The old count may have left some clue to its traditional hiding place. Until two, then.'

She went out as quietly as she had come in. Theo listened, but the board did not creak, which meant that she had deliberately avoided it. No fool, his cousin. No fool, but one hell of a complication.

Elinor sat down at the table in her room and stared unseeing at the plan. She had got her own way, she should be happy, not feeling hurt and confused and thoroughly hot and bothered.

It was not until she was inside Theo's bedchamber that it had occurred to her there might be any awkwardness in marching into a man's room two minutes after his mistress had left it. He could have been unclothed. He would certainly not be in any mood for a chat about hidden treasure.

But it did not seem as though Ana *was* his mistress any more— unless lovemaking was a much faster, tidier and less strenuous activity than she had been led to believe.

But it was different, being alone, both of them in their night-clothes, in a darkened bedchamber late at night. Different from that sunlit quarry where he had kissed her, different from his room at St Père where she had dressed his injuries and held him out of sheer thankfulness he was still alive. The shadows had hidden his face from her, veiling both the bruises and the familiar features.

Without his face to focus on, she had been burningly aware of his body under that exotic robe, of his hands, of his bare feet. And she had wanted to touch him. Was this desire? It seemed that being a confirmed spinster did not protect you from such feelings, nor could the application of common sense and intelligence stop you fantasising about a man. A man who might be quite willing to kiss her—men appeared to be thoroughly undiscriminating in that respect—but who certainly would not see her as a lover. Or anything other than a friend.

And then he had snapped at her, warned her quite clearly that he did not want to be found in a compromising situation with her. It hurt and she could not work out why. He was perfectly correct, it would be terrible to have to marry someone because you had compromised them. It was certainly no basis for a marriage. And she knew she was never going to marry, knew that those kisses had been all she was ever going to experience. She was a rational, educated, intelligent female—so why did Theo's words wound her so much?

You should be glad he is not a silver-tongued hypocrite, the voice of common sense chided. *And you should be very glad indeed he has no idea that you are lusting after him.* Because that was what she was doing, there was no hiding it from herself.

Elinor looked at the clock. Half past midnight. An hour and a half. Time to search this room thoroughly. The count was hardly likely to hide his indecent treasure in a guest room, but she might as well be thorough. Elinor removed her remaining old gown from the press and got dressed again. It was a deep bottle green, ideal for skulking about in the shadows, and was not such a bad fit as the others, so she might escape a lecture from Theo on how dreadful it was.

Theo's scratch on the door panels was so faint she would not have heard it if she had not been listening for him. He stepped back abruptly, straight on to one of the creaking floorboards, when she opened the door, knife in hand.

'Shh!'

'What are you doing?' he hissed.

'Searching my room. My painting knife is excellent for getting between floorboards, but none of them are loose.'

It was hard to see in the dim light of the dark lantern he carried, but she thought he cast up his eyes. 'Come on.'

The chateau was an eerie place at night. Sections of it were decorated and furnished to match their period, so one moment there was the comforting bulk of long-case clocks and armoires with vases on top, the next a suit of armour would loom out of the shadows or the mounted head of a wild boar would appear silhouetted against a window. Elinor resisted the urge to clutch Theo's coattails and padded along behind him in her light slippers, the knife still in her hand.

He found his way easily through the passageways to the study door. Elinor had thought she had committed the plan to memory, but she had become lost after the first staircase. He crouched down, removed something metallic from his pocket and began to pick the lock. It was a skill that Elinor did not think the average antiquities dealer would have. Could she persuade him to teach her?

They were inside faster than she would have believed possible. 'Check the curtains,' Theo whispered, unshuttering the dark lantern only when he was happy no chink of light would show.

They worked their way systematically around the room, testing panels and searching cupboards, Theo opening locked drawers and relocking them. 'How big is it?' Elinor asked, sitting back on her heels and pushing her hair off her face.

'This big, top to bottom.' Theo held his hands about eighteen inches apart. 'It is heavy too.'

'That just leaves the floor.' Elinor began to wriggle her knife blade between boards, but nothing shifted. It took twenty minutes to work across it, prizing at each long board with no result. 'Ouch!'

'Splinters?'

'In the heel of my hand.' She flapped it back and forth, muttering.

'Let me see. Theo opened the dark lantern and took her hand. 'One nasty big one. If I can just get it—hold on—there. Better suck it in case there are any little ones left.' He lifted her hand to his mouth and sucked on the swelling at the base of her thumb.

His mouth was hot and wet and the suction was strong and should have hurt—only instead it seemed to go straight to the pit of her belly, straight down to where that hot disturbing ache had started when he had kissed her. She looked at his bent head in the yellow light and felt a wave of fierce tenderness wash through her, so intense that she trembled.

Elinor was not aware of placing her other hand on his cheek, of cupping it gently against her palm, only of seeing it there and of Theo turning his head into the caress. Did she kiss him or did he kiss her? How did they get here, on the wide dark boards, limbs tangled, mouths hungrily together?

This time she knew the taste of him on her tongue, his scent familiar and arousing in her nostrils and she was aware for the first time of his body against hers, of the size and solidity against her softness, of the hard thrust against her belly that should have terrified her, but only added to the ache and the needing.

They rolled, bumping into furniture, too intent on each other, on exploring, to care. Her breast fitted into the palm of his hand as though it had been made for it and his mouth left hers to nuzzle down over the shrouding cloth. Her nipples were hard against the friction of her chemise and she wriggled, frustrated, wanting her flesh against his, needing his mouth where his fingers were rubbing in maddeningly slow circles until she thought she would scream.

Some rational thought surfaced, telling her that this, here, now, was madness and they should stop, and then his hand left her breast and she sighed, a great shuddering exhalation of relief and disappointment, not knowing which was which. And she lost that thread of rationality again when Theo's mouth sealed over hers, his tongue filling her with slow, heavy thrusts that made her clasp his shoulders for some anchor in this whirlpool of sensation.

The scrape of metal in the lock cut through her senses like a surgeon's knife. One moment there had been nothing but the delirium of his kiss, the next she was staring wild eyed at Theo as he pushed her towards the deep kneehole under the desk. Elinor scrabbled for it, finding the knife, scooping it up as Theo followed her, his fingers pinching out the wick of the lantern as he jammed into the space. It was a partners' desk, she realised, deep enough for two people to work opposite each other. Unless whoever was opening the door sat down and stretched out their legs, or bent to look, they were out of sight.

Theo's arms came around her, holding her tight so they were facing each other, knees drawn up, backs curved protectively towards the openings on either side. Her body was still shaking, her mind was reeling, but his calmness helped her keep still, breathe slowly and quietly. The door was open now. Over Theo's shoulder she could see the light of a candle, perhaps a branch—it seemed quite bright.

What time was it? What on earth was the count doing? In answer a clock struck the half-hour. It must be past three. Perhaps he had been unable to sleep and had come down to read. Then the quality of the footsteps struck her. Even a man in slippers should not be that quiet, surely?

As she thought it, she saw pale skirts pass and then stop. There had been a large inlaid box on top of the desk which they had left untouched because it was too small to hold the Chalice. The woman was opening that. Papers rustled, there was a soft exclamation, then the sound of the lid closing, the scrape of a key—or was it a picklock?

Who was it? She could tell nothing from the skirts, which looked like those of a heavy satin night robe. It could be any of the women who were staying. She was standing still as though in thought. Or was she listening? Could she hear them breathing?

Then, with a swish of skirts and the light tread of kid slippers, she was moving towards the door again. It opened, closed. Darkness, there was the scrape of metal again, then silence.

Theo's hand pressed against her mouth. Elinor counted in her head and reached twenty before he began to wriggle back out of their tight confinement.

'Who was that?' she asked, getting to her feet as he lit the lantern again. Her legs were shaking. 'It was a woman.'

'I have no idea.' He took out the picklocks and began to work on the box. 'She was using picklocks, or a hairpin, on the door.'

'Ana, then? Surely the countess would have a key.'

'Not necessarily.' He had the lid open, the papers in his hand. 'It's an inventory. My God—it is the wicked count's inventory for his secret society. See, here's the Chalice.'

He spread the crackling sheets of parchment on the table, Elinor struggling to read the ancient handwriting in the poor light. 'And a platter from the same goldsmith. Chains of gold and silver… whips of horse hair and leather… What is that, I don't recognise the word?'

Theo folded the list and put his hand on it. 'I'm glad to hear it and I have no intention of telling you.' He put the inventory back and closed the lid. 'So, there are more things to find. Whoever she is, she is welcome to it. All I want is to locate the Chalice and get out of here.'

'The inventory gave no hint about the hiding place?'

'Not exactly. It has given me an idea, though, for where to look. I must study the plan again.'

'We'll look tomorrow.' Now all she wanted to do was to curl up in her own bed, by herself, and try to sleep. Sleep and not think or feel or want. And somehow to subdue the heated intimate ache that Theo's kisses had aroused.

'We will not,' Theo said sternly, working on the door. He shuttered the lantern and opened it a crack, listening. 'Come on.'

'Why not?'

'Why not?' He looked up from relocking the door, his face grim. 'Because for some reason I cannot seem to keep my hands off you and I must. We are playing with fire, Nell.'

'Just then—before she came in—what would have happened?'

'Nothing more than a kiss,' he said abruptly, taking her arm and turning back towards the wing where their rooms were. 'I am still enough of a gentleman to be sure of that. But it isn't easy, Nell, not when what I want is to take you to my bed. To take your virginity.'

'Why?' she asked, determined to work this out. She had no idea what she felt, what she thought. But he was experienced, he understood, surely, what was going on? 'We are not in love. We are both intelligent, rational people. I do not understand why I am so confused, why I want to…to touch you, to have you kiss me.'

They were passing a deep window embrasure with seats built into the thick stone. Theo sat her down firmly, then sat opposite. *At a safe distance,* she thought, distractedly. 'It is desire—impure, but very simple, Nell. It is easy to stir into life, difficult to damp down.' He leaned forwards, elbows on knees, and ran his hands through his hair.

'I see.' Elinor tried to work it out. 'I can understand why I want to kiss you—you showed me how, I like you and I trust you.' *And*

I want you, but I must not say that. I shouldn't even think it. Theo groaned. 'You seem to like kissing me,' she ventured.

'Men like kissing women, full stop,' he said brutally, flattening any hope that somehow she was special. 'Nell, stop trying to apply your intellect to this. It isn't a set of grammar rules you have to learn and which then apply every time. Desire is very powerful, not logical and rarely convenient. It is not voluntary. It is especially inconvenient for ladies. Men can find mistresses. For ladies to take lovers and not lose their reputations into the bargain is almost impossible.'

'Bel—' she began and then clapped her hands over her mouth, horrified that she had almost said it.

'Bel and Dereham? Before they were married?' Theo, momentarily distracted, looked up. 'Really? Well, good for her after that prosy bore she was married to. But widows are different, Nell.'

'But I don't want a lover,' she said, trying to make herself understand as much as him. 'And you certainly don't want me, not when you can have experienced mistresses who don't need teaching and won't cause a scandal. So why can't we just—' She waved her hands about, frustrated at not being able to find the right expression.

'Turn it off like a tap?' Theo was smiling. It was a rather strained grin, but at least he was no longer frowning at her. 'Because it keeps surprising us and it is a very powerful instinct. You see why I don't want you in my bedroom?'

'Yes, indeed.' Her emphatic agreement had him smiling in earnest. He got to his feet and held out his hand. Elinor put hers in it and managed to smile back. 'It is such a…*crowded* feeling. I think it makes the Greek myths a lot easier to comprehend.'

Theo gave a snort of laughter, hastily choked back. 'Shh! We are getting close to the bedchambers. Do you want to explain to Aunt Louisa that we have been discussing mythology?'

On the threshold of her room he stopped and looked down at her for a long moment. 'I am not going to kiss you goodnight, Nell.'

'Very wise.' She put one hand on his shoulder, stood on tiptoe and touched her lips to his cheek. 'Goodnight, Theo.'

'Goodnight, Nell.'

The clock struck four and Elinor yawned, her jaw cracking, as she dragged off her clothes and stumbled into bed. Theo was wrong, she decided as she began to drift off to sleep. It *was* possible to understand this physical desire intellectually. The trouble was, it seemed impossible to make her body understand as well.

Chapter Eleven

'I don't remember you wearing this dress yesterday, Miss Elinor.'

Elinor looked up from her sleepy contemplation of her cup of chocolate to find Jeanie holding up the green walking dress, crumpled and dusty. The chateau's staff did not dust under desks, she thought, then caught herself before she said so. 'I couldn't sleep, so I got up and walked about,' she explained, stifling a yawn.

'What, in this spooky old place?' Jeanie shuddered dramatically. 'I wouldn't set foot outside my door in the dark, that's for sure, no matter what I heard outside.'

It took a moment or two for that statement to penetrate Elinor's drowsy brain. 'You heard something in the night? What, exactly?'

'Footsteps, and knockings and sounds like stones shifting,' the maid said, eyes wide, clothes brush suspended in mid stroke.

'Really? How odd. But then old buildings always sound odd if you aren't used to them,' Elinor said, suddenly no longer tired. She set her cup down. 'Where exactly are you lodged?'

Jeanie proved to have a poor sense of direction and even poorer descriptive skills. Eventually, with the help of the plan, Elinor pinpointed her room. 'You are on the ground floor?' That was odd for servants' rooms. Then she realised that it was part of the oldest wing and was immediately over the ancient cellars and dungeons.

Presumably all the family and guest rooms were in the more modern parts of the building.

'Is Mr Ravenhurst up, do you know?' She slid out of bed and went to look out of the window. The sun was already brilliant; Mama would probably want to spend all day in the chapel.

'I saw him as I was bringing your hot water, Miss Elinor. He pinched my chin and told me I was looking too pretty for a man to stand at that time in the morning.' Jeanie tossed her head, obviously delighted with the compliment. 'Cheek, I call it.'

'That's men for you,' Elinor replied, from her wealth of recent experience.

It seemed Theo and the count had been for a ride, for they were both in the breakfast parlour when she came down, both slightly windswept and apparently in better humour with each other. She had not known what to expect when she saw Theo again. Surely the fact that they had been so…intimate would show somehow? Would she even be able to meet his eyes?

And then, miraculously, it was all right. Theo was just her friend and cousin again, his hair tousled, his smile when he saw her, wide and uncomplicated. Or was he feeling like she was, very different inside? No—as he had implied, men hardly regarded a kiss as significant.

Elinor dimpled at the count, biting her cheek at Theo's comically raised eyebrows and took the opportunity to hiss as she paused beside his chair, 'Jeanie heard noises last night in the cellars. Someone else is searching.'

'It's a miracle we didn't bump into all the rest of the guests,' he murmured back, the scraping of chair legs as he resumed his seat covering the exchange.

'And what would you like to do this morning, Miss Ravenhurst?' the count enquired, placing a plate of very English-looking food in front of her. 'I still enjoy my English breakfasts,' he explained, sitting down to his own dish of kedgeree.

'Thank you. I will assist Mama, I expect. She will want to spend time in your lovely chapel, I am sure. The light will be good with so much sunshine.'

'And I cannot tempt you outside into that sun?' He was so hopelessly good looking, she thought. Those long lashes, those dark, stormy eyes, that beautifully chiselled jaw. And the intense way he focussed on her. It sounded as though his day would be ruined if she did not join him in the grounds.

'Oh.' Elinor tried fluttering her lashes. Her sister seemed to be able to do it to effect. She felt a complete idiot. On the far side of the count Theo raised his eyebrows, apparently in agreement with that assessment. 'That sounds lovely. But what I would *really* like to do is to see your dungeons. I *love* Gothic romances and they must be *so* atmospheric.'

Theo stopped pulling mocking faces and nodded approval. *Clever,* he mouthed.

'The dungeons?' The count looked wary. 'They are not very exciting these days, just cellars now full of wine barrels and old furniture. No hideous instruments of torture or skeletons in chains to send a *frisson* down your spine.' He did not seem exactly eager to take her, but then what host would be delighted at a request to tour his cellars on a bright sunny day?

'Please, Count?' Elinor tried wheedling. 'I am sure you could make it seem so exciting.' Theo, his mouth full of coffee, choked alarmingly.

'I cannot promise that,' he said, his eyes suggesting he lied. Elinor felt herself turn pink. Lord! Her inept flirting must be having an effect. 'But I will do my best. And you must call me Leon.'

'Oh, thank you—Leon.' Elinor reached for the toast, suddenly finding herself incapable of any more of this and terrified of meeting Theo's mocking gaze. 'I will come and find you when Mama no longer requires me, shall I?'

To her relief the others began to trickle into the room. Julie sat next to Leon, sending Elinor a cool, warning glance as though she had overheard her exchange with him. Laure and Antoinette fluttered in and sat down either side of Theo, exclaiming over the changes to the dramatic colouring of his bruises and managing to sound as though he had been injured in the course of some knightly endeavour. Elinor wondered about engaging him in conversation and then wickedly decided to leave him to deal with them as best he could.

His tactics appeared to be to treat them both as though they were about fifteen and he an indulgent and elderly uncle, an approach that won him an approving nod from his aunt when Lady James appeared.

The Traceys announced their intention of riding out and persuaded Monsieur Castelnau, and, to Elinor's surprise, Ana, to join them. Julie, she noticed, waited until Leon's refusal before refusing herself. *She's in love with him,* Elinor thought. *Poor soul, he sees only his mother's companion.* And companions, as she knew all too well, were so often invisible. But Julie was striking, with a slim dark elegance that matched the count's, and she hardly seemed lacking in self-confidence. They would make a handsome couple.

She waited for her mother to finish, sipping a third cup of coffee and crumbling a roll while she attempted to engage her hostess in conversation. The countess seemed heavy-eyed and strained. No doubt, Elinor thought compassionately, she was finding sleep hard to come by. Her husband had died in mysterious circumstances only a little while ago, after all. In fact, it was odd that she chose to entertain at all—perhaps she did so only at her son's insistence. Her gaze rested thoughtfully on Leon. He did not have the air of a man whose father had only recently died so tragically—had he and the previous count been on bad terms?

Lady James did not keep her waiting long. 'Come, Elinor, we have work to do.' Elinor turned to smile her thanks at Monsieur Castelnau, who had pulled back her chair for her, and blinked in sudden confusion. Who was that woman? Then she saw it was herself reflected in a long glass. She stared. Yes, of course it was her, only…

'I will just fetch my sketching things, Mama,' she said, leaving her mother to ask the countess about the key to the chapel.

Jeanie was folding clothes in her room and looked up with a smile as Elinor came in. 'Jeanie, do I look different?'

It was a bizarre question, but the maid did not seem to find it odd. 'But yes, Miss Elinor. You've got colour in your cheeks and your hair makes your face so much softer and you are wearing those pretty colours now.'

She stared at the mirror. She looked younger, or at least she looked her proper age and not years older as she sometimes felt. And if not pretty exactly—she did not have that sort of face—she might honestly claim to look quite attractive. She knew she had looked nice last evening, but then she had been wearing her lovely new gown and the jewels. But now… 'How odd. I suppose I have been getting more fresh air, and the new gowns and hairstyle, of course.'

'All those,' Jeanie agreed, coming to look over her shoulder. 'But its being in love that does it. Works every time.'

Elinor stared at her and Jeanie smiled back into the mirror, apparently unaware that she had said anything to shock her mistress. It took several attempts to make her voice work. 'Jeanie, I am not in love.' That did not seem emphatic enough. 'Not at all. Not with anyone.'

The girl actually winked! 'Of course, if you say so, Miss Elinor. You can rely on me not saying anything to her ladyship, we don't want to worry her, do we, not with all the things she's thinking about, what with her books and everything. It's ever so convenient over here, isn't it? Not like London. You can go around with him, just as you please.'

'Over here?' Elinor said faintly. 'Oh, yes. Very convenient.'

'And he's a lovely gentleman, isn't he? Not what you'd call handsome, not like the count. But what I'd call *manly*. And he's got lovely hands—' She broke off, looking thoughtful. 'Yes, miss, you definitely won't be disappointed in *him* for a husband.'

'Jeanie.' Elinor pulled herself together and spoke clearly, slowly and firmly, desperately ignoring the image of how Theo would not be a disappointment as a husband. 'I am not in love with Mr Ravenhurst. He is my cousin and my friend, that is all. There is nothing to keep secret from my mother.' *And may I not be struck down for lying!* she thought. *Lying about there being nothing to keep secret,* she amended. There was no secret about her feelings for Theo. It was ludicrous to think she was in love with him. That was not a rational emotion for her to have. And she was a rational female. Very rational, if unable to control the stirrings of physical desire. Nothing more than a kiss…that was no reason to fall in love.

'Yes, Miss Elinor.' Jeanie, not the slightest bit chastened, returned to her folding while Elinor, considerably flustered, snatched up her satchel and a folded copy of the plan and fled.

I am not in love with him, I can't be. 'Here I am, Mama—goodness, those stairs are steep! What would you like me to do?' *I desire him. That is a perfectly natural physical reaction over which I have no control. But I can control my actions and my thoughts.* 'Check the capitals for similarities with the basilica? Yes, of course.' *Falling in love is intellectual, surely? I do not* want *to fall in love, therefore I* cannot. *I have not.* 'This one, Mama, and that one there. I think they might be by the same hand.'

Falling in love turns your brain upside down. Look at Cousin Bel when she fell in love. Distracted, poor thing. I am perfectly in command of my emotions. I am perfectly normal.

'Elinor! What are you doing standing there, gazing into space? You have been looking like a moonstruck noddy for a good two minutes.'

'Sorry, Mama. I was trying to recall the basilica columns in detail.' *Focus, think.* She was terrified, she realised. Terrified by the emotions she did not understand, terrified that perhaps Jeanie was right, that she was in love with Theo. Because if she was, it was hopeless and it would hurt. It would hurt terribly and she had schooled herself to live life calmly, not expecting anything and never being disappointed. That way nothing wounded her any more, nothing was going to leave her raw and vulnerable and exposed. But this was going to, because it was quite hopeless, he had said so.

'Do you want me to draw, Mama?' she asked, praying the answer would be *no*. Her hands were shaking. 'Because I thought I would check for masons' marks, see if any match the ones in the basilica.'

'An excellent idea,' Lady James approved, beginning to pace out distances between columns. There, she could pull herself together and function after all. Elinor began to scan the walls closely, noting the cryptic signs the medieval masons had scratched on each block so their work could be identified and they would be paid correctly each day. It needed careful study and it meant she could check the walls for any sign of a hiding place as she went.

By the end of the morning her notebook was full of marks, her head was spinning and every inch of wall had been looked at. There was nothing in the least suspicious to suggest a secret.

A footman arrived with the message that luncheon was served, earning a frown from Lady James and a sigh of thankfulness from Elinor. 'Mama, can you manage without me this afternoon? I have such a headache. I could collate the marks against the ones for the basilica later if you like.'

'Very well. Come along, I suppose we must eat.'

* * *

Elinor wrestled with her problem throughout luncheon before she came up with a solution. She was seeing too much of Theo, and under circumstances that were so intense, it was no wonder she was becoming—she sought for a word—*engrossed* with him. All that was needed was contact with another man.

And there was an admirable candidate to hand. 'Miss Elinor?' The count was waiting to see if she was still hoping for a tour of the cellars. Yes, he would do perfectly. He was attractive enough to be diverting, sophisticated enough not to mistake her intentions or feelings.

'Leon.' She smiled back. 'I am relying upon you for some thoroughly spine-chilling stories.'

'Let me see what I can do to produce a *frisson*.' He took a lantern from a stand beside a small door off the great entrance hall and lit it. 'The dungeons date from the first castle, built by my ancestor, the Chevalier Guy de Beaumartin. He was a powerful war lord and needed somewhere to keep his many captives. Mind how you go on these narrow steps. Here.' He took her hand and led her down the spiral stairs.

It was no different from the way Theo helped her, his light grasp was quite impersonal, but Elinor freed herself with a murmured word of thanks as soon as they arrived at the bottom of the stairs. They were in a wide, stone-flagged passageway, vanishing into darkness and shadows and, on either side, small doors that she would have to stoop to enter. 'Cells?' she queried.

'Certainly.' Leon pushed one open with a rending creak of rusted hinges and shone the light inside for her to see. 'No windows, the damp runs down the stone walls. See the bolts in the walls that held the shackles? Imagine the despair of being chained here in the darkness, month after month, with only the rats for company.'

Elinor could imagine it only too vividly, and she did not find that sort of medieval barbarity romantic. But she had to maintain her excuse of wanting to see the Gothic horrors, so she produced an exaggerated shudder. 'Ghastly indeed.' Something scuttled across the edge of the pool of light: a vast spider. She gave an involuntary gasp and jumped backwards, to find herself being supported by Leon's arm.

'It is only a spider,' he said reassuringly, making no attempt to remove his arm. Elinor stiffened, but he did not try to take advantage of the situation either.

'Thank you. I have to confess to hating the things—so foolish.' She stepped aside as though to allow him to proceed and he dropped his arm away. The count's manner as he led her through the maze of underground passages and chambers was perfectly correct and yet Elinor was left in no doubt at all that he saw her as an attractive woman and that he wanted her to see him as a man, not just as her host.

How he achieved that intrigued her and she began to watch closely to analyse his technique. Leon touched her, fleetingly, always with a good excuse, always somewhere unalarming, such as her elbow or her hand, but frequently. His voice was husky, soft enough that she had to move a little closer to him to hear, and, when he spoke, he kept his eyes on her face as though hanging on her every word of response. He was, in effect, flirting in the most unexceptional manner.

Elinor decided to try responding. She laughed at anything he said that could be considered even faintly amusing, she leaned a little when he offered her support on the steps, she gasped in admiration when he told her tales of his ancestors' deeds of chivalry. In fact, by the time the narrow passageways opened up into a great chamber with a vaulted ceiling, they were both thoroughly at ease with each other and, she suspected, he might very well try to kiss her at any moment.

Oddly, Leon did not seem to want to linger, but took the direct path across the imposing space. 'Oh, please wait,' Elinor implored. 'What a strange room. Was it a guard chamber?'

'I have no idea,' Leon said, a trifle shortly. He wanted her out of there, she realised, staring round. The chamber was like a chapel with bays at intervals along the walls and rusted flambeaux holders. There were small metal hooks high up that she recognised as suspension points for tapestries, although the walls were stark stone now. There was a small stone platform at one end. It was too low for an altar.

Then she saw the ring bolts at all four corners of the platform and more on the pillars. She measured them by eye, cold chills running up and down her spine. They were the right height to tie the wrists of a woman to, if she stretched up. This, surely, was the room the wicked count used for his depraved orgies. And where better to house the ritual objects and the Chalice?

Leon set down the lantern, sending wild shadows flickering across the walls. As he walked towards her, smiling, his dark, lean features seemed devilish in the gloom. 'Do you find this gives you the thrill of horror you were seeking?' he asked her. And it seemed the light, bantering tone had been replaced with something more sinister. Almost she could believe he was the reincarnation of his ancestor.

'Oh, yes.' She tried to laugh. 'See, I am all of a tremble.' She held out her hand, surprised to see she was speaking the truth, and he took it, drawing her in to him. It seemed impossible to resist, as if he, or the strange atmosphere of the chamber, was mesmerising her. He was going to kiss her, she realised, almost fatalistically.

'Oh, Elinor, how I would like to make you tremble,' Leon murmured and lowered his mouth to hers.

Chapter Twelve

*T*hink, Elinor told herself fiercely, *see how this is no different from kissing Theo? See, all it is, is physical passion and my lack of experience.* She opened to the pressure of Leon's insistent lips, let his mouth mould hers, let his tongue explore, let him brace her hard against his lean body so she could feel his arousal. And she felt nothing, nothing but surprise that she could do this and feel only detachment.

But detached though she might be, this was enough. More than enough. Elinor put her hands on Leon's shoulders and pushed. It did not make him loosen his hold, but it threw her off balance. She took a step, the backs of her knees met an obstacle and she fell, Leon coming with her, to the low stone platform. He threw out a hand to take their weight, then let them both subside slowly on to the hard surface.

Now Elinor did start to feel uneasy. Surely he would not persist? He was a gentleman, her host—but she had held out her hand to him, gone willingly into his arms. Perhaps he thought that her unconventional lifestyle meant her morals were loose. With an effort she freed her mouth, pushing against the upper part of his chest with her left palm. From a distance of inches Leon's dark eyes burned into hers.

'No,' she managed. 'Enough!' Her outflung right hand met metal, grasped it, and she found she was holding one of the rings set at the corner of the platform. It was as though the panic and fear of those women from so long ago flowed into her body, lending her strength. She shoved harder and Leon stood up, catching her hand in his and pulling her to his feet as he did so.

He seemed neither put out by her rejection nor particularly agitated by what had just occurred. 'I am sorry we fell. Are you hurt?' he asked solicitously.

Elinor bit back the retort that it was rather late in the day to ask that and managed a bright smile. She did not want to expose her own inexperience, nor did she want to let him glimpse her fear, not of him, but of the place where they stood.

'I am quite all right, but I am afraid that this wildly romantic atmosphere has led us both further than we meant to go.' She heard her own voice sounding as cool and emotionless as though she was disputing a footnote in a learned journal. What was the matter with her? Her heart was pounding, but it was not the same as the way she felt after Theo kissed her. What did she feel? More than a little embarrassed, in the aftermath of that embrace, but not even slightly stirred by it. Shouldn't she be? He was an attractive man, his technique seemed perfectly assured. Wasn't she supposed to be aroused by what they had just done?

All she wanted, she realised, was Theo. She wanted to be in his arms and have him sooth away the terror that seemed to ooze from the stones; despite that, she wanted to join him searching the place, certain that here they would find the Chalice.

'Elinor!' Even distorted by the echo in the maze of underground corridors, his voice was unmistakable.

Leon smiled tightly. 'It appears your cousin desires to chaperon you. He does not like you being alone with me, I think.'

That was all she needed. The two men were prickly enough

around each other without them circling like two dogs over a juicy bone. The thought of herself in that light, when previously the best analogy would be to a rather overcooked and dried-up mutton chop, made Elinor's lips twitch in wry amusement.

'That makes you smile?' Leon asked. 'It amuses you to have two men desiring you?'

'My cousin most certainly does not—Theo! You have found us. Is this not the most atmospheric place? I swear I am going to try my hand at writing a Gothic novel, I am so inspired.'

'Aunt Louisa would have kittens,' Theo observed, smiling. In the light of the lantern his eyes looked like cold obsidian, utterly at odds with his voice and the curve of his lips. 'She is wondering, loudly, where you are. I gather you are supposed to be in your room, recovering from a headache.'

'So I am,' Elinor said. 'But it is much better now.' It seemed politic to move to Theo's side. 'You found your way down here all by yourself? How clever, I would be lost in an instant if it were not for Leon. Shall we go back the way you came?' She tucked her hand under his elbow, looking back over her shoulder at the count. Faintly, there was the sound of a low growl, then she realised it was Theo. Her smile was becoming somewhat fixed, she realised, urging Theo in the direction of the door. *'I've found something,'* she hissed. *'Can we please get out of here?'*

He had taken a shorter route and they emerged through a door into the inner courtyard of the chateau. The countess and Mademoiselle Julie were sitting in the shade, sewing. Elinor felt their speculative scrutiny and moved closer to Theo. 'How wonderfully atmospheric!' she exclaimed. 'Thank you so much, Count. I have to confess I would have been terrified to find myself down there alone—those spiders.' She gave an exaggerated shudder. 'Now I had better go and help Mama again. Theo, could you come and carry my easel, please? I left it in my room.'

* * *

When they reached the door she pulled him in, ignoring his protests about propriety and the damage she was doing to his sleeve. 'Theo, I think I know where it might be.'

'Sit over there.' He pointed a long finger at the window seat and took a stool by the door. 'If Aunt Louisa comes in, I want to be at a very safe distance from you. Now, tell me, what have you been doing, besides making love with the count.'

'I have not,' she began indignantly.

'The back of your gown is dusty, there is a slight red mark on your cheek. He needs to shave twice a day if he is kissing women.'

'He did kiss me, but that is all.' She had nothing to feel defensive about. Theo was not her guardian, certainly not her brother. Which was how he was sounding.

'Lying down?'

'I tripped. Theo, *listen.* You know I went down there with him to explore, so stop being so…sanctimonious. And why should I not kiss him if I want to? He is a very attractive man.'

Theo seemed to be counting silently. Eventually he said, 'So what have you discovered?'

'The room where you found us is very strange. Did you notice?' He shook his head and she felt a strange twinge of satisfaction that he had been so focussed on her. 'Look at the plan.' Her copy was still spread on the table and she went to trace her route. 'See? Like a chapel, with lots of deep alcoves, like side chapels. And there are rings on the walls.' She felt herself go pale and kept talking. 'And a low platform, like an altar, with rings at all four corners. That's what I fell back on to and I realised that it was probably used for…for…'

Standing on the other side of the table, looking down at the plan, Theo's face was grim. He probably knew, far better than she in her inexperience, the sort of activities that room had witnessed. 'You think it would be the place to hide the Chalice?'

'Surely there would have been somewhere to keep the silver and so forth, in the days when it was in use?'

'I think you are right. And look, the chamber is almost directly below the servants' lodgings.' He tapped a finger thoughtfully on the curling edge of the parchment. 'What do you think—someone searching, or someone checking it is still there?'

'Checking,' Elinor said, uncertain why she was so sure. 'What time shall we go tonight?'

'We?' Theo raised an eyebrow. Elinor mimicked him, earning herself a grin. 'You are not going anywhere, certainly not down into nasty, spider-infested dungeons.'

'Theo, if we don't go together, then I will go by myself,' she warned.

She thought he muttered, 'Give me strength.' Then, 'Very well. I will collect you at two. If you scream at spiders, I'll gag you.'

'Yes, Theo,' Elinor murmured with mock meekness. She liked the way he did not try to order her to do things simply because he said so—or, at least, he did *try* ordering her, but when she refused he did not bluster and get indignant, which she had observed was so often the male way when confronted with obdurate females.

Theo began to fold the paper and she watched his hands, wondering why she had an ache inside. He folded it meticulously, with exaggerated care, running his thumb down the creases, then standing with it in his hands, looking at it. Then he tossed it on to the table, took three long strides around it to her side and pulled her against him with one arm around her shoulders.

'Did he frighten you?' he asked, his voice gruff.

'No.' She shook her head, certain. 'No, it was very odd. There was something about that chamber, the atmosphere. When he kissed me I felt nothing from him, but I did feel fear—almost as though it was another woman's emotions.' Elinor gave an exaggerated shiver. 'Foolishness.'

'Perhaps.' Theo kept hold of her. She felt a pressure on the top of her head as though he rested his cheek there. 'Something is very wrong in this place, Nell, but I do not think it is ghosts from the past.'

Elinor let herself lean, indulging herself, realising that it *was* an indulgence and that revealed some truth about her feelings. And suddenly she did not care. Perhaps she was in love with him. What if she was hurt? Perhaps it was better to feel strong emotions than to go through life on a safe, dull, even keel. She lifted one hand and laid it on Theo's chest, just above his heart, feeling the strong beat pulse through her.

Yes, said the voice in her head. *Yes, he is the one. At last.*

'Nell? Are you all right? You sighed.' He let her go, setting her back a pace and holding her by the shoulders to look into her face. 'You know, you are damnably pretty in that colour.'

'For which you may take all the credit,' she said, making light of it. 'I freely acknowledge that my wardrobe was full of dreadful gowns. But you should not lie to me, Theo—I am not pretty.'

'No, you aren't, are you?' He frowned at her. 'That's too lightweight a word. I am no sure what you are, I will have to think about it.' He bent, kissed her on the lips with a fleeting pressure and turned abruptly to the door.

'Theo!' It came out as a somewhat strangled gasp, but at last she could still articulate. It hadn't been a proper kiss. It had been, she supposed, just a friendly gesture. No doubt he had got whatever *desire* he had felt for her out of his system with that kiss in the study and now she was just a friend to be reassured, and protected from the count. 'My easel? Mama will be waiting.'

'Lord, yes. I was forgetting, she wanted me to measure something high up—string courses, I think. Come on.'

At two in the morning Theo watched Elinor as she walked softly along the passageway in front of him, a lantern in her hand. They had decided to go the longer way to the chamber, the way she had gone with Leon in the afternoon, rather than risk opening an external door into the courtyard in the dark.

He had spent the rest of the afternoon balancing on stepladders holding measuring rods, while his aunt tried to make the dimensions of the chapel fit some mathematical formula dreamt up by a scholar whom Theo had no trouble stigmatising as being as daft as a coot. She had failed, something that appeared to give her great satisfaction, and had dismissed him until dinner, leaving him ample time to brood over what, exactly, was the right word to describe Elinor now.

She never had been plain, he had realised, his soup spoon halfway to his mouth during the first course, just smothered by drab colours and scraped-back hair and a life of dull regularity. Like the uncut gemstone he had likened her to, or perhaps a painting, languishing under layer after layer of ancient varnish.

The countess addressed a question to him and he answered her, half of his mind still on Elinor. Then it came to him as he saw her turn, laughing at something Sir Ian had said, her face lit up with amusement and intelligence and the lovely line of her upper body silhouetted against the baronet's dark evening coat. *Comely,* that was the word. And she always would be, even in old age, he realised, finding he was smiling.

He was still thinking about that revelation as he followed her into the hall, his eyes on the pool of light cast at her feet by the dark lantern. Distracted, he bumped into a chest. The sharp edge dug into his thigh, the lid lifted and banged down with a loud thud that seemed to echo round the great hall. He stopped, cursing under his breath and rubbing his leg.

'Does it hurt?' Elinor came back and held up the light to see.

'Damned chest.' The long-case clock they were standing next to chimed the half-hour, making her jump. 'We had better get a move on.' Elinor nodded, lifted the light and turned. 'Wait!'

'What?' She came back and looked where he was pointing. The great tapestry hung from floor to ceiling. It was in poor condition, moth-eaten and dusty from long years hanging close to the fireplace, but it was possible to make out that it showed the Chateau of Beaumartin in an earlier age. Around the borders were trails of vines, hunting scenes, vignettes of harvest and feasting. And in the middle of the left-hand border, the image of a chalice, half-hidden by a drapery.

'Is that it?' Elinor put the lantern on a side table by the sofa that stood in front of the tapestry and climbed up onto the upholstered seat. 'I can't see very clearly.'

'It is the right general outline. It doesn't show the detail, of course—that would probably scorch a hole in the fabric.' He could remember the effort it had taken not to react when the late count had finally taken the thing out of its case and handed it to him and he was able to study it for the first time. He had thought himself sophisticated and had been astonished to find himself shocked, enlightened and shamefully aroused, all at once.

Theo joined Elinor on the sofa seat, making it dip and forcing her to clutch at his sleeve to steady herself. 'If I lift this edge away from the wall, can you shine the light behind and see if you can see any kind of wall cupboard or opening?'

It took some doing. The tapestry was heavy, and without moving the weighty sofa, it was difficult to pull away from the wall. Sneezing from the dust, Elinor managed to get both the lantern and her head into the gap he created.

'Nothing, just smooth wall.'

'Good—I did not relish trying to drag this sofa out and then get it back in the right spot,' he said with some relief, helping her tuck the rucked tapestry back down behind the high upholstered back again.

It was smooth at last, and the two of them panting with the effort of doing it while balancing on the squashy and rather mobile cushions, when Theo froze. 'Someone's coming.'

It was just on the edge of his hearing, but it was definitely movement, the sound of someone trying to be quiet, and coming from the direction they had entered from. 'Hell, where can we hide?'

The heavily shadowed hall stretched out before them, singularly free of tables with heavy cloths over, cupboards or windows with floor-length curtains. It was quiet again. Theo had just decided he was imagining things when the door at the far end burst open.

It was too late to run—there was nowhere to conceal themselves. Theo fell on to the sofa, pulling Elinor down into his arms. 'Kiss me.'

He saw her grasp his intentions as fast as he spoke. With a ruthless hand she pulled open the top three buttons on her old gown, scattering them, then attacked the neck of his shirt. By the time he had her flat on her back his shirt was open to the waist and her hair was tumbling out of its pins.

It sounded as though half the village had erupted into the room. Theo sat up, pulled Elinor protectively against his chest and demanded, 'What the hell is going on?'

It might not have been the village, but it was certainly the entire house party, hastily bundled into night robes, candles in hand. 'I might ask you the same thing, Ravenhurst,' the count retorted, stepping in front of his mother and Julie as though to shield them from the shocking sight.

To one side Lady Tracey put her hands over her mouth and her husband appeared to be fighting the desire to laugh. Laure and Antoinette were agog, their hair in curling papers, their eyes wide at the sheer, wonderful, horror of what was occurring. From the shadows Ana looked on, smiling. When he caught her eye, she licked her lips like a cat delicately relishing a mouse she had just eaten

'Theophilus!' It had been too much to hope that Aunt Louisa was absent from this mob. 'What do you think you are doing?'

'I should have thought that all too obvious, *madame*,' the countess interjected in freezing tones.

'We were going outside. For a walk. But I am afraid our passion got the better of us before we got to the door,' Theo said, improvising rapidly in an attempt to come up with a convincing story. Crushed beneath him, he could feel Elinor shift. He tried to take some his weight off her without standing up. The image he wanted firmly in everyone's mind was one of lovers caught *in flagrante*, not of two people dressed to be creeping about the chateau on some clandestine errand. And the warm curves pressed against him were decidedly inspiring. 'Aunt Louisa, I had hoped to speak to you about this before now, but I fully intend—'

'You most certainly do,' she said. There was something in her tone that alerted him. She was not reacting as he expected her to. The others would not notice, they did not know her. But Theo knew that he could have expected to have been hauled off the sofa by his ear while she sent for a pair of blunt scissors, not subjected to a quelling stare down her imposing nose and utter, chilly, calm. 'You will attend me in my room at once. Both of you.' She turned to regard the others. 'Thank you, Count. I am sure there is nothing here to keep anyone else from their beds.'

Theo stood up and turned his back on the room, giving Elinor time to compose herself a little while the sounds of the retreating party diminished. Finally the door shut. She looked up at him, her face white. 'Theo, she is going to say I am compromised and insist—' Her fingers fumbled with the bodice of her gown and she looked up again. 'I do *not* want to marry you, Theo.'

'You don't?' He did not want to marry her, either, of course he didn't. The last thing he needed was a wife. But it shook him to realise his spinster cousin was just as adamantly unwilling to wed him. *Coxcomb* he jeered a himself for his reaction. *You are hardly God's gift as a husband, are you? A red-headed adventurer in disgrace with his family? Sensible woman.* 'All right, we will tell her the truth.' And that would be an act as courageous as any he had ever performed, explaining to his formidable aunt that he was involving her daughter in a perilous search for a pornographic artefact.

Chapter Thirteen

'What on earth were they all doing here?' Elinor asked, following Theo along the corridor as he tried to restore his shirt to some kind of order.

'I haven't the slightest idea—that damnable trunk lid banging down did not make so much noise it would rouse them from sleep, that's for sure.'

'Well, they were hardly likely to all be up recreating one of the famous orgies,' she said, shakily attempting humour. 'Not with Mama there. Can you imagine?'

'That was an image I am going to regret you placing in my imagination,' he said with feeling as they reached Lady James's door. 'Ready, Nell?' Elinor put back her shoulders and shook her hair out of her eyes. She felt as though she was going to face a firing squad.

'Ready.'

Mama was seated at her writing desk, her chair half-turned so she could scrutinise them as they came to stand in front of her. She did not ask them to sit down. 'Well, Theophilus?'

'I can explain, Aunt.' He did not appear either cowed or abashed by the situation. 'But first, tell me—how the dev—how on earth did everyone come to be in the hall at this hour of the night?'

'Those two idiotic girls decided it would be *fun* to creep around the chateau after dark in search of the Gothic horrors Elinor was foolish enough to speak of. They are addicted to sensation novels, it appears. They heard a loud bang as they approached the hall, assumed it was burglars—or a headless fiend, they are confused on that point—and rushed back, hammering on everyone's door and shrieking the place down.

'Normally I would have allowed the search to take place without me—most irrational and foolish, it merely needed the count to summon his male staff to search for the intruders. However, I was surprised to see neither of you coming out in response to the racket and looked in your rooms. Expecting the worst, I joined the group.'

'Mama, it was not what it seemed—' Elinor began.

'Nell.' Theo took her arm and guided her to one of the wing chairs by the fireside. 'I'll explain, you sit down.' She could not help but feel it was feeble of her to obey him. They had both got into this mess, she should be standing up to Mama at his side. But he looked cool and very confident and the smile he gave her was reassuring. Perhaps he could manage Mama better than she could.

He turned the other chair to face his aunt and sat down, uninvited. It was a good start—if she thought he was standing there to be carpeted like a naughty schoolboy, she was much mistaken.

'I have involved Elinor, and you, in an assault, a theft and a murder,' he began. The full frontal attack had the desired effect: Lady James's eyebrows rose, she reached for her eyeglass, but she did not speak. 'It began when I was commissioned to negotiate for the purchase of a unique, and utterly indecent, piece of precious metalwork…

'…and if you think I, or any other man, can stop your daughter when she decides to involve herself in something, then I am afraid you are much mistaken, Aunt,' he finished half an hour later.

Elinor could sense that Theo was making himself sit still in the silence that followed. Her mother looked at Elinor through her eyeglass, then turned it on Theo. 'I collect you two do not wish to marry?' she said calmly.

'No, Mama, I—'

'No, we do not.' Lady James opened her mouth to utter her next question, but he answered it before she could speak. 'Nor is there any pressing reason why we must. That scene in the hall was pure theatre.' He was, Elinor thought blankly, extremely convincing.

'Indeed? I am relieved to hear it.' She let the eyeglass dangle on its black cord and watched it swing for a moment or two while Elinor contemplated her toes and wondered just how crimson she was blushing. 'It would be prudent, I believe, to allow the impression that you are now betrothed. You will no doubt suffer considerable embarrassment for the remainder of your stay here, which I can only say is your just desserts. Once we are back in England, no more need be said—no one here moves in the same circles as we do.'

She waited, apparently for them to comment, then added with a certain malicious relish, 'It will certainly put your mistress's nose out of joint, Theophilus.'

'Mama!'

'Don't be mealy mouthed, Elinor. That unprincipled creature is one reason I was quite confident that Theophilus's amatory inclinations were directed elsewhere and not towards you.'

Had anyone ever tried to strangle the old witch? Theo wondered. But say what you might about her adder tongue, her attitude was an enormous relief. Or it should be. He was feeling unaccountably flat, but that, no doubt, was due to the shock of what had just occurred. Somehow he had been braced for an argument about marrying Elinor.

'Mama, Theo must find this Chalice or repay Lord X a great deal of money,' Elinor said, cutting across his musings. 'Even then, if he does not get the Chalice, there is no knowing what Lord X might do.' Lady James's gaze came up to scrutinise his bruised face.

'I did not suggest you stop looking for it,' she said. Theo's jaw dropped before he shut his mouth with a snap. Most of the time he felt confident he was in command of himself and of the situation—encounters with his aunt were a definite exception. 'One cannot allow murder and theft to go unpunished. As for his lordship, I suggest you tell me his name, Theophilus. I have powerful friends.'

'I do not break my clients' confidentiality,' he said, wishing he could in this instance. Goodness knows what, or who, Lady James Ravenhurst could summon to her aid if she wanted revenge upon someone. He shuddered to think, imagining a blood-crazed mob of Greek scholars pelting his lordship with heavy tomes.

'I intend helping Theo,' Elinor said firmly. He turned in the chair and smiled at her. Her chin was up and she was looking determined, despite the dark shadows under her eyes. He lov… He *admired* her courage.

'Of course,' Lady James said, startling them both. 'We are Ravenhursts, we do not abandon each other in times of trouble. However, I warn you, if she is harmed in any way, Theo, I will have your hide. Now, off to bed, both of you. I have work to do in the morning.'

'She called you Theo,' Elinor whispered as they stood outside in the corridor looking rather blankly at each other.

'I think we're dreaming,' Theo said, shaking his head. Elinor was still looking at him, the frown line between her brows furrowed. 'And don't do that.' He reached out and smoothed it with his thumb. 'Remember what your mother says about frowning.' Her skin was warm and soft and he ran the ball of his thumb along one arching eyebrow, feeling the elegant vault of the bone beneath. 'Goodnight, Nell.'

'Goodnight, Theophilus,' she said, suddenly grinning at him. 'I had better learn to address my betrothed with suitable deference.'

She was through the door before he could respond, although he thought he could hear her chuckle, floating behind her on the air.

Coming down to breakfast required a considerable amount of courage. The flash of amusement that had made her tease Theo evaporated as soon as she was alone in her room, leaving Elinor to toss and turn all night, alternately turning hot and cold with embarrassment.

It had never, ever, occurred to her that she might find herself compromised. Before Theo, men had not wanted to be alone with her for any other reason than to prose on about their translation from the Greek, to argue with her about Mama's latest controversial paper or occasionally to tell her at great length how miserable they were because their suit of some lady was not prospering.

Now—post-Theo—she did at least have the confidence that she looked well enough, and he had seemed to enjoy kissing her. But that they might find themselves caught, apparently locked in a passionate embrace… Every time her churning imagination presented her with the image of how they must have looked, she curled up tighter in bed and buried her head further into the pillows.

For some reason their exposure that night in a sham, and relatively mild, situation, was worrying her far more than the risk they had run kissing passionately—and very genuinely—in the study when they had been so nearly caught.

At this point Elinor got out of bed and began to prowl up and down, unable to lie still any longer. Her feelings in the study had been fuelled by ignorance, and the disorientation caused by the havoc Theo had wrought on her body and her emotions. This time they had been caught, and the appearance was everything. And it had just been appearance. He had been pretending; yet for her, even in the middle of that confusion and embarrassment, she had revelled in the feel of his hard body, his quick thinking, the instinctive way he had shielded her.

If Mama had insisted he marry her! She tried to imagine being married to someone she loved and who did not want to be married to her. It was too ghastly to contemplate. Ruin was infinitely preferable—after all, how much worse off would she be in disgrace than she had been before she bumped into Theo in the basilica?

Pride made her pinch her cheeks when she looked in the mirror in the morning and she sent Jeanie off to find rice powder to cover the shadows under her eyes. It was hard to find a manner pitched between shamefaced and brazen when she found the entire party gathered in the breakfast parlour, all apparently determined to make their meal last as long as possible in the hope that the errant couple would make an appearance together.

Theo, deep in conversation with Sir Ian on the subject of horses, got to his feet when she entered, walked to her side and kissed her cheek. 'Courage,' he whispered before turning and leading her to the chair beside his. 'Good morning, Elinor.'

Laure and Antoinette were staring. Elinor smiled warmly at them, making both drop their eyes to their plates in confusion, then extended the smile to take in the rest of the table. 'I am so sorry we disturbed you all last night, but I know you will all be happy for us—we are betrothed.'

That at least had the effect of taking the wind out of their sails. If they thought she was going to creep around, blushing and humiliated, they had another think coming. Elinor gazed up at Theo and tried to look like a woman in love. It was apparently more convincing than she expected. Lady Tracey gave a sentimental sigh, Mademoiselle Julie looked pleased—presumably because she would no longer take any notice of Leon—and even the countess's severe expression softened somewhat.

'When do you intend to wed?' Monsieur Castelnau enquired.

'We have not decided—' Elinor began, but Theo cut in smoothly.

'It will be a while. Naturally we want my father, the Bishop of Wessex, to marry us and I would hope our cousin the duke will be able to attend, although he rarely travels south. And her Serene Highness, the Grand Duchess of Maubourg, who has recently joined our family, is naturally subject to many commitments.'

'A large Society wedding, then?' Sir Ian asked.

'Huge,' Theo said expansively, warming to his theme. Elinor sat quietly eating while he talked. If anyone there had not fully comprehended just who Theo was, and how well he was connected, they knew now. And, as his cousin, they must realise this applied equally to her. He was taking out insurance, she realised, making it very clear that anyone who harmed or insulted them would have the entire Ravenhurst clan to deal with.

She allowed herself to fall into a daydream of walking down the aisle of the cathedral on Theo's arm, as his wife. The organ would be filling the space with joyful sound, the entire family would be beaming, she would be looking beautiful in cream silk with almond trimmings. The scene ground to a shuddering halt at this point, as though the actors had been turned to stone. She was never going to make a fairytale bride, the bishop would never agree to marry them, the family would be aghast at Theo making such a poor match as a spinster bluestocking. And, above all, Theo did not want to marry her anyway and this was all pretence.

To her horror, tears began to well up in her eyes. 'Oh. Oh, forgive me, I feel a little—' She bolted from the room, hearing Ana's voice, rich with mock concern, just as the door closed behind her.

'I *do* hope she is not feeling sick.'

Oh my God, she means morning sickness. Elinor found herself in the inner courtyard and sat down, trembling. *Well, they'll see, I'll be fine every morning after this.*

'Elinor?' It was Theo. 'What is it? You were doing so well.' He sat down and took her hand. The warm, familiar grasp made the tears gather again and she jerked it away, furious with herself.

'Have you got a handkerchief?' Wordlessly Theo produced a large white square and she blew her nose.

'I am just tired and I do not feel very…very…' She ran out of inspiration and sat twisting the linen between her hands, forbidding herself to produce one more sniffle.

'Oh, that,' Theo said calmly. 'I've got sisters, I'm quite used to regular, um, moods.'

He thought she was having her courses! Elinor was not sure whether to simply melt into the ground with embarrassment or seize thankfully on the excuse for her loss of control. Theo seemed to be taking it in his stride, so she decided to simply ignore the whole thing. She blew her nose again, conscious that it had probably turned pink, and folded the handkerchief away. 'What are you going to do today? We cannot search during daylight hours.'

'I was going to take advantage of the count's invitation to browse in his library. There probably isn't anything there, or he wouldn't be so open about it, but there might be some volumes of value I might be able to persuade him to sell.'

'Can you afford it?' Elinor asked. 'If you have to repay Lord X, that will be very expensive won't it?'

'Very,' he agreed grimly. 'I won't be able to afford a wife, I'm afraid.'

He was joking, of course, despite his very straight face. 'Well, that will give us a good excuse to break it off,' she said. 'I don't wish to figure as a jilt—not that anyone would believe I would be so foolish.'

'Really?' Theo looked bemused. 'Why on earth should anyone imagine I would be a good catch?'

'Don't fish for compliments,' Elinor said, her lips twitching, amused despite herself that she had made a pun.

Theo grinned back. 'Go on, flatter me, my morale needs boosting.'

'You are very well connected, healthy, intelligent, well-off—provided you do not have to repay Lord X—and moderately good looking, assuming one discounts the hair of course.'

'I suppose I should be glad of the *moderately*,' he said with mock gloom. 'Go on—is there anything else on the plus side of the account?'

'You are a talented artist, have good taste and a sense of humour. And you—' She broke off, confused at where her list was taking her, and bit her lip.

'And I what?' Theo was watching her mouth.

'You kiss very well.'

'Thank you,' he said gravely. 'And might I ask what basis for comparison you have, Miss Ravenhurst?'

'None, except Leon, but I do not think he can be very good. He kissed me and I did not feel a thing.'

'Indeed? Excuse me for a moment while I fight the urge to feel smug. But I feel bound to point out that he was kissing you in a dark and gloomy dungeon, which might well have dampened your feelings of ardour.'

'You kissed me on a study floor,' Elinor pointed out. 'And that was very stimulating.'

'For both of us.' Theo got to his feet. 'Are you going to stay here and rest?'

'Rest?' It took Elinor a moment to remember he thought her to be feeling delicate. 'Goodness, no. I think I will escape for a walk before Mama finds me and gives me something dreary to do indoors. Those woods look beautiful. I thought I would climb up through them and see if there is a view of the basilica from the top.'

'May I come with you? The library can wait for a wet day, if one ever comes. The weather is so beautiful it seems set to be like this for ever.'

'I will see you at the front door in fifteen minutes,' Elinor said. 'How lovely to get out of here and away from all those sharp tongues and prying eyes.'

She was before him, hurrying through the hall, enjoying the freedom of her new divided skirt and not noticing the other figure standing there until she was almost upon them.

'Marquesa.' Ana was wearing the original of Elinor's garment.

'Miss Ravenhurst. And where did you find the pattern for your habit, might I ask?'

'Theo drew it for me,' Elinor said cheerfully. 'He was able to describe it in detail.'

'So I should hope, he has removed it often enough.'

'Were you his mistress for very long?' Elinor enquired, refusing to gratify the woman by showing any embarrassment.

Ana drew in her breath in a sharp hiss. 'He is my lover—I was never his mistress. There is a difference.'

'I am sure there is.' Elinor gave no sign that she noticed Ana's use of the present tense, although a sharp stab of jealousy knotted her inside. 'What fun for you, to find a man so much younger than yourself.'

'Comparing fashion tips, ladies?' It was Theo, his satchel over one shoulder. He reached out and took Elinor's easel. 'Come on, my love, let's take advantage of this light.'

He nodded to Ana as he swung the heavy door open and Elinor went through, not looking at the other woman, but hearing her indrawn hiss of angry breath.

'*Not* tactful to call one woman *my love* in front of another who has just declared you are her lover. Present tense.'

Theo swung the easel on to his back and grimaced. 'She isn't.'

'You don't have to justify yourself to me.' Elinor walked through the arch under the gatehouse and turned uphill along a steep track. She was feeling decidedly flustered. She had stood up to Ana on instinct; now she was realising that she was way out of her depth, sparring with a woman of the marquesa's experience. 'We aren't betrothed. Remember?'

'What you think matters to me.' Surprised, Elinor looked back over her shoulder and slowed her pace. 'I respect your opinion and your judgement.'

'She is a beautiful woman and an intelligent one. I imagine she is stimulating company.' Elinor tried to be fair. 'You must enjoy the freedom you have. I imagine it exceeds even what a gentleman might expect in England.'

'Yes.' Theo climbed beside her in silence for a while. 'Freedom, of course, is everything.'

Elinor was about to retort that it was not, that, precious though it was, there were other equally important things in life, and then the edge of bitterness in his voice struck her. How many lovers, how short a time with each? So much intimacy of the body—how much of the mind? No ties, no responsibility. No one to care about and no one to care about you.

'I don't agree,' she said. 'Not at the price of love.'

'Who do you love?' he asked harshly.

'My mother. I loved my father. I love my friends and our cousin Bel.' *I love you.* 'Don't you love anyone?'

He was silent so long that she thought he was not going to reply. They climbed on, up through the woodland, past a group of foresters stacking logs, up the last steep pull and out on to open scrubby meadow.

'I do not intend ever to marry,' Theo said abruptly. He stood still, shading his eyes, apparently orientating himself, then strode off along the crest.

Confused, Elinor stared after him. He had not answered her question. But that statement was clear enough. Why not? She bit her lip, watching him. It could only mean he loved someone he could not marry.

Chapter Fourteen

Elinor watched Theo walk away. Should she follow him? Did he want to be alone with his thoughts? So he was in love. Not with Ana. Not with herself, obviously. A hopeless love, then, one that was not returned. Or perhaps she was a married woman. No wonder he sought companionship from lovers and felt no attachment to any of them. It was lonely, unrequited love, she was discovering. At least Theo was not being tormented by daily contact with the object of his affections as she was.

It was better, she decided, not to marry at all rather than to marry someone one didn't love, while all the time there was someone you did care for and could not have. No wonder he had reacted so strongly when she had come to his room, and had been so clear about their present masquerade being merely for convention.

He had stopped, dumped her easel and his satchel on the ground and was standing, hands on hips, looking out over the view. Elinor straightened her back, adjusted her own bag on her shoulder, and walked to join him, indulging herself with the opportunity to study the tall figure unobserved.

When she reached him, she realised he had found a fine view out towards the basilica perched on its hill. 'Do you want to sketch?' he asked without looking at her.

What she wanted was to talk. But did he? She studied his unresponsive profile. 'Not just yet. That was a steep climb, I think I'll sit over there on that outcrop of rock and enjoy the view for a while.'

It took almost quarter of an hour before he joined her. Elinor lifted her chin from her cupped hand and smiled at him. 'Hello.'

'Hello.' He folded down on to the turf at the foot of her perch, presenting her with the unreadable back of his head. 'I must apologise.'

'For what?'

'Brooding. You did not come up here to put up with me moping.'

If she reached down, she could run her fingers through his hair, smooth it down where the breeze had caught and tossed it into disarray. If she slid down the smooth rock, she could be in his arms. Elinor sat still and made herself smile so her voice would sound cheerful. 'I would hardly call that moping. Or brooding. I'm your friend, Theo, we can talk to each other about things that matter to us, or we can be silent in each other's company. It doesn't matter.'

His shoulders dropped, as though he had relaxed. 'There is someone, isn't there? Doesn't she love you? Or can't she marry you?'

'Doesn't love me, doesn't want to marry me,' he said, tipping his head back against the rock. 'Not that I'd ask. Can you imagine the sort of married life she would have to put up with, stuck in England while I'm away so much?'

'Naval wives put up with it,' Elinor said. 'And in any case, why wouldn't she travel with you? I would.' Theo went very still. 'If I was in love with you, that is. Or wanted to marry, for that matter.'

'You, Nell, are unique. I can't imagine any other woman I know living out of a trunk for months at a time or pulling a pistol on a pair of thugs. And what about the children?'

'You would just have to get a bigger travelling coach,' she said robustly. 'Or a second one for some of the children and the nurse, so they could rotate with you. Of course, as the children got older, you'd need a schoolroom coach as well.'

'So you wouldn't put all the children together to give my wife and I some peace and quiet?' He sounded as though the fantasy was cheering him up. 'I thought you didn't like children.'

'I'm not over-fond of my nephews and nieces, they have been thoroughly spoiled and indulged. I wouldn't mind mine, and I'm sure yours would be delightful.' *And ours would all have red hair and tempers to match and would be a complete handful in a coach! But such fun...* This was edging into dangerous ground. 'I think I'll draw now. Can you pass me my things? Not the easel, I'll just use my sketchbook.'

Theo found himself a rock to sit on and balanced his own sketchbook on his knee. God! That had been dangerous and painful and very illuminating, that flash of realisation at the top of the hill. *Of course* he loved Nell, his red-headed cousin who just wanted to be his friend. Why hadn't he realised it sooner? Perhaps he had and had simply denied it to himself. She was perfect for him, in every way, but she was not in love with him, did not want to marry him.

Was it worth risking asking her? What would happen if he told her the truth, convinced her he meant it and it was nothing to do with compromising her? But she would say *no,* and their friendship would be spoiled and he would lose even that. He glanced across at her and found Elinor was sitting biting the end of her pencil and looking at him. She grinned, tossing back the heavy plait that hung over her shoulder.

There was no point in entertaining false hopes. If she felt anything for him, she would never have reacted so violently to the suggestion they might have to marry and she would never have discussed his love for another woman with such frankness. Nor would she be so open with him about sex—it was obvious that she had none of the self-consciousness on the subject he would have expected if her feelings for him were involved.

He squinted at the landscape and found no inspiration there. Then he began to doodle in one corner, the image taking shape with speed under his hand. After a few minutes he moved to another part of the sheet and began another sketch, then another, aware that his spirits were lightening, too focused to see any danger in what he was doing.

Soon the pages were filling with a procession of travelling carriages of all shapes and sizes, luggage piled on top and falling off behind and from each window a child was hanging, dropping toys, waving, fighting with a sibling. The top of two adult heads were vaguely discernible in the chaos and a pack of dogs ran behind, barking madly. In the middle was his self-portrait looking desperate, his arms full of precariously piled precious objects while infants rampaged around his feet.

'Show me what you have done.' It was Nell, somewhat tousled from having slid down the rock.

'No.' He flipped his book shut, realising he must have filled five or six pages with his fanciful sketches.

'But I want to see.' She tried to tug it out of his hands, but he held firm, pulled it free and sat on it.

'No,' he said, reaching to pick up her sketch book.

She too had been caught up in the foolish fantasy. There, on the first page, was Elinor's impression of his travelling family, a circle of carriages drawn up like a gypsy encampment. Children of all ages had been sketched in, noses in books, playing with kittens, chasing each other in a wild game of tag over and under a collection of scantly draped classical statues, the subjects of which looked on in frozen marble hauteur. In the middle, in front of a camp fire with a kettle suspended over it, was a woman drawn from the back, her sun bonnet tipped back, her feet on a box, a fan in her hand. A wickedly accurate sketch of himself showed him sitting in one of the carriages, head in hands.

He flipped the page and found the children sitting in a circle, solemnly listening to Elinor herself, perched on a box while she read to them from a book. Her hair was dishevelled, she was wearing the divided skirt and she had dotted in a fine array of freckles across her own nose.

'Give me that back!' She made a grab for her sketchbook and missed as he held it over his head. 'I thought perhaps you would employ me as a governess,' she explained.

'They seem to be paying you a great deal of attention,' he said, finding his voice was, inexplicably, not quite steady. 'Elinor.'

'Yes?' She was a little pale, but that was probably explained by the time of the month. He shouldn't have let her come on this strenuous walk, he wanted to wrap her up and cosset her. Even as he thought it, he realised that she would hate it, that what she wanted was freedom, the freedom he had. The freedom he could give her. Hell, he would risk it.

'Elinor, why don't we get married. Really get married?' He dropped the sketchbook and pulled her to him. 'There is no one else for us. We are friends. We have this.' She was so still in his arms that she seemed frozen.

Her mouth under his was warm, tremulous. He coaxed with his tongue, slid his lips across hers, trying to show her how he felt without saying the words that would place such an emotional burden on her.

For a moment she melted, swaying into his body, her lips parting to let him in and he was dizzy with triumph, then she pulled back so she was straining against his grip. 'No, Theo. No. I do not want to marry you. I told you, I meant it.' He let go and she took three steps away from him, her back turned. 'There has to be love, Theo,' she said over her shoulder. 'I am a fool to be such a romantic when I thought myself rational, but there you are.'

All the laughter had gone from her, all the trust, replaced by regret and wariness. He should have listened to his head, not to his heart. Listened and settled for what he had, not what he hoped for. She could give him friendship and laughter and her courage. But not her love.

And now she was miserable and he was lonely again. So lonely. He had not realised how wide and deep that hole had been until she had come into his life and filled it. Now it gaped blackly under his feet.

'I'm sorry, Nell.' She did not move. 'Compromise is not right for us.' A nod. 'I just thought it would be companionable, you and I together. Can we be friends again? Have I ruined things?'

'No. No, of course not.' She turned and walked back to him, put her arms around as much of him as she could manage and hugged hard, then stepped back and smiled. *Well, that settles it. Hugged like a brother.* The smile was a little wary, but it was genuine, he saw it in her eyes.

'What have you got to eat in that bottomless satchel of yours?' she asked. 'Or do we have to snare a rabbit if we aren't to go hungry?'

'I went and charmed some food out of the cook. That was why I was late,' Theo confessed.

'Good.' She nodded towards a dense thicket. 'I'll just go and, um…'

Theo knelt down and began to unpack the food. Nell's sketchbook lay open where it had been dropped. He reached across and tore the sketches clean out, looked at them for a long moment, almost hearing the ghost of the children's laughter, then slipped them inside his own book, tying the strings into a knot it would be impossible to open without a knife. All the portraits of their children who would never be.

Elinor reached the shelter of the bushes before her legs gave way and she sank down on the turf. To have a good weep was tempting, but pointless. She would have to emerge, nose red, eyes bleary—and what could she say? *I love you, of course I'll marry you, even if you love someone else? I'll marry you because you want a companion and feel sorry for me so I'll do?* She prided herself on common sense and stoicism; now was the time to exercise those qualities.

After all, she was no worse off than she was a few weeks ago, she told herself, selecting a nice dense bush and checking for thistles, adders and stinging nettles.

Adjusting her clothing again, she decided that actually she was worse off. Much worse. If you had never eaten strawberries, you had no idea what you were missing. But once you had, you never forgot the taste and always yearned for them. Theo was strawberries and cream and every sensual pleasure she had ever experienced and he was here, now. Not safely out of the way, but a constant reminder, a constant temptation.

There was only one way to get through this and that was to stiffen her backbone and just endure until they parted company. 'Well,' she said brightly as she emerged from the thicket, chin up, shoulders back, 'I hope you did well with the cook, because I am starving.'

They ate chicken legs and crusty rolls, cheese and apples, all washed down with cider. 'I'm sleepy,' Elinor confessed.

'Sleep, then.' Theo took off his coat, rolled it up and set it down as a pillow. 'Go on.'

'You, too.' Elinor stretched out on the short grass in the shade of the big tree where Theo had laid out the food. 'We both need our sleep if we are to search that chamber in the cellars tonight.'

Theo stopped, halfway into a sprawl, and propped himself on one elbow, looking at her. 'I am searching alone, you are not...well.'

'I am perfectly well. It isn't an illness.' Elinor shut her eyes and snuggled into the Theo-smelling soft wool. 'And it certainly isn't an excuse for missing the fun.'

'Fun?' She could hear him yawning. Perhaps he had managed

as little sleep as she had last night. 'And what are we going to say if we are caught down there, pray?'

'That we are rather, er, sophisticated in our tastes and wanted to make love at the scene of the infamous orgies?' she suggested sleepily.

There was a gasp of laughter from Theo. 'Now that is another image you have put into my imagination that I really, truly, did not want there.'

A person would need to be not sophisticated, but downright perverse, to want to be anywhere near this chamber, let alone making love in it, Elinor decided, shivering in the semi-darkness at two the next morning. Theo was pacing, muttering under his breath; she was perched on the unpleasant stone slab, waiting to do something useful.

'If I was conducting a semi-ritualistic orgy,' he announced at length, 'I think I would want as much drama as possible.'

'I agree,' Elinor nodded vigorously, trying not to speculate about what was making scuffling noises in a far corner.

'So—I produce the Chalice and all the other items of plate with a flourish. From where?' He frowned at her. 'Would you mind very much lying down?'

'As the sacrifice?' He nodded, looking as happy about it as she felt. 'All right. Like this?' Elinor lay down and stretched up her hands to catch the iron rings. Theo seemed to tower above her in the flickering light, the shadows making a mask out of his face and the focused light from the dark lanterns setting his hair aflame. It took an effort of will to remember that this was play-acting. He threw up his arms dramatically as though commanding an audience.

'Now what? I wouldn't bend down, that loses impact. There is nothing in front of me…' He spun on his heel, coat tails flaring out behind him, and flattened his upraised palms against the stonework. There was silence. 'Elinor, come and help me—there is something here.'

She came and stood beside him, the two of them feeling the stone, running their fingertips along the mortar lines. He was right—there was something odd about the feel of that patch of wall, but whatever it was, it was well hidden.

'I give up,' Elinor said after ten minutes, standing back to suck at a torn nail.

'Damn it.' Exasperated, Theo thumped the wall with his clenched fist, then swore with the pain of it. There was an odd grinding noise and there, in front of him, was wood. 'That's a keyhole.'

She saw the gleam of his teeth as he smiled at her, then the picklocks were clinking in his fingers and she stepped back to give him room. It seemed to take for ever, and it seemed too that the ghosts of the chamber were crowding in behind them, eager to see their treasures again, rustling and breathing in the darkness.

Fighting her lurid imaginings, Elinor kept her gaze firmly on Theo's hands until the panel swung open on to the gleam of precious metals, the sparkle of gemstones and the dull sheen of leather. 'Is it there?' She craned to see past his shoulder.

'Yes. You should not look at it.' He sounded oddly breathless.

'Well, I am going to! For goodness' sake, Theo, you cannot expect me to close my eyes now.'

'Very well.' He reached in and lifted it out, a vast vessel that took both his hands to bear, and set it down on the stone platform. 'Just don't ask me to explain anything.' Elinor crouched down and studied it.

From the square base four columns, uneven and yellowish white in colour, rose from pairs of great oval opals to support the silver cup itself. There were six sides, each etched and chased and each with a scene in almost full relief of small figures sculpted in gold,

The arched lid rose above it, ribbed, with sprawling figures tumbling down in utter abandon.

Elinor reached out a hand and touched the supporting shafts. 'Ivory, with a pair of opals at the base of each.' The shafts were oddly veined and ridged and she ran her hand down one, marvelling at the tactile finish. 'It's a—' She got a grip on her voice, even as she snatched her hand back. 'They are all male, er…members.'

'Yes.' She could not look at Theo, but neither could she tear her eyes away from the object. The tiny, perfectly detailed figures were men and women and—animals? Some scenes she could understand, some, as she turned the object slowly around, mystified her. It was arousing, disgusting, beautiful and beastly. She wiped her fingers on her skirts as though they were sticky. The sound of Theo's breathing was harsh.

'Are the receipts there?'

'Yes.' He had gone back to the cupboard and was staring into it, some papers in his hand.

Elinor ducked under his arm. There were cups, a great platter, coils of leather she realised with a jolt were whips, and more ivory objects. 'More male members?' she queried as Theo shut the door, twisting the picklock to make it fast.

'Don't even think about it,' he said tersely. 'Help me wrap this thing up in my coat.'

They were crouched over it, padding the stem with the coat sleeves, their backs to the room, when the attack came. Filthy sackcloth descended in a smothering blanket, she heard Theo swearing and struck out with her nails, ripping against the cloth, then something hit her head, hard, and she went down into even deeper blackness.

Chapter Fifteen

'Nell! Nell, wake up.' Someone was calling her, which was most unfair when her head hurt so. Besides, she could not have overslept, it was still dark outside and the candles were lit.

Consciousness came back with a rush. She was sitting on something cold and hard and her hands were at full stretch over her head, which ached abominably. She was in a small stone chamber lit by guttering candles set side by side against the far wall and she wanted, rather badly, a drink, a privy and to ease the desperate ache in her arms.

'Nell!' It was Theo. Somehow she managed to turn her head and found he was chained beside her, his arms shackled as hers were, although as he was on his feet he was able to lower them so his elbows were bent.

'What happened?' she managed and saw raw relief on his face as she spoke.

'Someone hit us over the head—two people, it must have been.' So, it hadn't been her imagination or the ghosts of the past she had heard behind her after all. 'Are you all right?'

'My head hurts and I would kill for a drink, but otherwise I'll feel better if I can just stand up.' The relief when she scrambled to her feet, pushing up against the rough wall to help her shaky legs, was enormous. The chains sagged and she could clasp her hands together in front of her. 'Oh, that's better, my arms were coming out of their sockets. How are you?' Theo looked very white and there was blood on the shoulder of his shirt.

'I'll do,' Theo said, his mouth grim. 'At least they didn't want us dead.'

That was true. 'And we'll see who they are when they come back,' Elinor pointed out, nodding towards the candles. 'Two people—does that mean it is the Traceys after all?'

'Or Leon with a servant. Or Ana, with John, her groom, who has been noticeably absent from sight.'

'Even if we knew, it doesn't get us much further forwards, and it doesn't help us get out of here. What I don't understand is why they didn't just knock us out, take the Chalice and leave.' Elinor lifted her hands and peered at the heavy metal cuffs around her wrists. 'Where are your picklocks?'

'In my coat pocket.' And the coat was lying beside the candles.

'Oh.' Elinor reached out for him, finding that the chain ran freely through whatever it was secured to, high on the wall above. If she let one arm rise, she could straighten the other, almost as far as Theo. 'Can we hold hands for a little while? I'm feeling a bit shaky.' His hand clasping hers was warm, the fingers reassuringly strong and steady. 'Mama will want to know where we are.'

'That's true. And Hythe. He knows we are searching. I wish now I'd risked having him help me, but it would have been even harder to explain him if we were found than it was with you.' Theo's smile was obviously meant to be reassuring, but she was not at all sure he placed much confidence on his aunt thinking to search the dungeons, which was where they must be. 'It will take a while, though, for Aunt Louisa to start to worry and then to think of speaking to him. Plenty of time for you to tell me all the family news.'

It was a good attempt to keep her spirits up, although nothing was going to happen for a few hours, she was certain. Meanwhile, given the number of Ravenhursts, telling the news was a task that would take some time.

'And both Bel and Eva were expecting when we left England—the babies may even have been born by now,' Elinor was saying when Theo stiffened.

'Listen!'

Someone was coming. A key grated in the lock and the door swung open. '*Madame*, Julie—thank goodness!' Elinor slumped back against the wall in relief. 'You've found us. Someone hit us, dragged us in here…' Her voice tailed away as she saw them more clearly. Both looked grim, both were clad in old, dark clothes and neither made any move to approach them. 'Please, let us out of here.'

'You will be going nowhere, Mademoiselle Ravenhurst,' the countess said harshly. 'You have chosen to pry into my business, now you pay for that.'

'You took the Chalice from Theo?' Beside her he was silent, but she could feel the tension running through him as though he had touched her. If they came close enough…

'I did.' It was Julie. 'I had been following him ever since Paris. He did not know me, even if he had seen me. And, of course, he did not expect me.'

'Then what happened to the late count?' It was hard to believe these two elegant Frenchwomen could be responsible for this, but there seemed no denying the evidence of her own eyes and ears.

'My late husband would have dragged us into notoriety and scandal again, releasing that dreadful, sinful, object on to the world. My son Leon is the first de Beaumartin for decades about whom one hears no sniggers, no repetition of the gossip. At last the past was buried, we could hold our heads up once more—and then Charles drags it out into the open again.'

'Scarcely, Madame,' Theo spoke at last. 'The Chalice was to go to a private collector.'

'Who would brag to his *select* friends, I have no doubt.' The countess took an angry pace closer, still a wary distance from their reach. 'Charles would not listen, would not hear my plans for a suitable marriage for Leon.'

'To Mademoiselle Julie, no doubt?' Theo waited until the younger woman nodded, her thin face intent and tense. 'No doubt he wanted a better match for his son?'

'She is like a daughter to me and she will make him a good wife—and one who will work to restore the family name. Charles would have him marry some society girl with no backbone, no commitment.'

'And your husband sold the Chalice to restore the family fortunes despite your objections and fear of scandal?' Elinor stared at the countess's implacable face. 'Did you kill him?'

'It was an accident,' Julie said passionately. 'We were arguing in Paris, when I was trying to help her convince him it was wrong to sell the Chalice. He shouted that I was a nobody, that Leon should marry someone worthy, someone with a title and wealth to bring to the match. But I love Leon,' she said in a whisper, 'God help me, I love him.'

'So who killed the count?' Theo asked. Elinor was beyond words, staring at the two women in disbelief.

'It was an accident,' the countess said, her voice harsh. 'We struggled over the receipts, over the money. He tripped. When we saw he was dead, Julie followed you and took back the Chalice.'

'And where is it now?'

'Back in its hiding place, where it will stay for ever. Now I have found the inventory, I know nothing else is missing.'

'And you expect us to keep quiet about this?' Elinor demanded. 'Even if the count's death was an accident, you owe Lord X the money, you have assaulted us—'

'You will stay here,' the countess said, her voice eerily calm now. 'We will lock the door and we will not come back.'

'You would leave us here to die of hunger and thirst?' Elinor could hardly say the words.

'Let Elinor go,' Theo spoke over her. 'Let her go and she will promise to say nothing and I will give you access to all my money.'

'No! Leave you here? No!' She reached out for him, the chains tearing into her wrists as they stopped her, inches from him.

'I am not a cruel woman,' the countess said, placing a pitcher on the floor just within reach and stepping back. 'There is enough poison in there to kill you both, quickly.'

'Without blood on your hands?' Theo demanded.

'Exactly. I have no confidence I could kill you humanely by any other method.'

'You are a monster,' Elinor said with conviction. 'But *my* mother is not, and she will search for me and never stop.'

'I would do anything for my son's name.' The countess turned towards the door. 'And everyone, your mother included, will believe you two have eloped. In the morning all your clothes and possessions will have gone.'

The door closed behind her and the key rasped in the lock. Elinor turned and faced Theo, struggling to find calm somewhere in the sick turmoil of panic. 'Mama knows we do not want to marry, she will know something is wrong at once.'

'I agree. And together with Hythe they make a formidable team—but I do not intend staying here for however long it takes them to find us.'

'Good.' Elinor swallowed hard. 'Because I have to confess I feel just a touch…apprehensive.'

'When we do get out of here,' Theo said, smiling at her, his mouth a little crooked, 'remind me that you said that. Now then, let us be certain we cannot reach my coat and the picklocks.'

Fifteen minutes later, their wrists raw, they gave up every possible combination of stretches. The coat remained inches out of reach.

'Right.' Theo leaned back, peering up through the gloom at the point where their chains were suspended. 'I think these have been dropped over a hook, not run through a loop.'

'Which means if we can unhook them we can move about the cell and get to the picklocks.' Elinor tried to throw up the chain, but it slumped back, jarring her sore wrists. 'That won't work, it is too heavy.'

Theo stood, thinking, then knelt down, one knee raised. 'Climb—if you can get high enough, you might be able to do it.'

She could get her feet on his knee all right and up to a crouch, her fingertips scrabbling at the wall for purchase. 'Now what?' He held out his clasped hands. Gingerly Elinor put one foot on to the linked fingers.

'Hold on.' Then he was beginning to stand, lifting her weight from a kneeling position with only the wall to lean on for balance. Elinor could see the veins standing out on his temples, hear the breath hiss from his teeth. But he was rising and she was higher, higher, until he was standing upright and she was swaying on her perch, her arms outstretched. 'Now, try and throw the chain over the hook.'

She tried, and failed, three times, constantly aware of the strain on his arms, of what would happen if she failed. The cell was cold, yet perspiration was trickling down her forehead and into her eyes. *Once more,* she told herself. *I'll do it this time.*

The chain snaked up, caught, hung poised for a moment, then fell, its weight pulling her with it to land sprawled on the stone floor. 'Nell. Nell, for heaven's sake, say something!'

'Ouch,' she ventured, sitting up and rubbing her knees. 'That hurt. Nothing is broken though.'

Theo wondered if he was going to faint. He never had before, but he supposed, leaning back against the wall, the periphery of his vision closing in and his ears full of buzzing, there must be a first time for everything.

He wasn't sure whether it was the pain—his arms felt as though he'd been racked—or the relief. Probably both.

'Theo? This is not the time to go to sleep,' Elinor said severely. He opened his eyes and found her standing right in front of him, her face white. 'Are you all right?' she managed when she saw his eyes focus.

'Yes. Get the picklocks.'

It took half an hour to fumble her shackles open and then, with her holding his in the best position, to free himself. At last the chains swung back against the wall and he was able to flex his arms. 'Are you still apprehensive?' he asked as she fell against his chest, wrapped her arms around his waist and pressed her face into his shoulder.

'No.' She looked up, her smile valiant, if a little tremulous. 'Why?'

'Because I thought it the bravest thing I ever heard,' he confessed, unsurprised to find his voice husky. 'To be chained in a cellar with a pot of poison to drink and to own yourself merely a little apprehensive.'

'I was lying,' she confessed, tipping back her head to look up at him. 'I was terrified. But I knew you'd get us out.'

'Let's get this door open first before we congratulate ourselves.' The old lock was so large and crude he needed two picks to work it, but they were out into the passage in minutes. 'I'll lock it again.' He had to keep going, to think ahead and not back to what might have been. If Hythe and Lady James had been attacked, if they had not found the cell in time. If… Somehow he had to starve his imagination until they were safe away. 'We'll take the candles. I wonder if she would ever have opened the door again.'

Beside him Elinor shuddered. 'She must be mad. They both must be. You know, I've had a horrible thought. What if Leon marries

Julie and they have a son—and then Leon does something to upset them? What do you think his life is worth once there's an heir those two can fully control?'

'Not much. I'll write to him once we get clear. He may need some convincing, though. Would you believe such a thing of *your* mother?'

He did not wait for her answer, striding to open the secret panel and take out the Chalice. This time he did not wrap it when the hiding place was secure again, merely grabbed it by the stem and put his other hand under Elinor's arm. 'Come on.'

'Where to?' she asked as they slipped out into the silence of the great hall.

'To the bedchambers.'

'But we can't take anything or they'll realise we are free.'

'We need to speak to your mother, let her know what is going on.'

Aunt Louisa was, all things considered, extremely calm about finding her daughter and her nephew in her bedchamber at four in the morning, both of them filthy, battered and clutching an artefact of such indecency she had to examine it twice with her quizzing glass before she was prepared to believe the evidence of her own eyes.

Alarming in nightcap and flannel robe, she listened to their story in silence. There was, Theo admitted, something to be said for the scholarly turn of mind.

'The woman is insane,' she pronounced when they had finished. 'So, what do you propose we do now? Call in the authorities?'

Theo had been thinking about that. A descent on the *mairie* with a demand to see the mayor and order the arrest of the most powerful woman for miles around seemed doomed to failure. It would take some time to convince Leon of his mother's appalling crimes and, even if convinced, he might act to cover them up, rather than to restrain her.

'There is no one we can trust,' he concluded and saw from her nod of approval that she fully agreed. 'I will take the Chalice and get it back to England.'

'And what about me?' Elinor demanded.

'I can drop you off with Madame Dubois; you can hide in my old room. Aunt Louisa will pretend to believe we have eloped and will set off in pursuit, collecting you from St Père on the way.'

Both women regarded him in silence. Finally Elinor said flatly, 'Very well. I do not like it, but I would be a burden to you on the way, I can see that.'

He expected his aunt to agree, but she looked at her daughter incredulously. 'I never thought to hear you so feeble, Elinor! I am not happy with you hiding with some woman I do not know, and I am not convinced of our safety if they should find us together. You will go with Theo.'

It was like someone handing him an unexpected gift. Days with Nell, just the two of them, the gypsy existence on the road they had joked about. The life those sketches had pictured so vividly. He looked at his aunt, the incredible suspicion forming that she was quite deliberately throwing them together. Surely she did not really want him to marry Elinor? Did she?

Elinor looked at him and, just for a second, he thought he saw his own desires mirrored there. Then she said, with no colour in her voice, 'If you feel it better, Mama.'

'We will go to Maubourg,' he said, the idea coming to him from nowhere. 'It is closer than Paris and the coast and you said Sebastian and Eva have gone back there for the baby to be born.'

'Very sensible,' Lady James approved. 'You can send that hell-begotten object to your patron in the diplomatic bag.'

'I think not,' Theo said, imagining some clerk in the Foreign Office unwrapping it and requiring medical attention. 'I will write to Lord X from there, though.'

'Maubourg?' Nell was frowning at him.

'Where better to be safe than a castle surrounded by guards? We will get down to the stables and wake Hythe. He must take the carriage and drive to Avallon to have Lord X's men set free. He will also provide a false trail, setting out to Paris. Goodness knows if those two will ever check on us, or move the stone panel again and find the Chalice gone, but if they do then my carriage is distinctive enough to give them something to chase. We can drop off on the road to Avallon and hire a chaise.'

He felt invigorated now, despite the lack of sleep, the blow to the head, the horror of believing he had brought Nell to her death. They were alive, relatively unscathed and he had days in her company ahead. Not that she seemed very happy about the prospect. *My poor love. She must be exhausted*, he thought, wishing he had the right to take her in his arms and carry her off to his bed. To sleep. Just to watch her sleep.

'Right. I imagine we must get a move on,' Lady James was saying briskly. 'I will find a spare toothbrush and soap and underthings from my wardrobe so it will appear nothing of Elinor's is missing. That is a weakness in their little plot, is it not? If *I* were eloping, I would certainly pack a bag!'

The thought of her mother doing such a thing at least produced a faint smile on Elinor's lips. Theo watched her with concern. Had he finally found the limit of her courage and endurance? Or was she appalled at the thought of spending days alone with him after his insane proposal up on the hill?

'No, they had thought of that, apparently. I'll see what I can find of mine that won't be noticeable,' he said, thankful for an excuse to leave Elinor alone with her mother for a few moments. She was probably desperate to cry on her shoulder.

He was back in the room only minutes later to find that, far from weeping in a maternal embrace, Elinor was briskly packing a small valise. 'They've been in my room, as they said they would,' he announced tersely. 'There's a valise gone, drawers pulled out—it looks as though I packed in a hurry. Yours—unless Jeanie left it in a mess—is in the same state.'

'They may be wicked,' Elinor remarked, 'but they are not stupid. Have you found anything you can bring?'

'Here.' He handed her a rolled shirt with his spare razor inside. 'If I take a valise now, they may spot it. I'll buy more as we go. By some miracle they didn't find my money.' She took the things, pushed them into her bag and snapped it shut.

'Mama?'

'I find myself more diverted than I have in many a year,' Lady James remarked. 'Now, look after Theo—he appears to be managing very well, but one can never tell with men—and do not worry about my researches. I will pretend to set out for Paris, then double back once I am sure I am not being followed. I shall go down to Avignon—you may meet me there.'

'Of course, Mama. We can always complete the Burgundian work later,' Elinor agreed colourlessly.

'Come on, Nell.' He picked up the valise. 'We haven't much time before the servants will be up.'

'Yes, of course. Goodbye, Mama.' She kissed her mother and followed him out, into the unknown. *No,* he thought, sending a penetrating glance sideways at her face as they slipped through the trees down to the stables, *she hadn't reached the limits of her courage and endurance. She will keep going as long as I ask it of her.* The realisation left him strangely shaken—what would it be like to be loved by this woman?

Chapter Sixteen

Elinor sat in the jolting coach while Theo washed and dressed her raw wrists. He had dismissed her protests that his were worse and should take priority with a curt, 'Do as you are told', and for once she found she had no will to argue back. It was taking all her strength to stay awake and upright and she had to manage that, at least to tend to his wounds in her turn.

She should be feeling relieved that they were alive, that they had a plan and were heading for safety, but all she could feel was wave after wave of paralysing horror at what they had escaped. If Theo had been less resourceful, less strong, less…Theo, they would be in the dark by now, the candles gone, facing the prospect of dying together. Theo had sounded full of confidence, but they had both known what would have happened if Hythe and Mama had not found them in time.

Would she have told him then that she loved him? Probably not—it would only have added another burden to his shoulders for the sake of indulging herself.

She would have died never knowing what it was like to lie with a man, to show him with her body how much she loved him, to learn passion and tenderness from him. She would have died a virgin and Theo would have been lost to her for ever. Hazily she wondered if she had been given a second chance.

'Nell,' he said gently. 'You can lie down now.'

'No, I will bandage your wrists.' She forced her eyes open and reached for the basin with the stained water that was slopping around on the carriage seat.

'Nell—'

'No! Stop fussing. Just let me…' She dragged down a steadying breath and controlled the urge to babble of her terror. 'Just let me do this.' In the face of her outburst he was silent, holding out his hands for her to clean the dirty, raw scrapes and wrap the bandage around each wrist. 'There,' she said, tying the last knot. 'That's done.'

The carriage seemed to be swaying wildly, the lamps on their gimbals were fading, surely? And she was falling. 'Nell, my love,' said a voice gently and then everything faded and was gone.

Elinor woke to broad daylight, to even wilder swaying. 'Theo?' She was alone in a small carriage, wrapped up in a rug on the upholstered seat. Sitting up was an agony of bruises, stiff joints and, when she knocked her wrist, sharp pain. Doggedly she unwrapped herself from the rug, pushed her hair back from her face and made herself remember. It had not been a nightmare, then. But where was Theo?

The window let down on a strap. Elinor leaned out precariously and caught a glimpse of him up on the box, the reins of a pair in his hand. He looked relaxed, happy almost. 'Theo!'

He reined in and jumped down. 'You're awake—about time, Miss Ravenhurst, I thought you were going to sleep the clock round.'

'You said were going to hire a chaise—I thought you meant one with postillions. And where did you get those clothes?' He was dressed in a drab frieze coat and a rather battered hat.

'They're Hythe's. I thought it would attract less attention hiring just a chaise with no men. We couldn't wake you up—are you all right?'

'I'm fine. I think,' she added, trying a few experimental stretches. 'Are you?'

'Sore,' he admitted with a wry grimace. 'And I'll be glad to sleep tonight. But I'll live.'

'What time is it?' Elinor took the opportunity to study Theo as he dug his pocket watch out and checked it. He had said something as she had slipped into sleep, something that touched the edge of her consciousness, but which now she couldn't quite reach out and grasp. She wanted to hold him, hold on to him, needing comfort and wondering if he, too, felt the same hideous twist of fear when he remembered what might have happened. But you could not ask a man if he felt fear, and he would never admit it if he did.

When he looked up she saw there were dark smudges under the clear green eyes and the lines either side of his mouth were deeper. He looked older, harder and somehow different.

'It is half past two,' he said, pushing the watch back into the fob pocket. 'We'll stop at the next reasonable inn and get something to eat.'

'Where are we heading for?' Elinor asked.

'Arnay le Duc, but we may not make it tonight. I'm trying to take a direct route for Maubourg without using the most obvious main road.' He opened the carriage door, but Elinor shook her head. 'You want to come up on the box? I won't let you drive, you know.' The smile creased the corners of his eyes and she made herself smile back as he gave her his hand to help her climb up.

'Will they follow us?'

'The countess and Julie?' Theo untied the reins and gave the pair the office to move. 'Difficult. I doubt very much if they'll check on the cell—much too squeamish. What if they found us still alive? But they might check on the Chalice, worrying about whether it was safe to leave it there. Foolish to keep revisiting it, but people aren't always rational when they've something on their conscience. I prefer to be cautious for a day or two. I've given Hythe a letter for the count, and I have to hope he acts upon it, but one can never be certain.'

'What about Lord X's men? They'll be furious at being locked up.'

'Hythe is going to tell them to go back and tell his lordship we have the Chalice and will be getting it back to England. If they decide they don't trust me and come looking, it'll take a while to cast around before they pick up our trail.' He looked at her. 'Don't worry, Nell.'

'I'm not. I'm just making sure I understand where everything, and everybody, is,' she said, trying to focus on the practicalities and not on the fact that she was alone with Theo, not just for an hour or two, but for several days.

'Well, the Chalice is under the seat wrapped up in a horse blanket and without a scratch on it, which is more than can be said for us.' There was an edge to his voice, which made her want to take his face between her palms and not let him go until he told her what was wrong. That was not possible as they drove, but she could try just asking.

'Theo, what is wrong?' He shot her an incredulous look, one eyebrow arching up. 'No, I don't mean the fact that we are careering about the countryside with a valuable erotic art work hidden in the carriage and have left Mama with two murderesses. There's something else.'

He had his eyes back on the road, his gaze focused on the road ahead and for a moment or two she thought he would not answer her. Elinor slipped one arm through his. 'Theo?'

She did not receive a very warm response. He neither pulled away, nor, as she hoped, squeezed her arm against his side. 'It occurs to me that I have not been taking very good care of you, Nell.'

'You saved my life,' she protested, incredulous.

'I put it at risk in the first place. And besides, if you weren't so determined and brave we would never have got out of there. I have dragged you into this mess, I made love to you and now, as you say, we are careering about the countryside in a thoroughly improper manner.'

Something hot, confused and miserable turned over in Elinor's chest. 'I have free will and a brain! You did not drag me anywhere, I went where I wanted. After that first kiss—if you can call it that—I wanted what we did at least as much as you did, and if I hadn't, I'd have told you so. I thought we were friends, Theo. I thought we were in this together. But, no, I am just a woman who was apparently dragged along at your coat tails, who was waiting passively to be kissed, or not, who—'

'Stop! Nell, I can't argue with you while I'm driving. You'll have to wait until we get to an inn if you want to scold me.'

'Scold you?' She dragged her arm free and clenched her fists in her lap. 'I don't want to scold you, you idiot man. I want you to treat me like an equal.' And that was the heart of it, she realised. She loved him, admired him, wanted him. But she did not want to be treated like someone he had to cosset and protect. She wanted to be with him, not safe in England. She wanted to share the dangers and the adventures. She wanted, she realised with the clarity born of hunger and exhaustion and desperation, to live his life with him.

'How, exactly?' he asked warily.

'Treat me like a man. One who is not as strong as you, of course. One who doesn't have a good right hook in a fight. But I'm as intelligent as you are,' she asserted. 'I can take responsibility for myself.'

Theo looked at the slim, dishevelled, determined figure on the box beside him. Treat her like a man? Oh, no, never that. But treat her like an equal? That was an intriguing thought. He thought he had been, but his feelings for her were so overwhelming that she was probably right. His instinct was to protect Nell, cherish her— and all he had achieved so far was a variety of sexual experiences that had doubtless been highly unsatisfactory from her point of view, a fight from which he had had to be rescued, a scandal and a near-death experience.

'All right, I promise,' he said, meeting her stormy gaze. 'I can't treat you like a man, but I can treat you like the independent, intelligent woman you are. From now on, if I do not respect your decisions, you may remind me of that pledge.'

'Good.' Her nod was decisive, yet there was something else that was troubling her, he could sense it. But he couldn't force her to confide. 'Look, an inn. Theo, I don't care how disreputable it is, I am *starving*.'

As it turned out, the Coq d'Or was modest but clean, and the girl who came out as they entered from the yard was pleased to offer them a choice of rabbit casserole or a cut off yesterday's leg of pork, to be followed by cheese.

They made short work of the rabbit and still had appetite to attack the cheese, washed down with a *pichet* of the local red wine. 'Where are we?' Elinor asked the girl.

'Eschamps, *madame*. Do you have far to go?'

'Autun,' Elinor said promptly. It was a good answer, he conceded mentally. Prompt, with no hint of mystery or concealment, and quite plausible, given the road they were on. Theo tipped his glass to her, to acknowledge the tactic, and she smiled back, turning his heart over in his chest.

He wanted her. He wanted *this*. This companionship, this meeting of minds. This enjoyment. That he also wanted her in his bed, stretched out under him while he took that slender, agile body to heights of delight, while he buried himself in her, while he showed her, again and again, how much he loved her, was something he had to deny to himself, had, at all costs to resist.

In the event the road was better than he expected and the horses stronger than he had hoped and they drew into Jouey, just north of Arnay le Duc, as the light was beginning to fade. And there, by the side of the road, was exactly the sort of inn he had been looking for. Large, respectable, with stabling and grooms and the strong possibility of bedchambers that would give them both the good night's sleep they needed.

What he had not foreseen was the enforced, almost domestic, intimacy of the private parlour. Nell was delightfully wifely about the whole thing, insisting on checking the beds to see they were aired, frowning over the choices of food presented, consulting him, then ordering, sending the maid for more candles—creating, very successfully, the impression they were an established married couple. And, again, he had not thought to discuss the need to play-act with her in advance.

But admiration at her ingenuity was no protection against the insidious yearnings that were stirring in his breast. What if every day could be like this, travelling around the continent, searching for things to buy and patrons to sell to? Having adventures and having, every evening, the contentment of being together, sharing the day. Sharing the night.

'What is it, Theo?' He looked up with a start to find Nell, elbows on the table, chin on cupped hand, regarding him with a twinkle in her eyes. A bath, a change of linen and another good meal had restored her, both in spirits and in looks. He could have wished she had fallen asleep the moment her feet were over the threshold. 'You were smiling,' she explained. 'Wistfully.'

'That sounds maudlin,' he said, trying to make a joke of it. 'Don't I often smile?'

'Not like that. Not as though you had just seen something you loved very much, something in a daydream.'

'Very maudlin,' he confirmed. 'Just thinking about something I can never have.'

'Of course. I'm sorry.' She looked embarrassed and he suddenly realised she thought he had been thinking about the words he had let slip on the summit of the hill above Beaumartin. No doubt she had assumed he was pining after some unobtainable love. What would she say if he told her he was dreaming about her?

'Look.' The crackle of unfolding paper had him snapping out of his self-absorption. 'I asked the waiter for a map. It's a bit dirty and creased, but it shows Maubourg. How much longer do you think it will take us?'

'Four days, three nights, unless we hit bad weather or problems on the road or the horses weaken. I'm not intending to force the pace.'

Nell's face lit up. 'Four days? Oh, good. Theo, I'm enjoying this so much now.'

'You are?'

'Of course. Mind you, we need to shop.' That smile, the one that went right to the base of his spine, lit up her face. 'I never thought I'd hear myself say it, but I really, really, want to shop for clothes now. I never enjoyed it before—it was a chore when everything had to be so practical and, anyway, I was convinced I looked plain in anything I bought. You have given me pleasure in dressing up.'

'It's a good thing I've got plenty of money, then,' Theo teased, warmed by the thought he had done something so simple that had given her pleasure. He indulged a fantasy of playing at husband and wife, of shopping together, buying her presents and little luxuries. He would wager that frivolous indulgences, small pieces of frippery nonsense, had never entered Elinor's life. Well, they would now. 'Arnay will be fine for the essentials, I am sure.'

And Lyon for the luxuries. He would keep that as a surprise, find a modiste who could deliver in two days. It would delay them a little, but Nell would arrive at Maubourg with a wardrobe befitting the cousin by marriage of the Grand Duchess, whether she liked it or not. And he firmly intended that she would like it very much.

'Excellent, I'll make a list, then.' To his amusement she produced notebook and pencil in a most domestic manner. 'Linen, a robe. A plain walking dress. A cloak, I think. Yes, that's all.' Theo hid an inward smile at the modest list. 'What do you need?'

'More linen. Shoes—I've spent too long in these boots. Toothpowder.'

Elinor stopped writing and looked up. 'Brushes? A nightshirt?'

'Yes, those too,' he conceded. 'You are being very housewifely. I thought you had no talent in that direction.'

'I am merely being practical,' she said severely. 'Someone has to worry about toothpowder.'

'No,' Theo said, straight-faced, suddenly feeling relaxed and warm and in the mood for teasing. 'No one should have to worry about toothpowder, and certainly not the intellectual Miss Ravenhurst, who has a mind above such matters.'

'Beast.' She threw the notebook at him, missing by a country mile. Theo stretched out one arm and caught it.

'Why can't women throw?' he enquired, with every intention of being provocative.

'Because we do not waste our time in childhood chasing balls,' she retorted. 'Give me my notebook back.'

'No. I shall read it. Perhaps it contains your diary and every secret you possess.'

'You, Theophilus Ravenhurst, are no gentleman.'

'So I have been told.' He began to flick through the pages, not at all sure what he expected to find. What he did not anticipate was a pencil sketch of his head and shoulders. He was looking away, utterly focused, eyes narrowed. He could not place it, then saw the suggestion of a slender arch in the background and realised she must have done it that morning in the church at St Père, while they were sketching.

'Give it back.' She sounded tense. 'That is private.'

'It is very good. What are you so worried about? I've got all my clothes on.'

'Oh! You—' She dived for the book as it hung provocatively from his fingers, managed to get a grip and then was pulled firmly on to his lap and locked there by his arm. 'Let me go, Theo, or I'll bite you.'

'You wouldn't—ow! You little hell cat.' She was off his lap and round the other side of the table, eyes sparkling, her laughter a positive incitement to any red-blooded male. Theo gave chase, dodging, feinting, always his fingertips a fraction of an inch behind her until they faced each other from opposite ends of the rectangular polished wooden table. Theo vaulted up, took one long step and slid on his knees to her end, arriving just in time to snatch her into his arms and crash off the table on to the settle beyond.

'You idiot!' she managed, whooping with laughter.

'I have always wanted to do that,' he confessed, hiccupping faintly himself. 'I read about it in some novel and decided it was exactly the sort of thing a hero should be able to do, like swinging from the chandelier with a cutlass in my teeth. Naturally, not being a hero, I have never found a use for it.'

'You are a hero,' Elinor said, no longer laughing. 'My hero.' She was very still in his arms, her eyes wide on his face, their colour darkened to a complex green, far more subtle than their usual hazel.

'Nell,' he began, all the caution knocked out of him. 'Nell, my—'

'Monsieur?' The door banged open. 'Are you all right? I heard a crash. *Oh, pardon monsieur.*' The waiter went out again, pulling the door shut behind him with exaggerated care.

'I must go to bed.' Elinor slid off his knee, her face averted, every line of her body stiff. 'I'm very tired.'

'Yes, of course.' He sounded equally constrained to his own ears. What had he almost blurted out? *Nell, my love? My darling?* 'Have you everything you need?'

'Thank you, I will be fine.' She was not fine. She had never been like this with him, but there was nothing to be said that would not make matters worse. Theo lit a candle and passed the chamberstick to her. 'Sleep well.'

As the door leading to the stairs to their two bedchambers clicked shut, Theo sat down on the settle and stared at the notebook that had fallen to the floor. It lay open at the small sketch of him. His own profile was intent, focused. It was the face of a man completely unaware his life was about to be turned upside down. Whatever happened he must not touch her again, not like that, not in any way but the most everyday and fleeting, because he very much doubted if he could control himself if he did.

Chapter Seventeen

Theo sat for a long time after the footsteps on the boards above his head ceased. Sat while the candles guttered and sent wild shadows across the room. Finally he got to his feet and climbed the stairs stiffly, like a man in pain.

On the small landing that served only their two rooms, light was still visible under her door. He raised a hand to knock, to ask if she was all right, then opened his fist and laid the palm against the door, listening, trying to feel Nell's presence.

The door jerked open so suddenly he almost fell into the room. 'Theo?' She was dressed in her mother's nightgown, several sizes too large and trailing on the boards, a shawl wrapped tight around her shoulders.

'Sorry, I had something caught on my boot and I was freeing it.' He rested a hand on the doorpost and tried to look casual. 'Is anything wrong?'

'I can't sleep,' she said tersely. 'Every time I close my eyes I'm in that damnable dungeon. I am so *cross* with myself. We escaped, we won, we are all right, for goodness' sake. So why am I afraid of the shadows?'

'Because we could have died,' he said. 'And you are intelligent enough to know that and have enough imagination to realise what it would have been like.'

Elinor made a brave attempt at a smile. Theo's fingers tightened on the door frame. 'I'm frightened of having nightmares. Eva told me she used to suffer from them, but Sebastian made them go away, by being there. Theo, I'm not used to being frightened of things I can't do anything about. It is different if you can fight back, but now I'm terrified of sleeping, and I must sleep, sooner or later.'

'Leave your door open a crack, and I'll do the same to mine. Then if you cry out in your sleep I'll hear you and come and wake you,' he offered. He would fight dragons for her, but how could he fight the ones in her mind?

'Thank you,' she said, the smile rather more convincing this time. But she was still frightened, he could see it in the very way she squared her shoulders and her chin came up. This was the woman who had faced death by his side, who had tackled two ruffians for his sake and, now she was afraid, all he could offer was to leave his door open.

Over her shoulder he could see the big bed with its heap of blankets and puffy goose-feather quilt. The landlord had given her the big bed and him a smaller one, presumably calculating that the husband would cross the landing to visit his wife and not the other way around.

'Would it help if I slept with you?' Her pupils widened so her eyes went dark. '*Sleep*, Nell. That's a big bed with lots of covers. You get into the bed, I'll lie under the quilt. If you are aware of my breathing, know I'm here with you, you will not dream.'

He had no idea whether that was true or not, but if she began to show signs of distress at least he could wake her instantly. 'I'll just go and undress.' He went into his own room before she could say anything and before his own will weakened. It was going to be sheer hell lying next to her, unable to touch her, kiss her, love her.

But he had told himself he would fight demons for her. This scaly monster would be his own desires.

Elinor stripped all but one blanket and the sheet off the bed, slid in and turned over, as close to the far edge as she could get. It was a warm night, but now she felt fevered. She had not expected this. She had expected Theo to give her a brisk, reassuring, lecture to the effect that there was nothing to be afraid of, to pull herself together and not be foolish. That was what Mama would have done. It was what she had been telling herself, with singularly little effect, come to that.

The thought of making love with him was beginning to haunt her, but he would never risk touching her like that again, she knew. She loved him so much, and yet she was never going to be able to show him—not without him guessing her feelings. Then he would pity her, perhaps feel he had to renew that offer of marriage, and she would have to refuse again.

He was quick. Her tumbling thoughts unresolved, she lay listening to the sound of bare feet passing over the boards, the click of the door shutting, then the rustle of him sorting through the pile of discarded bedding. The far side of the bed dipped, there was some scuffling and a flapping sound as he shook the cover over himself. Elinor closed her eyes tightly, aware that the candle had been extinguished.

'You do not have to cling to the edge you know.' He sounded amused. Elinor shuffled back towards the centre a little. 'That's better. I'm told I don't snore.'

Ana wouldn't tolerate snoring, I'm sure, Elinor told herself, then smiled, feeling a little better. 'I'll prod you in the ribs if you do,' she replied, trying to make this sound normal. She had feared she would never get to sleep alone; now she was convinced she would be lying awake all night out of sheer embarrassment. 'Goodnight, Theo.'

'Goodnight, Nell.' He turned over once, then seemed to settle immediately, his breathing evening out. She rolled over on to her back and turned her head on the pillow. Beside her in the gloom the big body seemed completely relaxed. There was nothing to be afraid of, nothing that Theo would not protect her from. With a sigh Elinor closed her eyes and willed herself to sleep.

She woke to find herself lying on her back, hot, pinned under the covers by a heavy weight and with hot breath fanning the back of her neck. *Theo*. Had she dreamed at all last night? She could not remember. All she could recall was feeling safe and dreadfully self-conscious. Now, in the dreamy after-sleep state she still felt safe, and not in the slightest bit uncomfortable.

Elinor blinked her eyes open and turned her head on the pillow. It was still early, she could tell from the quality of the light through the thin cotton curtain. It shone on the bed, turning Theo's hair the red-gold of autumn leaves and highlighting the dark stubble over his chin and cheeks. It would not take much for him to grow a beard, she thought fondly, wondering how it would feel if she touched it.

He was very soundly asleep, lying on his side facing her, his right arm thrown over her waist. She liked the feeling of it, the sense of being claimed and held, but she wanted to touch him. She wanted, she admitted, to kiss him. Was it possible without waking him?

Cautiously she began to turn within the curve of his arm, sensing new things as she became wider awake. She was more conscious of the scent of him: clean, hot male. One shoulder was visible above the blanket, protruding bare from his shirt. There were old bruises on it and fresh scrapes, bringing vividly to mind the way she had scrambled and clutched at him as she had struggled to free the chain in the dungeon.

Then she was over, almost nose to nose with him. His lashes

were long, even darker than his beard. There was a small, sickle-shaped scar just below his right eyebrow. He did have freckles after all, she realised, they just didn't show as much as hers because his skin was lightly tanned. *My love.*

Could she? Dare she? Elinor leaned in, her lips close to his so that they were breathing the same air, so close she could feel the heat of his skin warming her. Only half an inch more. She puckered her lips and he moved, just enough to bring their mouths together.

Was he awake? His eyes were still shut. Elinor held her breath, her lips against his, then he shifted his weight over her and kissed her properly, an open-mouthed, utterly sexual caress. His tongue thrust and claimed and explored, demanding she respond, and she followed, unafraid of anything, but not matching what he wanted. Wide-eyed, she held her gaze on his face, but his eyes were still closed. His weight on her was troubling and exciting, both at once. She wanted to struggle simply to feel his strength holding her, but she kept still, sensing that he was not fully awake.

It probably meant he did not know who he was kissing. Perhaps he was deeply asleep and thought she was someone else. Was he dreaming of the woman he loved hopelessly, the reason he would not marry? Or Ana? It should have made a difference to how this felt, the rational part of her brain tried to say, but her body was taking not the slightest bit of notice.

Theo's hands came up to cup her face, to hold her still as he plundered her mouth. Pinned under him, she could feel his erection, thrillingly, terrifyingly large. Her own body was on fire now, melting, twisting, aching. Between her thighs she felt the moisture, understood hazily what it was preparing her for. All she knew was that she needed his hands on her, his body possessing her.

He was not fully conscious, she was sure of that now. Was this the second chance, the opportunity to experience a man's loving after her brush with death? If she was careful, did not speak, he might make love to her without even realising. *Without knowing it is me. No.*

No, that was not how she wanted to be loved by Theo and it was wrong. It would be using him, just as shockingly as if he had seduced her while she lay asleep and unknowing.

Elinor turned her head away from the seeking mouth and pushed at his shoulders, her hands meeting linen on one side, bare flesh on the other. He grumbled, low in his throat, like a big dog whose bone has been taken away, and she smiled despite herself.

'Theo, Theo, wake up.'

His eyes opened full on her face and she saw him go white, watched as the colour literally drained from under his skin as realisation struck him. 'Nell. Nell, what the hell have I done?' He threw himself away from her, hurling back the covers, and sat on the edge of the bed, shoulders bent, his back to her.

'Nothing,' she said prosaically. 'You just kissed me, that's all. It was very nice, but I thought I ought to wake you up because you obviously didn't know who I was—'

'That's flattering for you, isn't it?' he said, back still turned, voice bitter.

Lord, he is going to start blaming himself for this. I can hardly tell him nothing would have happened if I hadn't tried to kiss him myself. 'Theo, look, it is not as though we had made love last night, is it? I mean,' she persisted, despite the fact that the back of his neck was becoming decidedly pink and her tongue was getting in a tangle, 'if that had been the case, obviously I would have been insulted you didn't remember who you were in bed with. But you were only in bed with me because I was frightened and it worked, I had a wonderful night's sleep.'

'Good. No dreams?' He sounded slightly happier now. She wished he would turn round, then remembered what little he must be wearing and how his aroused body had felt against hers. Better to get out of the situation as smoothly as possible.

'No dreams. What happened a moment ago, that was just, um, a reflex, I expect. I really don't think of it as anything else.' She turned over and pulled the covers up around her ears. 'I'll be lazy for a little longer while you go back to your own room. Could you ring for water?'

'Right.' She waited until the door closed, then sat up, arms round her knees, chin resting on top. It was a comfortable thinking position and she needed, above all, to think. Her body felt alarmingly alive, achingly unfulfilled. It was obvious that making love was pleasurable, otherwise people would not do it. But there was more to it than she had realised. It was as though Theo had been taking her body on a journey, but they never got there and that left a deep yearning for completion. Making love was apprently not like having a delicious meal where, provided one was not starving, one could stop after one course, having enjoyed a satisfactory experience. One needed to eat all the courses, or whatever the sexual equivalent was.

Her plait was tangled in the neck of her overlarge nightgown and she pulled it out, nibbling the very tip in a manner that would have earned her a severe telling-off from her governess, who had cured her of that childish habit years ago. Obviously it was perfectly possible to go through life without experiencing physical love, it was just that it was becoming very clear to her that she did not want to.

A few weeks ago she could have gone through life, aware she was missing something, quite happily. But now she knew Theo, knew she loved him, she did not want that ignorance. She wanted to know what it was she would never have.

Men, it seemed, were quite happy to make love to women they didn't love. So were some women—Ana, for example—but she had gathered that it was a very different emotional experience for the two sexes. So Theo might not be exactly appalled if she asked him. He might not guess her real reasons if he thought he had simply physically aroused her. After all, he had kissed her in the old quarry to answer her curiosity…

'Just the once.'

'Madame?' The chambermaid stood in the doorway with a steaming jug of hot water. 'I did knock, *madame*, but *monsieur* said to take the water in.'

'Yes, thank you. Has *monsieur* ordered breakfast?' Elinor smiled at the assurance it was all in hand and went back to brooding.

But how to persuade him when he was fully awake and aware of what he was doing? And persuade him without him guessing why she wanted him. Would he accept that it was intellectual curiosity? Not that that was very flattering to him. She would just have to play it by ear when the opportunity arose.

Breakfast was substantial. Elinor could not decide whether Theo was simply hungry or finding an excuse not to speak to her. His single-minded demolition of steak allowed her to study her emotions with a mind somewhat cleared by two cups of coffee.

She loved Theo. She was not just in love with him, although she had not realised that these were two separate things until she experienced them both. He loved someone else, she was certain, someone perhaps from long ago. Certainly someone unobtainable. Despite that impetuous declaration on the hilltop, he obviously did not wish to marry *her.* Not when he was thinking clearly. He might want a companion, perhaps, but that was all.

So whatever she did, she must not allow him to feel trapped. Elinor poured two more cups of coffee and pushed one over to Theo, then began to butter a slice of bread before realising she already had a neat stack of three pieces sitting on the plate. Theo accepted two of them with a nod of thanks and addressed himself to his food again while she spread preserves on the remainder.

And becoming pregnant would certainly trap him. But there were ways to make love without that happening, she was certain. She had heard whispers. Bel had been Ashe's lover for some time before their marriage and Bel was not a reckless woman. At least, she had not been until she fell in love. Theo would know.

'What are you brooding about?' he asked so suddenly she dropped her bread. 'You look as though you have a knotty problem in translation to puzzle through.'

'Things I want.' It was a miracle that she had not blurted out, *you*, he had made her jump so.

'Oh, shopping.' Theo pushed back his plate. 'We'll stop in Arnay le Duc first thing, then push on to Mâcon for the night. Then it's a relatively easy drive down to Lyon and after that Grenoble, the last stop before Maubourg.' She nodded, reassured that she had three days to decide what to do, and how to do it. 'You know what you want, then? Are you going to put it on the list?'

'No. I'll remember without any trouble.' She looked up and smiled but Theo was already on his feet, ringing for the waiter.

Arnay behind them, their valises reassuringly full of essentials, Theo sent the horses down the long road to Mâcon at a steady pace while Elinor packed things away and tried to snatch sketches from the bouncing seat.

After lunch she climbed back up on the box again, ignoring the effect of wind and dust on her complexion and the hardness of the seat under her. 'Why only a pair? Must we be careful with money?'

'No. I thought we would be expected to take four, and in any case there is no great hurry. I could buy another pair, I suppose, and make up a team.' He flicked the whip down to discourage a small pack of village dogs that had come tumbling and barking out of a farm gate. 'I might do that after Lyon, the hills will be steeper.'

'Is it difficult driving a pair?' He was still only using one hand for the reins, his whip hand only coming across when he needed to loop a rein to take a corner. She frowned at his fingers, trying to work out what went where.

'More difficult than a single horse, as you'd expect. Why? Do you want to drive?' He turned his head to grin at her. 'It will make your shoulders stiff.'

'I'll try for a bit. They seem steady enough.'

'All right.' He moved over to the right. 'Come into the middle as much as possible—now open your hands.'

It took five minutes of fumbling, and considerable confusion for the pair, before she was settled sitting snug against Theo, the length of his hip and thigh pressed against hers, his left arm round the back of her, resting on the rail. 'I'll keep the whip and help you with the reins when we come to a bend.'

Somehow, as they bowled along, the Burgundian countryside unfolding green and gold on either side, the rows of vines stretching like the marks of a giant comb up every south-facing slope, his arm came up and round her shoulders and his right hand came over and guided hers more and more until they were driving together. There was no need to talk, no need to do anything but feel the companionship and the shared pleasure in what they were doing.

It was like that first walk along the river bank. Theo would nudge her and she would look round to see a vivid patch of flowers in front of a cottage, or children playing tag in and out of the puddles around a public wash house. She would murmur and he would look up as a buzzard swept overhead, mewing, or a white horse in a field galloped down to whinny at their pair as they passed.

'There's Mâcon ahead.' Theo took the reins back. 'I don't remember a day when I've spent more time doing virtually nothing and yet enjoyed myself so much.'

'No.' Moving back to her side of the box and smoothing down her skirts before they reached the streets, Elinor nodded in perfect comprehension. 'It was like a day from childhood, taking sights and experiences as they came with no worries, nothing to do but be.'

Beside her Theo chuckled. 'I like that: *Nothing to do but be.* You are taking years off me, Nell. Hold tight, here we are.'

As he swung the team through the gates of the inn, Elinor watched his face: focused, intent, strong. No, they might have taken a day out of childhood, but this was not a boy. This was a man.

Chapter Eighteen

Maĉon, and a night spent chastely in their own beds lay behind them, Lyon was just ahead in the late afternoon sunlight. Theo had kept the reins the whole way, saying he wanted to get to Lyon before evening and Elinor had secretly welcomed the chance to recover from yesterday's stiff shoulders and aching back.

She stretched as they climbed down into the courtyard of the Phaison Blanc. Theo was negotiating with the landlord for rooms and ordering hot water immediately. 'Come along, upstairs for a quick wash, then we are going out.' He was up to something, she could tell. Some excitement was bubbling underneath. Willing to indulge him, Elinor hurried to do as he asked, reappearing in the courtyard to find him hat in hand, hair ruthlessly combed.

'Where are we going?' Without thinking she tucked her hand under his elbow and allowed herself to be guided along the crowded footway.

'We will be in a Grand Ducal court soon.'

'Yes, I know.' That was not news.

'I intend we look the part.' Theo stopped in front of a discreet green-painted shop window displaying a length of figured silk, a pair of kid gloves and a fan. 'In we go.'

* * *

Ten minutes later Elinor found herself abandoned to the mercies of a team of interested semptresses under the direction of their employer, who had received detailed orders from Theo. Bewildered, Elinor saw large amounts of money change hands while she struggled to keep up with the rapid-fire exchange of French.

'Theo—what on earth—?' She managed before he was out of the door.

'I'll be back, just going to find a tailor.' Then she was staring at a closed door and hands were tugging her gently towards screens at the back of the shop.

'Madame, s'il-vous plaît.' Abandoned, and not at all sure she knew her way back, Elinor surrendered to having her outer clothes stripped off, to the accompaniment of much interested comment on her divided skirt, and being comprehensively measured, prodded and subjected to length after length of fabric being held up to her face.

It was like being gently assaulted by a flock of small, but very determined, birds. Just why measuring her for one gown, which she supposed was Theo's intention, should take so much fuss, she had no idea, but she was tired and her French vocabulary failed her.

Theo reappeared over an hour later when she was sitting with her feet on a petit-point footstool, sipping a tisane and leafing through copies of *La Correspondance des Dames*. This was the sort of thing her friends Bel, Eva and Jessica did, not her.

'Having fun?' Somewhere along the way he had acquired a cane and a smart tall hat and his breeches and coat had been brushed and sponged.

'No! Well, yes, in a way. But, Theo, Eva and Sebastian won't mind us turning up with just a valise between us, not once we explain. And one of Eva's ladies will be sure to be my size and won't mind lending some things, I am sure.' She looked him up and down as he stood in front of her surrounded by the shop girls. 'You are looking very much the thing.'

'Wait until tomorrow. *Merci, madame, à bientôt.*' Theo held the door for her and ushered her out. 'Now then dinner, a bath and an early night.'

'Yes, but I'm not—'

'Not tired? We've a busy day tomorrow.'

'Theo!' Elinor dug in her heels in, stopping in the middle of the square. 'Talk to me! I thought we were going on to Grenoble tomorrow.'

'No, we are going to Grenoble *next*,' he said patiently, steering her firmly across the road. 'Tomorrow we shop. We need clothes and I want to indulge myself.'

'By dressing me up? Theo, how many gowns have you ordered?'

'One or two,' he said evasively. 'It is a very stylish court, I don't want either of us to feel out of place.'

Elinor set her lips tight together and walked back to the inn in silence. Theo had cajoled her into new clothes in St Père, and he had been proved right. She *had* looked a dowd and it was gratifying to look one's best and have a pretty gown or two. But they were not in London, she was not attending court for social reasons and she was baffled by why Theo should want to continue encouraging her to shop.

She held her peace until after dinner, maintaining a flow of cheerful conversation that Theo obviously found disconcerting. When the waiter cleared the board and brought in a bottle of brandy he half-rose to his feet, expecting her to retire.

'Oh, no, you don't.' Elinor settled down across the table where she could watch his face, pulled a glass towards her and splashed brandy in the bottom—she rather thought she might need its support. 'Now Theo, why, exactly, did you take me to that *modiste* this afternoon? And what shopping are we going to be occupying valuable travelling time with tomorrow?'

He did not answer her immediately, pouring himself a glass of brandy and pushing his chair back so he was sitting at right angles to her. Elinor waited patiently while he loosened his neckcloth, stretched out his legs and generally made himself comfortable. If he thought she was going to be put off by such obvious tactics, he had another think coming.

'I've risked your life, dragged you across France, made you thoroughly uncomfortable. I thought you deserved a treat. I thought I did, come to that. I thought I would enjoy buying you pretty things.' He turned from his contemplation of the brandy to look directly into her eyes. 'I wanted to take you to Maubourg and show you off.'

'As your creation? You wanted to buy me things as you would your mistress?' She thought she was angry, but the mixture of emotions churning round inside her were difficult to interpret.

'As I would any lady I was fond of, who had taste, who I thought might enjoy it,' he said, his eyes narrowing as he tried to assess her reaction.

'Oh.' Put like that, it was hard to be cross. 'I am not used to being brought presents of that sort.' And, of course, no lady could accept any article of apparel from a man as a gift, not so much as a pair of gloves. 'I should pay you back when we get back to England.'

'This is a present,' he said, his voice level. 'I would be gratified if you would accept tomorrow as a present.' There was emotion behind the calmness, feelings she did not understand. Unless her fear the other night had shaken him, made him feel he needed to make reparation for that terrifying time in the dungeons.

And if that was how he felt, could she throw it back in his face? She could hardly be much more compromised than she was already and it was not as though anyone need know how she had come by whatever it was Theo was determined to give her.

'Thinking again?' he enquired, not unkindly, as she sipped her brandy. She was not certain she liked it, but it warmed right down to her toes. 'I love your mind, Nell, but I wish you'd let your emotions out sometimes.'

'Yes. Yes, I would very much enjoy for you to take me shopping and buy me things, Theo, thank you.' *There, is that emotional enough for him? He loves my* mind*? But I don't want him to love my mind, I want him to love* me*! Just how startled would he be if I showed him my emotions, asked him to make love to me?*

'Right.' He grinned at her, suddenly looking happier than he had all day. 'Drink more brandy, it is obviously good for you. I told them that I wanted the gowns ready for a first fitting before noon. I will go to my tailors at the same time. Then there are all the other things, the frippery things—we can fit those in around the fittings.'

'Frippery things?'

'Do-dads. Bits of nonsense men aren't supposed to talk about. Absolutely nothing sensible or practical, Nell, I warn you.' She found she was smiling back, carried away by his enjoyment of his plans for her. 'Now, bed and an early morning.'

Theo lounged, with a total lack of concern for propriety, on the chair in Elinor's bedchamber and watched her unpacking their purchases on the bed. Four gowns: morning, walking, half-dress and full dress; a froth of Swiss lawn undergarments and night things; gloves and stocking; fans, slippers and shoes; two shawls, a pelisse and three hats.

'Oh, my goodness.' She sat down on the end of the bed and looked at him, breathless, and apparently in two minds whether to laugh or cry. 'Theo, I just don't believe all this now I see it all together. It is so beautiful. Thank you. I have never been shopping like this before.' She whisked off the bed and was kissing him, her hands on his shoulders, before he could brace himself.

Oh, God, the scent of her. It had been torture all day, being with her, watching her enjoyment as he coaxed and teased her into trying things on, choosing between pairs of gloves and then buying them all for her anyway, seeing an utterly frivolous, fun-loving, playful Nell emerge into the sunlight.

She had accompanied him, shockingly, into bootmakers, had insisted on checking the quality of the neckcloths he bought, dabbed cologne on the back of her hand and then on his new hand-kerchiefs and teased him into buying a waistcoat all the colours of autumn, which she said would go with his hair.

'I'm glad you like them,' he said mildly, exercising considerable control of his breathing. 'I think I can hear the new luggage being brought up.'

'Shall I pack for you?'

'No. I can manage, thank you.' The thought of her bent over the valises, folding his shirts, acting like the wife he wished she was—that was one torture too far.

It was as well, he thought wryly over dinner, to be careful what one wished for. He had fantasised about a day spent with Nell, indulging his desire to buy her pretty things and now he was having to live with the consequences. She was happy and sparkling and light-hearted. Which was wonderful. She was also treating him like an indulgent brother, which was not.

She left him after dinner with a gesture towards the brandy bottle. 'That gave me a headache, I think I will leave you to it, Theo.' Something of the sparkle had gone out of her mood; she looked serious as she stood, the door handle in one hand, a copy of Petrarch's poetry she had insisted on buying in the other. How like Nell, he thought tenderly, off she goes to bed to read four-teenth-century Italian in the original.

'Theo.'

'Mmm?' He was not sure whether he did not like her best when she was serious, her brow furrowed over a book, or deep in thought. The laughter was never very far away and the look in those clear hazel eyes…

'Theo, wake up! Will you knock on my door when you come up? Say goodnight? I'll be reading.'

'If you want me to translate, I can't, my Italian is strictly the modern variety.'

'No.' Her smile was oddly tense. 'No, I won't ask you to translate.'

How long had she got to wait? Elinor wondered, washing with the tablet of fine-milled soap that she had picked up to smell in the perfumers and which had been immediately added to the pile of Theo's purchases. She could change her mind, right up to the point where he tapped on her door, expecting to say goodnight.

Her new nightgown slithered over her shoulders, a virginal pure white that should have prodded her conscience. She tied the ribbons loosely at the neck, for the first time in her life thinking about dressing to please a man. *No,* she corrected herself firmly, *seduce him.* It had a matching robe, hardly more practical or modest. She slipped it on, wondering if it was as translucent as it felt.

Theo had seemed to like her hair loose, she thought, remember-ing the way he had weighed it in his hands before plaiting it on the river bank. Freed from its ribbon, the braiding shaken out, it rippled over her shoulders and down her back, a shifting veil.

A more assured woman would have scent and know how to use it, would place a jewel strategically, might use lamp-black to lengthen her lashes, or the petals from those geraniums on the window sill to redden her lips or cheeks. But she had none of those arts, or those accessories. Either he wanted her or he did not. All she could do now was to wait and see whether her nerve held.

The book she had bought was hard to translate, forcing her to concentrate as she struggled with the meaning. But it was not a good choice for the love-lorn wrestling with conscience and desire, filled as it as with sonnets written by the poet to his unfulfilled love, Laura.

'*Wherever I wander, love attends me still, Soft whispring to my soul, and I to him.*' That was lovely, and, sadly, implied that love would never let you alone.

'Sighing?' She had not heard the tap on the door. Theo was standing just inside, regarding her with affectionate amusement. He had taken off his boots, which was perhaps why she had not heard him. 'That is heavy stuff for this time of night. Are you having trouble with the grammar?'

'No, it isn't as bad as I feared. Theo—' Now was the moment to make up her mind, take that second chance. 'Would you come in and close the door?' He raised his eyebrows, but did as she asked, putting his chamber stick down on the dresser and watching her in the candlelight.

'Are you afraid of sleeping again?'

'It isn't that.'

She put the book down with care and stood up. How difficult could it be? He only had to say *no*. Theo's eyes widened as he took in her loose hair, the fragile white lawn garments. As though his gaze was being dragged, it travelled down her body to her toes, bare under the lacy hem.

'I want you to stay with me tonight, Theo, and make love to me.' A frank demand, not one of the careful phrases she had rehearsed, but at least it was said, even if her stomach did seem to have shrunk to a tight knot of apprehension and she could feel the colour rising in her cheeks. He was standing there, watching her, his face a mask, yet she sensed anger, not any of the other emotions she would have expected—embarrassment, alarm, pity.

'You do not have to pay for what I bought you today,' he said finally, and the rage was there, clear and cold in his voice. It was the tone she would have imagined one man would have used to another in the moments before rapiers came sliding out of scabbards. And something else. Pain.

'Oh, no! Theo, I would never… I was going to ask before today, before I knew what you intended.' She was normally so calm and articulate and now the words were tangling in her mouth and she found that, confronted with pure emotion, she had no idea how to put right what she had done. This was Theo and she was losing him.

Elinor fought down the panic and took a deep breath. 'I realised the night before last, when you slept in my room, how much I wanted to…' Her resolution died away in the face of his implacably blank expression. She tried again.

'Theo, I know I'm not going to get married, I have always known it. I would never settle for anything other than a love match, and I know I'm not going to find one of those. But I find I don't want to live the whole of my life not knowing about—' She swallowed hard. 'Not knowing about physical passion. It is not something a single woman can seek out, not without terrible risks, not unless there is someone she can trust, as I trust you.'

The anger was leaving him, she could sense it, although she was still surprised by how quickly it had flared up in him, the hurt she sensed. Was it simply touchy male honour? Surely not.

'As you say, there are risks,' he said steadily, his eyes watchful on her face. 'Your reputation, if word gets around that we have been travelling together, is ruined anyway. But with your mother's connivance and the Maubourg court as cover, there is no reason why it should ever get out. Unless you become pregnant—and if we make love, then that is a very real risk, and one I am not prepared to take.'

Because, if that is the consequence, you will be trapped? one part of her mind asked. *He is quite right, said her common sense. You would* both *be trapped.*

'It is possible to make love without that risk, is it not?'

'Ah.' Theo came fully into the room, leaning against the bedpost, a faint smile lifting the corner of his mouth. 'My very well-read and very innocent Elinor, you are quite correct. But there is one proviso—you have to trust the man who is making love to you not to get carried away in the heat of the moment.'

'And you do not trust yourself?' she queried, sceptical. 'What exactly were your intentions those times you kissed me, might I ask? Were they completely dishonourable? Were you confident things would go no further than a kiss? Or were you going to risk the consequences and rely on disappearing back into your wandering life afterwards?'

'I intended to give you pleasure,' Theo said slowly, his eyes locked with hers, 'and I intended to take pleasure myself from doing that. You would still have been a virgin at the end of it. And the intensity of it made me realise that I should not involve myself with virgins and I resolved, somehow, to keep my hands off you in future. Don't blush like that, Nell, you cannot initiate this sort of conversation and expect it to continue in euphemisms.'

'I see. I beg your pardon for having implied any lack of honour on your part.' The apology came from stiff lips, but something warmed the cold green eyes and she sensed him relax a little. The wise thing would be to say goodnight, to stop this now while she was still safe from the emotional consequences of what she wanted so much. But she no longer wished to be wise. Or safe.

'Could we not pretend we are still in that study?' she asked. 'Could we not finish what began there?' His lids lowered, hooding his eyes, hiding his thoughts from her. She wanted to shake him, make him realise how much she was suffering from the need he had ignited in her.

'Theo, I know men have ways of dealing with frustration.' His expression of mingled shock and amusement had her smiling back for the first time since this fraught encounter had begun. 'Well, I do read, as you say, and all kinds of journals, including medical ones, find their way into the study at home, and I am bright enough to read between the lines. But you have made me want something I do not understand. And I want to understand it and I don't want to ache like this any more.'

He was going to refuse her, she was certain. Theo walked to her side, his face serious. 'Nell.' His big hand curved under her chin and tipped her face up. 'I am not sure about revisiting the study. That floor was dreadfully hard and this one looks just as bad. Would you settle for the bed?'

Chapter Nineteen

'Yes, I will settle for the bed.' It was difficult to keep her tone light to match his. The bed suddenly seemed very large, Theo seemed very close and it did not seem as though she was wearing very much at all, not with the way he was looking at her now.

'Just tell me if you want to stop, Nell. This is all about you, about your pleasure.' He had shed his coat and was loosening his neckcloth while she stood there like Pandora, wondering what on earth she had just let out of the box.

'That is rather selfish,' she demurred, reaching up to take the ends of the long muslin strip from his hands.

'I didn't say I wouldn't enjoy it, too.' Theo bent his head to help her pull off the neckcloth, then added encouragingly as she hesitated, 'I would like it if you took off my shirt as well.'

It was all rather leisurely, in contrast to that explosion of passion in the study. Elinor began to unbutton his shirt, her fingers fumbling a little. But the tension this slowness engendered was very real, knotting in her stomach, aching down the inside of her thighs. Between her legs a pulse began to throb with intimate urgency. Then her fingertips brushed skin and Theo caught his breath and she forgot to analyse how she was feeling.

As she pushed the linen off his shoulders, he pulled at the shirt so it came out of his breeches and fell to the floor and then she was standing, her palms flat on the naked chest of a man. It felt…wonderful. He looked wonderful. She had thought she had known what to expect, but it was not the tactile smoothness of tanned skin over hard, defined, muscle or the strangely arousing tickle of crisp hair or the intriguing way his nipples hardened when she accidentally brushed against one.

Theo moved his hands to push her robe open and the muscles of his chest shifted, rippling under her hands and she smiled, caressing down to explore as the fine lawn fell to catch at her elbows.

'Are you sure you haven't done this before?' Theo asked as her fingertips slipped into the tight waistband of his breeches. 'You seem to know all the right places.'

'Quite sure!' Worried she would do something wrong if she went any further, Elinor snatched back her hands and the robe fell to the floor at her feet. Theo made a complicated noise, somewhere between a growl and a sigh and pulled her against him, his hands sliding down her back from her shoulders to cup her buttocks, lifting her against the wonderful evidence that she was doing something very right indeed.

Then he shifted his grip again and the next thing she knew her nightgown had gone and she was quite naked against him, feeling his heart hammering as his hands skimmed over her back and her buttocks, caressing with a gentleness she did not realise a man could possess. How she got on to the bed she could not say, but Theo was removing his breeches, drawers and stockings in one movement that a part of her brain which was still functioning recognised as honed by long practice.

He was even more beautiful naked than clothed, she realised, staring at him with unabashed interest, not even the startling jut of his erection deterring her. Then she saw his eyes and realising he was looking at her in just the same way. *I ought to be shy, I ought to be hiding under this sheet,* she thought, wondering at herself, but all she could do was bask in the warmth of his gaze.

'I knew I was right about what was under those dreadful gowns,' he murmured, lying down beside her and gathering her in close for a kiss. That felt safer—wonderful and exciting and inflammatory, but at least familiar, as his mouth worked over hers. But then he moved, slid down against her, and that wickedly knowing mouth was doing things to her breast and to her nipples and she arched up off the bed with a gasp as he nipped the tense buds between his teeth.

'Theo! Theo?' She caught at his head, her fingers threading into the glorious red mane, but he kept moving, his mouth hot and wet now on her belly. Under his tongue the flesh was sensitive, responsive and she tried to move, only his hands cupped her hips, steadying her. 'Where? *Theo!*' He was nuzzling into the dense red curls at the apex of her thighs and she knew she was wet and hot and aching and it was the most shocking thing she could imagine. And then it became even more shocking as his tongue tip found something, found *her*, and teased and stroked while his hands pushed her unresisting legs apart and his fingers searched and probed and slid inside just as the complex knot of sensation deep in her belly unravelled itself into something that sent her spiralling into an explosion of feeling that was anguish and was delight and was everything.

'Theo.' That must be her voice, murmuring. Somehow she was in his arms again and the thud against her cheek was his heart.

'Nell?' He was stroking her, gentling his hands down over her hot skin, stilling her quivering. Now, at last, she realised that *making love* meant just that. He might not love her, but he had pleasured her with loving care, was holding her with tenderness.

'That was…beautiful.'

'Good,' he murmured into her hair. 'Are you tired?'

'I'm not sure,' Elinor answered honestly. 'Why?' In answer, his hands began to move with more firmness and he turned her in his arms until he could kiss her, while those clever, wicked fingers searched out that hidden part of her and began to touch and tease while she gasped against his mouth and realised that, no, she was not in the slightest bit tired.

But what about him? What about his pleasure? Experimentally Elinor slid one hand down between their bodies to where his heat was most intense and curled her fingers around him. It stopped his mouth on hers and his moving fingers stilled. 'Yes,' he said, his voice husky. 'Like that. Move like that—ah, Nell!'

She was clumsy, unskilled, she knew, but he didn't seem to mind and to feel the powerful urgency of his body responding to her while he drove her to the brink, brought her back, over and over, was utterly delicious madness. Then that tightening knot broke, shattered again, just as he surged in her grasp, his groan mingling with her gasps and she collapsed, limp, into his arms as he fell back shuddering with the force of his release.

Theo woke to find himself in a hot sticky tangle of sheets, hair and soft feminine limbs. He lay looking up at the ceiling in the faint morning light and wondered if he had ever felt better. Beyond the moment, beyond this bed chamber door, was a reality he did not want to think about yet. Time enough to face it. Half on top of him, her face burrowed into his chest, Nell slept, her breath stirring the hair on his chest in an arousing tickle. He thought about waking her, then contented himself with stroking her hair.

He had roused her once in the night, loving the way she responded to every caress with delighted surprise. And then he had been the one to be surprised when he had woken from a deeply erotic dream to find her small hand caressing him into total arousal. Half-asleep as he had been, he had almost forgotten the overriding need to preserve her virginity, had caught himself just in time as he brought his weight down over her.

Had he satisfied both her and her curiosity? he wondered. Was she going to put away this awakening, this knowledge, and become once again the respectable bluestocking spinster? She was so vulnerable, trembling in his arms. Would it take so very much to convince her to marry him?

A hand slid down his belly, its fingers teasing into the coarse hair, then tiptoeing up the rapidly stiffening length of him. 'Good morning, Theo,' she said, turning up her face to smile at him.

'You, Nell, are a hussy. Don't you want your breakfast?'

'No.' She had learned not to handle him as though he was breakable. In fact, Theo thought, abandoning himself to her wicked exploration, she learned everything, very fast. And if he didn't do something, now this moment, it was all going to be over very fast, too.

'Nell, *slowly*. Oh, my God…'

Elinor curled up at the foot of the crumpled bed and ate toast, heedless of the crumbs. Theo, up at the pillow end, had wedged steak between two halves of a large roll and was demolishing it, wolf-like. It had been his idea, this decadent picnic breakfast when she had declared herself too indolent to get out of bed.

'We've got a longish drive ahead of us, we will eat in bed and then you must get up' he had said firmly, ringing the bell despite her protests. 'What? They think we are married, stop blushing.'

But she hadn't really been blushing, she rather thought she had lost the capacity to, all in one intense night of pleasure. Of course, there was that one thing still not experienced, Theo had not taken her, claimed her body, possessed her. But he had taught her, shatteringly, the pleasure that a man and a woman could give to each other. There was one more night before they reached Maubourg. Would he come to her bed again, or would he take her literally and make last night the one and only?

Theo had demolished his steak, and his third cup of coffee, and was watching her while she daydreamed. 'What is it?' she asked. He looked so right there in her bed, his chest bare, the sheet draped precariously, with unselfconscious provocation, over his hips.

'Nell, won't you think again about marrying me?'

No! So he had not listened to a word she had said last night. Now he was going to be noble and honourable and want her to marry him. No wonder he had been so reluctant, he had known he would feel this the next morning.

'No, Theo. Thank you, but no. I cannot marry without love, you see. I know it was wicked of me to want to experience this, but I did mean what I said last night—please do not make me feel bad by trying to do what you see as the honourable thing.'

'Honour be damned,' he retorted. 'Nell, I love you—'

'Yes, I know.' She had to reassure him, the words tumbled out. 'You couldn't be a more loving friend and cousin. And I love you, just the same way.' *Lies, I love you in every way there is.* 'But you told me you would never marry, and I realise that must be because you love someone else, hopelessly—no, don't interrupt—and I know it is sad because she doesn't love you, but two wrongs don't make a right. Given my feelings, it would be wrong for us to marry. Truly, I don't think I could *stand* it,' she added with as much con-viction as she could muster.

'I see. Thank you for being so clear about it.' Theo put his plate down and threw back the sheet. Shy all of a sudden, Elinor looked away, keeping her eyes on the pile of hat and dress boxes while behind her she could hear Theo hunting through the strewn clothing for his breeches and shirt. 'I'll send the maid up with water and to help you to dress, shall I?'

'Yes, please.' How painfully polite they were being to each other. Last night, this morning, there was not an inch of each other's body they had not caressed, kissed, explored. Now they would be discussing the weather in a minute.

The road to Grenoble was long, Theo, reserved, and the horses, tired. The magic had gone out of the journey and Elinor knew she had only herself to blame for that. How could she have failed to anticipate the emotions that would be unleashed by intimacy of that kind? He had been so right, back at the chateau. She kept trying to understand desire intellectually and all the time it was far too complicated for that.

Theo suggested that she must be tired and might prefer to travel inside where she could sleep. Elinor translated this, without much difficulty, as meaning that he wanted to be alone and could very well do without her company.

She sat in the chaise surrounded by the pretty boxes full of Theo's joyful purchases and felt very much like weeping. Which was not helpful, she decided, waiting in an inn while Theo had a local livery stables change the fittings and harness another pair to the carriage. She had got into this mess by thinking too much; now an excess of sensibility was no way to get out of it.

The only thing to be done was to keep reminding herself that she was actually better off than she had been before Theo had come back into her life. She looked better, she felt more confident, she had had adventures and experiences and she had learned that risking letting herself feel led to both the expected disadvantages and to undreamed wonders.

If she could just manage to school her awakened body into accepting that it had experienced quite enough sensuality and was now satisfied, she was certain she would soon feel very much better.

The unexpected touch of Theo's hand on hers made her flinch. As she got to her feet, he stood well back to give her room, and, instead of explaining that he had simply startled her, she found there was nothing she could say. Perhaps, she thought with sadness as she climbed into the carriage, there never would be again.

That night Theo had professed himself tired from so much driving and had retired with the brandy after an hour of very stilted dinner conversation, leaving her to the dubious pleasures of Petrarch and the private parlour with a view of rain-soaked rooftops. Even the glorious August weather had deserted them, making the last ten miles a miserable drag along muddy roads.

Elinor shut her book with a snap, rang the bell for a glass of red wine, wrapped her shawl tight around her shoulders, put her feet up on the fender and gave her future some serious thought. It would not hold Theo, she knew that, but she was beginning to wonder whether it would bear any relation to her life with her mother so far either.

There was nothing she did for Mama that a competent secretary who could draw could not do. She had her own money—not that she ever touched it or questioned the decisions of her trustees. Well, that would have to change if she was going to stop simply existing and start living.

She could afford her own companion, could afford to travel. Elinor stretched out a hand for her notebook and began to scribble.

Half an hour later the wine was untouched at her side and she had filled a page with tightly packed notes headed, *How Much Money Do I Have?* and finishing, *ITALY!*

She read it through slowly, stretched out a hand for the glass and fought down the rising knot of apprehension. Yes, she could do it. One tear rolled down the side of her nose and she scrubbed it away with an impatient hand. She was going to be lonely, but she rather thought she had been lonely since she was a child. Now she was going to be lonely on her own terms and in that, surely, there must be some happiness. It was just a pity it had taken her heart being broken to make her realise it.

Theo came down to breakfast dressed in cream pantaloons, shining Hessians with gold tassels, brand new linen and a coat of immaculate dark blue superfine.

'You are never going to drive dressed like that, surely?' Elinor asked, putting down the coffee pot. She had put on her new carriage dress in heavy Lyon silk, taken a good deal of trouble over her hair, and had chosen a pair of exquisite kid gloves in honour of her first appearance at the Maubourg court.

The words had escaped before she had given any thought to the fact that things must still be somewhat constrained between them, but Theo shrugged amiably enough. 'I've hired a groom to drive. I did not think my arrival looking like the driver of the London-to-Brighton stage would add to our consequence. We might be relatives, but we've got to get in the front door first.' He accepted the coffee she passed him—strong, black, one sugar, just as he liked it—and added, 'You look very fine.'

'Thank you.' Elinor scrabbled around mentally for things to talk about, then realised they were going to have all day shut up in the carriage together and stilted conversation was not going to be enough. 'I don't suppose you have a travelling chess set on you?'

'No, but I can buy some cards from the waiter. Do you play whist? No? Let me teach you, then when we get to Maubourg Sebastian can teach you how to be a sharper.'

'Sebastian? Is he really? From his days as Jack Ryder, do you mean? I wish he would talk about his adventures as a King's Messenger, but he is desperately discreet.'

'Rather more than a King's Messenger,' Theo remarked, slicing ham thickly. 'And still is, from time to time, when the government needs him. Although don't, for goodness sake, repeat that.'

'And Eva knows?'

'Apparently she says that so long as it doesn't involve beautiful young women, he must do as he sees fit.'

'What would she say about the marquesa?' Elinor stole one of Theo's slices of ham, beginning to relax a little.

'Ana? Eva has more sense than to fret about Sebastian's past—after all, her first husband was one of the most notorious rakes in Europe. But I would not fancy any woman's chances of escaping with a whole skin if they decided to set their caps at Sebastian now.'

Elinor envied the Grand Duchess her strength and her certainty. If she could be like that, then an independent life would be easy to achieve. And then she remembered Eva's confidences about her nightmares, recalled seeing the way she looked at Sebastian when she thought she was unobserved—perhaps Eva was not so self-assured. Perhaps it was a matter of application and holding one's nerve after all. They would be in the castle of Maubourg tonight and she would talk to her cousin by marriage, ask her advice. Not about Theo, of course—she was certain that she could never speak about what had happened to a living soul—but about making a break from her past and becoming independent. Eva would understand.

Chapter Twenty

It was past seven in the evening when the rumble of the carriage wheels over cobbles woke Elinor. She had been dozing in the corner of the carriage for an hour, worn out by a day struggling with the rules of whist and Theo's ruthless acquisition of a vast, if imaginary, fortune from her. Her lost wealth was represented by the litter of vowels on the carriage floor.

'Wake up.' Theo reached out and shook her arm, gently. The first time he had voluntarily touched her, she realised, since he had left her bed. 'Put on your hat, we are almost there. Here.' He held out her pelisse and helped her into it For a moment his fingertips brushed along the nape of her neck, then he was sitting back in his corner, gazing out of the window, leaving her to button up the garment and twitch her skirts into order as though nothing was amiss and her breath had not hitched in her throat with the shock of his touch.

The light still lingered in the sloping square before the wide sweep of steps. At the top the massive double doors, studded with knots of medieval ironwork and with a dragon's-head knocker in the centre, frowned down at them. The shadows from the tall houses were long and Elinor shivered as she stepped down into shade, suddenly a prey to doubts. 'Is it going to be all right, just turning up like this?' she whispered, as Theo turned from giving the driver instructions and came to take her arm.

'Yes, of course. This is Eva and Sebastian, don't forget.' He walked across the cobbles, ignoring the curious stares of passers-by.

'Yes, but I don't know Eva at all well, not really,' she worried. There was an imposing pair of guards in full silver-and-blue uniforms with plumes in their helmets and pikes in their hands at the foot of the steps and another pair at the top. As Elinor and Theo approached, the pikes clashed together in an unmistakable signal to stop.

Theo kept going, arrived at the foot of the steps and addressed the right-hand guard in French. 'Mr and Miss Ravenhurst to see Her Serene Highness and Lord Sebastian Ravenhurst.'

One of the top pair of guards pulled a large metal knob, producing a sonorous clanging from inside. Elinor, her still-sleepy brain conjuring up scenes from Gothic novels, stifled a nervous giggle. A wicket gate opened, words were exchanged with someone unseen inside, then both doors were thrown wide, the guards saluted smartly and they were climbing the steps to be met by a tail-coated major domo with a long staff in his hands and a footman on either side.

'This is very formal,' Elinor hissed in Theo's ear. 'But they seem to accept who we are.'

'Mr Ravenhurst, welcome to Maubourg. Their Serene Highnesses will be delighted at this unexpected pleasure. *Madame*.'

'Monsieur Heribaut, it is a pleasure to see you again.' So they knew him; she should have guessed. 'This is Miss Ravenhurst, Lord Sebastian's cousin. I regret, but there has been an incident that has forced us to seek the hospitality of the Grand Duke without notice. Elinor, this is Monsieur Heribaut, the Chamberlain of the castle.'

'If you would care to come in sir, *madame*, I will—'

'Papa, please let me hold him!' The Chamberlain swung round as a boy walked backwards into the great hall talking to the man who followed him. 'I won't drop him, I promise, Mama said—'

The man, tall, broad shouldered, elegant in black evening dress was, Elinor realised, her cousin Sebastian, holding a very small baby against his shoulder and patting it on the back. Her mouth dropped open—this was not at all how she would expect to see him. The boy stopped walking and began hopping up and down on the spot, allowing a small flock of what Elinor assumed were nursery maids to catch up and hover anxiously behind them. 'Papa…'

'Your Serene Highness, Lord Sebastian.' The Chamberlain managed to cut through the chatter of the women and the boy's wheedling voice without raising his own. 'Mr and Miss Ravenhurst.'

Elinor, who was always rather in awe of her magnificent cousin Sebastian, swallowed as he turned. Then he grinned and strode over, an incongruous figure with his exquisite clothes and the baby, which had begin to dribble, she noticed, clasped to his shoulder.

'Theo! My dear cousin. And…' he stopped and stared down at her '…Elinor?'

'Yes, that's Elinor,' Theo said cheerfully, holding out his hands and receiving the baby with an easy competence that almost struck her speechless. 'We're on the run and need sanctuary and a good strongroom. Is this the latest Ravenhurst, then?'

'This is Charles James Oliver Ryder Ravenhurst,' announced the Grand Duke, aged ten, ducking under his stepfather's elbow and thrusting out a hand. 'He's two weeks old and has no hair yet. Welcome to Maubourg Miss Ravenhurst. Sir.'

'Your Serene Highness.' Elinor took his hand and produced her best court curtsy.

'Freddie,' the Grand Duke said, grinning. 'We're sort of cousins, aren't we, if you're a Ravenhurst?'

'My goodness, Theo and Elinor.' The lightly accented, richly feminine voice cut through Theo simultaneously talking to the baby and Sebastian and Elinor trying to explain to Freddie how she was related to his stepfather. The Grand Duchess, in full evening dress, sailed down the hall, her hands held out to them. 'My dears, how lovely. Are you eloping?'

'We most certainly are not,' Elinor began hotly.

'We are trying to give the appearance of doing so,' Theo said. 'Eva, you grow more beautiful every time I see you and your new son is utterly charming.'

'He is, isn't he?' she said smugly. 'I do think it was clever of us. Now Freddie, you take Charles very carefully and carry him up to the nursery and have your dinner.'

'But, Mama, you said I could eat with you—'

'We need to have a business dinner, Freddie. Papa's business, hmm?'

'I see. Secret stuff,' Fréderic said with a grin. 'I'll see you tomorrow then, Cousin Elinor.'

Elinor was not quite sure how Eva did it, but in two crowded minutes the baby and its attendants had been despatched to the nursery, a message had gone down to the kitchens to delay dinner, the Chamberlain was organising rooms and Sebastian's valet had materialised and was sponging dribble off his coat.

'Come along.' Eva tucked one hand under Elinor's arm. 'Come up to my rooms and have a wash and then we can eat while they take up your luggage.'

'I'm so sorry, arriving like this,' Elinor tried to apologise as they climbed the stairs.

'I am delighted. Now tell me, how did you come to look so lovely? You were such a little brown mouse whenever I saw you before. Except for the hair, of course.'

'It was Theo.'

'Oho!' Eva's chuckle was enough to make Elinor blush to her toes.

'No! I mean he nagged me into buying new clothes and doing my hair differently. And we've been having adventures recently, which seems to have improved my complexion. Or something,' she added doubtfully, not at all sure herself why these days she seemed to be glowing. Unless Jeanie was right and love did that to you.

'But you *are* going to marry him?' Eva swept into the room, startling a middle-aged woman who was folding clothes on the bed. 'Hortense, this is Miss Ravenhurst, Lord Sebastian's cousin. She will be staying and requires a maid. Now she needs hot water, if you please.' The dresser bobbed a curtsy and hurried out. 'Do you want to change? Don't feel you have to, it is only us tonight.'

'Thank you, if it is all right, I'll just wash my hands and face.' Elinor sat down with a thump on the dressing-table stool. 'Eva, I am not marrying Theo.'

'No? But you are compromised, are you not?' Eva picked up a comb. 'You have been travelling with him. Here, let me take your hat, your back hair is coming down.'

'Yes, but Mama knows about it and I do not have to. I mean, I am still—' Goodness, but this was embarrassing.

'A virgin? Not such a rake as he likes to make out then, our Theo. But you are blushing like a rose! Only just a virgin, perhaps? So, he is a very careful rake.' She was teasing, but gently, and her smile was warm.

'Eva! We'll tell you all about it at dinner. No, I do not mean *that*,' she added repressively as the Grand Duchess's smile became positively wicked. 'I would like to talk to you later, though, just the two of us,' she added, suddenly shy now the urgency of assuring Eva that she did not *have* to marry had ebbed away, but realising she did need a woman to confide in. 'And, please, do not tease Theo about me, he keeps having attacks of being all honourable and noble and saying we should get married and he obviously doesn't want to. Nor do I, naturally.'

'Naturally? How very odd of you,' Eva remarked through a mouthful of hairpins. 'I think he is very attractive. Not beautiful like Sebastian—no one else is *that* beautiful—but so masculine. No? And intelligent, which you need.'

Elinor was saved from answering by the arrival of the dresser with a maid in tow. 'Annette, *madame*—she will look after you while you are here.'

Walking down to dinner twenty minutes later, Elinor wondered uneasily whether Theo had been having an equally embarrassing talk with Sebastian. It was too much to hope that Theo's arrival with her, unchaperoned, would not provoke his cousin into some kind of enquiry, if only a teasing one. And the last thing she wanted was anyone reinforcing Theo's conviction that he must offer for her.

Thank goodness Eva had dropped the subject. She was talking about fashions, admiring Elinor's carriage dress and marvelling that she had managed to have it made in such a short time. 'Even for Lyon, that is good work. Obviously Theo has shopped there before.'

'I am sure he has,' Elinor responded brightly. 'It is equally obvious he has a great deal of experience shopping with ladies. Women,' she corrected herself after a moment's thought.

'If you will accept one word of advice from me…' Eva slowed and stopped as they approached the doors flanked by liveried footmen '…it would be to forget the women who came before a man meets you. They will have taught him many lessons, for which you may be grateful, but it is only the ones in his life after you have met him that need concern you.' Her eyes flickered up to the portrait of a rakishly handsome man in ornate uniform hanging at the head of the hallway. 'And not even then.'

'Did it not hurt?' Elinor asked, greatly daring, remembering the tales of Eva's first husband and his legendary *affaires*.

'There is hurt pride and there is love betrayed,' said Eva drily. 'They are not necessarily the same thing. When you marry a man like Louis Fréderic there are many compensations, but the price is learning not to give your heart. But we are not talking about Grand Dukes here, are we? Marry for love, Elinor, or not at all.'

'That,' she retorted with conviction, 'is my view entirely.'

The dining room was small, obviously the space used for eating *en famille*. Sebastian and Theo rose to their feet as the ladies entered, Sebastian nodding to the butler. 'Bring the wine to the table, then you may all leave us.'

Theo pulled out a chair for Elinor, then circled the table to sit opposite her. Before them dinner had been set out *à la française*, but in a much reduced form with the desserts on a sideboard. She had been fearing a formal court service, full of pitfalls for the unwary and with no opportunity to relax and talk. This was perfect. Or it would be once she had got over the butterflies in her stomach that Eva's frank remarks had produced.

With everyone served, Sebastian put down the carving knife and looked round the table. 'Now,' he said with a smile, 'you must sing for your suppers.'

Elinor let Theo talk, occasionally chipping in a comment, but mainly eating and watching the faces of the listeners. Sebastian, she decided, must be a superlative card player, possibly even have the skills of a sharper as Theo had suggested, for there was not a flicker of expression on his face when Ana's name was mentioned.

Eva was less guarded, although she betrayed her recognition only by a slight narrowing of her fine, dark eyes. Then she laughed, a gurgle of genuine amusement. 'So, you keep your mistresses in the family, you Ravenhursts?'

Sebastian, well used to his wife, merely smiled lazily. Theo retorted, 'She was never my mistress, that would be like trying to domesticate a wild cat. As I was explaining, having visited the chateau…'

'And you decided to visit us rather than make for the coast?' Sebastian leaned over and cut himself a corner of cheese as Theo reached the end of the tale. 'That seems a wise choice to me, if the countess had discovered your escape and decided to give chase.' They had demolished both courses and now the port decanter was circulating and Theo was cracking walnuts between long fingers.

'I wonder if they did realise you had escaped,' Eva pondered. 'By now your man will have delivered the letter you left with him to the count. He will have to decide what to do about his mother.'

'Unless he has resolved to keep it quiet and not risk scandal,' Elinor pointed out.

'He will have your mother to deal with in that case, with Hythe at her side. And I was frank with him—if he does not deal with her, I will tell the tale all over Paris.'

'So, the excitement is probably over,' Eva said with regret. 'Now, where is this Chalice? I want to see it.'

'No, you do not,' Elinor retorted with a shudder. 'It is a work of art and absolutely horrible, to look at and to touch.'

'In that case, it can stay where it is. We will find you some large outriders to guard it on its way back to England. How long can you stay with us?'

'Until Hythe arrives.' Theo swirled his port and looked into the ruby wine. 'He can escort Elinor to meet her mother in Avignon, I will go north for England.'

And that will be that, the end of my adventure.

'But you have been travelling alone with Elinor,' Sebastian pointed out. 'You cannot just waltz off and leave her.'

'Apparently I can,' Theo said, not lifting his eyes from the glass. 'Our cousin will not have me.'

'I don't have to marry you,' Elinor snapped, suddenly wanting nothing more than sleep and nothing less than a pair of men trying to tell her what to do. 'And I am not going to be pushed into a marriage of convention I don't want with an unwilling man just to satisfy everyone else's sense of honour, respectability and propriety. And don't look at me like that,' she added for Sebastian's benefit, 'you aren't head of the family, the Duke is, and he isn't about to appear from Scotland and order us to marry, is he?'

Eva cleared her throat. 'I think the ladies will retire now, gentlemen. I wish to go to the nursery and Elinor is sorely in need of her bed, I am sure.' She stopped by Sebastian's chair as she passed, pressing down on his shoulder to prevent him rising, and bent to kiss him on the mouth.

Elinor averted her eyes and met Theo's. 'Goodnight.' She lifted her chin and swept out in Eva's wake.

'I apologise if I was rude,' she said as Eva led the way to the guest chamber.

'Sebastian can look after himself,' Eva said. 'If there is no risk of you being with child, then it will be a simple matter to cover up those days you two spent together. Naturally, you will mention if asked that, with my invitation to visit, I sent one of my ladies to chaperon you. Now, here we are.'

Elinor doubted she would ever find her way back through the maze of passages and staircases, but as there were liveried retainers around every corner that was probably not too much of a problem. 'That little door leads to a circular stair up to the west battlements. There is a range of chambers up there opening out on to the battlement walkway that we give to single male guests. There is room for them to walk up and down smoking their cigarillos and telling *risqué* stories. Theo is the only occupant at the moment.'

Now why had she explained all that? Elinor wondered as she looked round at the cosy bedroom that had been fashioned from the unpromising beginning of a stone-vaulted chamber. Even in the winter it would be snug, with its thick carpets on the flagged floor and the Aubusson tapestries lining the walls.

'This is lovely, thank you.' She decided not to comment on Theo's whereabouts; it was probably her own over-sensitivity to any mention of him. Eva was merely making conversation. 'Eva, I would appreciate your help in finding myself a suitable companion. I have decided that I want to travel and I would rather face Mama with a *fait accompli*.'

'This is rather sudden, is it not?' Eva perched on the edge of the bed, looking less like a grand duchess and more like a young woman contemplating mischief. 'Is it because of Theo?'

It would be easy enough to lie. Elinor found she was tired of dissembling. 'Yes. That and the fact that I find I cannot contemplate going back to the way things were.'

'Very well, I will help you find a companion. There is a very pleasant and cultivated widow in her forties living in the town. She dines here occasionally—her husband was one of the court physicians. She may be a possibility. But why don't you do the obvious thing?'

'What is that?' Elinor plumped down beside Eva. Something obvious would be rather a pleasant change.

'Why, marry Theo, of course.'

'But he doesn't love me, that's what I meant at dinner.'

'He doesn't?'

'No, he says he will never marry. The way he told me, I am sure there is someone he loves, but whom he cannot have. He keeps proposing, of course—but I think that's a mixture of loneliness and guilt and this maddening male honour.' Eva looked decidedly puzzled. 'He is by himself so much, except for lovers, of course, and I don't think he has become attached to anyone other than this woman he cannot have. And we get on very well, most of the time, so I expect he thinks I would be pleasant company. And the guilt—well, he knows he has compromised me and we were rather, er…'

'Was he good?' Eva enquired, ignoring Elinor's gasp.

'Very. He made me feel wonderful. And special,' she admitted finally 'Not that I have any basis for comparison. Eva, men don't talk about—I mean, Theo and Sebastian?'

'Theo is far too much the gentleman, and Sebastian would never ask. Women are far less inhibited about these things.' Eva smiled her wicked smile. 'But who is this woman he is in love with, I wonder? Not the marquesa, surely?'

'Lord no. He threw her out of his bedchamber at Beaumartin. She's like a cat, she whisked her tail and stalked off to find another mouse to play with.'

'Pretending she wasn't at all put out? The lady has style, that is obvious. But Elinor, my dear, you love Theo, don't you?'

The quiet question caught her unawares, still smiling at the thought of Theo's rejection of Ana and the way she had reacted. 'Oh, yes,' she murmured, then caught herself. 'Far too much to marry him like this,' she added firmly.

'Oh, dear.' Eva put an arm around Elinor's shoulders and hugged. 'And you don't want to tell him and the idiot can't see it.'

'He isn't an idiot—'

'They all are when it comes to love,' Eva said with authority. 'Mind you, women are too. I proposed to Sebastian, and a complete mull I made of it. Then Bel put her oar in and that made it worse. Too much pride on both sides, of course, but we came to our senses in the end, thank goodness.'

'You are so happy. And Bel and Ashe, and Gareth and Jessica. Perhaps I am just infected by the Ravenhurst fashion for marriages and I'm pining for something I don't really want,' Elinor said, trying hard to sound light-hearted about it.

'You sleep on it.' Eva slid off the bed. 'Ring if you want anything, Annette will come. I must go and look in on the nursery. Theo's good with children, isn't he? Goodnight.'

Elinor sat looking at the closed door for some minutes after Eva had taken herself off with that airy observation, seeing not the solid wood panels, but the image of Theo with the gurgling baby in his arms.

Chapter Twenty-One

To Theo's decidedly jaundiced eye Eva was up to something. His mood, he readily acknowledged, was considerably depressed by a crashing hangover. Sebastian had rung for a second bottle of port, declaring that they were both in need of an exclusively masculine evening and somehow that had emptied in short order, only to be replaced with brandy.

Quite why Sebastian, who appeared to be in the best of spirits, should need to indulge in what turned out to be a solid evening's drinking, Theo had no idea. In the end he knew himself to be so disguised that he took considerable care to hug the inner wall when he came out of the spiral stairs on to the battlements and Bachelors' Walk.

He was aware of the conversation turning to women and the problems they caused a man, and could remember wondering if Sebastian was trying to pump him about Nell. But he had quite as hard a head as his cousin, and probably almost as much experience keeping his mouth shut. So why, this morning, he had the uneasy feeling that he had given away more than he intended, he was not sure. A guilty conscience, probably.

His mood was not improved by the presence at the breakfast table of the castle's librarian, a slender young Englishman with blue eyes, blond hair, a classical profile and considerable address. Theo wanted to strangle him, if only to stop him discussing, with every appearance of interest, Gothic architecture in Italy with Nell.

'He is such an intelligent young man,' Eva murmured in Theo's ear. 'Lord Finchingfield mentioned him to us when we were last in England—Phillip is the third son, you know—and he is working wonders in the library. It had been dreadfully neglected. I was sure Elinor would find him entertaining, and I appear to have been correct.'

'Indeed?' Theo applied himself to his ham and eggs, trying not to glare at Mr Finchingfield, who was making Nell laugh now. Nell never laughed at breakfast. And why did she have to look so damnably lovely this morning?

'If you have finished, Elinor and Phillip, there was something I wanted to discuss in the library.' Eva gestured to the footman who sprang to pull back her chair and left with the others behind her, still laughing over some shared joke.

Nell had hardly spared him more than a polite *good morning* when he had come in and had then pertly enquired whether he would like her to ring for a powder for his head. When he had growled at her, he had seen her bite the inside of her cheek to keep from laughing at him. Did he look that bad? A glance in the mirror opposite confirmed that he did. His skin was pale under the tan, there were shadows under his eyes and he had made a hash of shaving that morning.

Sebastian, to be fair, did not look much better, but at least he had the decency to eat his breakfast in silence.

'My lord. There is a lady at the front door.' The Chamberlain looked as though he was not certain that *lady* was the apt word.

'She has presented her card?' Sebastian raised one eyebrow at Theo, who shrugged. Whoever it was, it was nothing to do with him.

'My lord.' The Chamberlain proffered a salver. Sebastian lifted the rectangle of pasteboard and studied it with a perfectly expressionless face.

'The Marquesa de Cordovilla. Now, which of us do you think she is visiting?'

'The lady enquired for Miss Ravenhurst, my lord. Apparently she has a message from her mother.'

'Miss Ravenhurst is in the library with her Serene Highness and is not to be disturbed. Show the marquesa in here, Heribaut. Interesting,' Sebastian remarked. 'I wonder if she really does have a message from Aunt Louisa or if it is simply a ruse to get entry.'

'To what end?' Theo felt the first stirrings of amusement he had felt all morning. 'I am looking forward to seeing the meeting between Ana and Eva.'

She was as dangerous as a snake and as difficult to handle as a flock of cats, but Theo found no difficulty in understanding why he had entangled himself with this woman. Her sheer nerve, let alone her looks, made her stand out like a diamond in a tray of paste stones.

And she was on her best behaviour. 'Lord Sebastian, Mr Ravenhurst.' Her curtsy was immaculate, her carriage dress perfection and butter would not melt in her mouth. 'I do appreciate the honour of a reception. And I see I am interrupting your meal— my apologies.'

'Please, join us, Marquesa.' A water ice wouldn't have melted in Sebastian's mouth, let alone butter. Theo resumed his seat as she took hers, smiling at the footman who set a place before her.'

'Coffee only, I thank you.'

'You have come from Beaumartin? Our aunt is well?'

'Indeed, yes. Your letter put the cat amongst the pigeons with a vengeance, Mr Ravenhurst. But perhaps I had better wait until Miss Ravenhurst can join us?'

'Heribaut, please enquire if her Serene Highness and Miss Ravenhurst are free.'

It seemed none of them could find a topic for conversation. Ana consumed black, unsweetened coffee, Theo pushed back his chair so he could see the door and Sebastian steepled his long fingers and sat, apparently deep in thought.

Theo suspected Heribaut had informed Eva who the unexpected guest was, for she came through the door first, a warm smile on her lips and her hand extended. 'Marquesa, how delightful. I have heard so much about you, such a famed connoisseur and expert in art.'

'Your Serene Highness, you are too good. I merely love handsome—I mean beautiful—oh, my English!—things.' As she sat again, Eva cast her husband a glance and winked. Sebastian's eyes crinkled in an appreciative smile, then he was serious again as Elinor entered. 'Ah, Miss Ravenhurst, I come with a message from your mama.'

'So kind,' Elinor murmured, waiting until the staff had filed out and the door had closed. 'Our cousins know everything about events at the chateau before we left.'

'As you may imagine, there was a great to-do once your flight had been discovered. Lady James was most affecting, reproaching herself for having spoken to you so severely that you felt elopement was preferable to the rigours of a society wedding. And so we continued, some of us grieving, some vastly entertained,' And I know which you were, Elinor thought appreciatively, 'Until breakfast the next day, that is, when Theo's man arrived with a missive for Leon.'

Theo had always thought the expression a cliché, but now, as they all sat around the breakfast table, the tension could have been cut with a knife.

'Hythe went to stand behind Lady James's shoulder, which I thought odd, until I glimpsed the pistols in his belt. Leon read the letter, twice, I believe, each time becoming a little paler. Then he asked Lady James and Monsieur Castelnau to join him in his study. Well, we were agog—at least I was, and the Traceys seemed most interested—so no one went out and we were all making the most dull conversation in the salon when down comes Leon and asks his mother and Julie to join them.'

Ana broke off to take a sip of coffee, quite deliberately prolonging the suspense in Theo's opinion. 'So we sat a little longer, none of us quite liking to comment on what our hosts must be up to—and then the screaming began.'

'Naturally, good manners must have held you in your seats,' Eva commented. 'How frustrating.'

'But, no! How could we resist—off we all went, up the stairs, the noise getting worse by the second, and there, outside the family suites on the *premier étage*, was Leon, in the act of locking his mother's door and Julie, biting and screaming, in the more than capable grip of Hythe. She was bundled into her room and by this time all the servants were there—you may imagine the chaos. To cut the story short, a messenger was sent to the family doctor, the servants informed that the countess had been taken ill with some sort of brain fever and that Julie was hysterical with worry.'

'Did anyone accept that?' Theo enquired. Thank God, Leon had believed his letter. The count should be safe now, whatever happened to the two women.

'The servants did, why should they not? The poor woman, grieving over her husband until it all becomes too much to bear? And the two young girls guess nothing—Leon packed them both off home in the company of his elderly relative. And Julie was known to be devoted. But myself and the Traceys? No, of course not. So, Leon tells us the whole story—he did not have much choice, I think. We all went down to the dungeons and found the scene of your imprisonment—and there was the poison. My blood ran cold, believe me.' She gave a theatrical shudder, but Theo saw the darkness in her eyes. Yes, that horrid chamber had affected her, more than she was willing to betray.

'And the rest of the treasure?'

'He showed us that too, before locking it away and asking us all to swear on the bible that we would keep all this secret, except from you.'

'But what will happen to the countess and to Julie?' Elinor asked. They were the first words she had spoken since she had sat down. Sebastian and Eva had murmured comments, but Nell had sat impassive throughout. He wondered if she was finding it hard to listen to.

'The family doctor has found that the countess is deranged by grief and she will be confined at the chateau—for ever, I suppose. Julie will be sent back to her mother with an annuity, which will cease if she ever tries to contact the family again, or leaves Brittany where her mother lives.'

'How neatly it is possible to dispose of murder and attempted murder,' Nell said softly.

'How kind of you to come out of your way to tell us this, Marquesa,' Eva remarked. 'You must, of course, stay the night.'

'Thank you.' If Ana was offended by being asked for only one night, she did not show it. 'And it was not out of my way at all, I am travelling to the coast to take ship for Italy. Lady James had already sent to Avignon to arrange her lodgings, so it would have been inconvenient for her to detour.'

Inconvenient, but natural, Theo thought, protective of Nell's feelings. At least if she had any concerns about her mother's safety, they were now put to rest. He watched her while the others asked more questions, sorted out just what had occurred to their own satisfaction. She sat still, her hands folded in her lap. For a while he was deceived into thinking she had reverted to the way she used to deal with her mother, passively allowing it all to wash over her. But then she lifted her head, listening to something Ana said about her plans in Italy, and he saw he was wrong.

She was not happy, but she was thinking, planning—he could

see it in her eyes. His Nell was making a decision, and she was making it with no reference to him. But then, why should she? he thought with a bitter jab at his own feelings. He had made love to her when he knew he ought not to have done and yet he had failed to give her whatever it was she truly needed.

'Theo!' It was Sebastian, who appeared to have been talking to him for some time.

'Sorry, I was miles away.'

'I was asking if you wanted to ride out with me, see the agricultural experiments I've introduced.'

'Of course, although you do realise I wouldn't know a turnip from a potato, don't you? Nell, why don't you come too?'

She was at the door, exchanging a word with Eva who was bearing their latest guest off to her bedchamber. 'No, thank you, Theo. Mr Finchingfield is expecting me in the library.'

'Bloody librarian,' Theo muttered as he found himself alone with Sebastian in the breakfast room.

'You didn't take to him?' His cousin looked surprised. 'Very competent, good family and all that. I wonder if Eva is matchmaking—he's a excellent choice for Elinor, I'd have thought.' Apparently not noticing Theo's snarl, he added, 'Let's see if Freddie would like to come with us. I'd value your opinion on the pony I've just bought him.'

A librarian? For Nell? A pattern-book pretty young man with respectable bloodlines and a sound knowledge of the classics? She would be bored to tears. Safe, no doubt, no dungeons or pistols or scandalous lovemaking with Mr Finchingfield, that was for certain, but where would all that fun go, that courage?

'I'll get my hat and gloves.' He took the spiral stairs to his roof-high chamber at a run, two at a time, all the way up, arriving with his breath tight in his chest and a burn in his thigh muscles and still wanting nothing more than to ruin the line of the librarian's perfect nose for him.

* * *

A day spent in the panelled library was soothing, Elinor found. It was light and airy and well organised and she admired the young librarian's enthusiasm for his task.

'But there is still so much to do,' he said with a groan, waving a hand towards the back of the room where stacks of books, dusty and disorganised, still crowded the shelves. 'The late Grand Duke was not interested, except for sporting subjects and, um…certain rather indelicate volumes. But he bought widely, just as he did works of art. The only trouble was, he neglected to replace the librarian when the last one died twelve years ago. And as for the archives, I haven't even touched them. They are a full-time job.'

He opened a door into another chamber, with stone walls and vaulted ceiling. Bundles of documents, rolls of parchment, tin boxes and wooden chests were crammed inside with great ledgers balanced on every flat surface. 'Goodness, what a treasure trove.' Intrigued, Elinor lifted the nearest scroll off its shelf and peered at it. 'This is fascinating.'

'I am glad you think so.' It was Eva, her skirts lifted clear of the dusty floor. 'I did wonder whether you would like to spend a little time here as our archivist. It would allow you to consider your plans and to make a considered choice of companion for your travels.'

Mr Finchingfield effaced himself and tactfully went off to his desk while Eva waited for Elinor's response. 'Naturally, we would pay you the same salary as Phillip. And you only need stay as long as you wish—just make a start and help me find a permanent archivist is all I would ask.'

Taken aback, she considered it. 'It would make things easier with Mama. I am sure she would be less anxious if I came here rather than taking off by myself.' Actually she probably wouldn't be anxious at all. Irritated at having to find a new secretary, that was all. But it would stop Theo fussing. She might even see him from time to time if he knew where she was. 'Thank you, yes, I would like that very much.'

'Excellent. We must find you a desk. Phillip! You have a colleague,'

At dinner she found herself seated next to Mr Finchingfield with the castle's Anglican chaplain on her left. Perhaps to dilute the impact of Ana, Eva had invited a number of people, including the widowed Mrs Massingham, whom she had suggested as a possible companion for Elinor's travels.

It made it easier to avoid Theo. Why she wanted to, Elinor was not certain, but instinct told her that he would not be happy with her plans and that having an argument with him would be more upsetting than she could cope with just now.

When the gentlemen rejoined the ladies and Eva presided over the tea tray, Theo finally cut through the group around her. 'Elinor, I was hoping for a word with you.' Next to Phillip's slight elegance and the chaplain's comfortable roundness he looked big, masculine and decidedly commanding. He also looked thoroughly irritated, although she doubted anyone who didn't know him well would notice.

'Why don't you join us?' she asked, knowing that was not what he wanted. 'Mr Finchingfield was just explaining his new classification scheme for the library, which sounds most comprehensive, only I am not certain how it would work for theology. What do you think, Dr Herriot?'

'Indeed, comparative religion may be the stumbling block with your ideas,' the chaplain began.

Theo shot her a look that showed he knew exactly what she was up to, combined with something else she could not fathom. Surely he was not hurt by her evasion? He must know she would only refuse him again if that was his intention in speaking to her.

'Theology is not my subject, you must excuse me.' He turned and went back to join the rest of the group clustered around the wide, empty hearth.

But that look, that darkness behind the clear green eyes, haunted her. Was she imagining things, projecting her own unhappiness at the relationship between them on to him, manufacturing feelings for him he did not have? But he did not look happy—there was a tension about him even when he was joking with Sebastian or engaged in a barbed flirtation with Ana.

She watched, half her mind on him while she tried to keep up with Dr Herriot's arguments. There he was, the man she loved, funny, brave, attractive, heart-stoppingly sensual, and she was sending him away. It was the right thing, of course it was. Only it seemed to be making neither of them very happy.

When the clocks struck midnight—a somewhat prolonged matter in a castle the size of Maubourg, despite the best efforts of the official clock-winder—Elinor was still awake.

She had gone up at eleven, washed and changed into her night-gown, thanked her maid and settled down in an armchair with an extravagant number of candles and a sensation novel from the pile that Eva had sent up. It had been a long day; she was convinced she would soon want to climb into bed. But despite the best efforts of the valiant heroine, trapped in a tower by her wicked guardian for reasons that were not entirely clear, she could neither concentrate on the tale nor fall asleep.

Assuming that he and Sebastian had not had another late-night session, Theo was in his bedchamber somewhere above her head. Was he asleep already, or reading? Perhaps he was planning the journey back to England with the Chalice, or his next buying trip, somewhere in Europe. Or perhaps he was sitting like she was, a book disregarded on his knee, just thinking.

Had that strange darkness gone from his eyes? Had he realised that he did not need to worry about her?

What she wanted, she realised, more than anything, was to be close to him. Not to do or say anything—what was there left to do or say? Just to be close.

Elinor scrambled out of bed and opened the clothes press, searching for something she could wear that she could fasten herself. The shabby old gown she had explored the chateau in was the only thing, and it was warm. Despite the time of year, it would be cool up on the battlements.

Tossing a drab cloak around her shoulders and pushing her feet into slippers, Elinor peered out of her door. Down at the far end of the corridor stood one of the guards who patrolled the castle night and day, but his back was to her. Soft-footed, she crept to the doorway Eva had pointed out and was through it without a sound.

The stairs spiralled up, opening out on to a paved walkway, perhaps ten foot wide, with the battlements on one side and a wall, broken by doors and small windows, on the other. There was no sound except the hoot of a hunting owl drifting over the river far below and distantly, faint music from the town. And all was dark, but for the spill of light from under one door and from around the edge of the heavily curtained window.

Theo was still awake, then. Elinor leaned against the door, flattening her cheek and her palm on the warm old wood as though against his body. She knew she could not stay there all night, sleeping across his threshold like a medieval page, but she did not want to leave.

Interspersed with the regular gaps of the battlements were darker areas, which proved to be alcoves with stone slabs for seats, perhaps to allow sentries to rest or shelter in bad weather. Wrapping her cloak tight around her Elinor sat down in one, put her feet up and leaned back. It was surprisingly comfortable and it gave her a clear view of Theo's door. She would stay until he snuffed out his candles and then she would go back down to her own bed and try to sleep too.

How long she dozed there, warm in her corner with only a cold nose and toes to betray the deepening night, she had no idea. Nor was she sure what brought her completely awake. The light was still showing under Theo's door, but there was no sound from within his room.

Then she heard it again, the brush of leather on stone as the sole of someone's shoe met an uneven slab. The person halted. Elinor could sense, rather than hear, breathing and muffled her own in a fold of the cloak. She saw the person move across the spill of light from under the door, silk gown swishing faintly.

The door opened, throwing the woman into silhouette. Elinor craned to recognise who it was and saw, before she hid it in the folds of her skirt, the long blade in her right hand, sparking silver in the candlelight.

Chapter Twenty-Two

'Ana.' Theo had recognised the intruder, but he had not seen the knife. His voice, just reaching Elinor, held only resignation and faint amusement. 'What the devil…?'

She tore off her cloak and wriggled out of her niche, running without any attempt at concealment to the door, throwing her shoulder against it as Ana tried to close it from the inside.

The force of the push sent the other woman staggering off balance. Elinor swirled the heavy wool cloak in her hands and threw it, enveloping Ana in folds of cloth. 'She's got a knife,' she gasped, trying to hang on to the flailing figure.

Theo seized her by the shoulders and pushed her unceremoniously into the corner of the room. 'In that case, leave her to me.' He dragged off the cloak and Ana emerged, blinking and furious.

'You stupid little witch,' she hissed at Elinor. 'Sleep with him if you want. Do I care? I have had him, I do not want him back—so you take care not to attack me again or you will be sorry.' She advanced towards them, the long knife glinting in her hand as she prodded it towards Elinor to emphasise every word.

'Ana—' Theo was edging to one side, attempting to keep his body between Elinor and the furious Spanish woman. 'Put the knife down—we don't want anyone to get hurt, do we?'

'Don't we?' she enquired ominously, then tossed the weapon on to the bed where it lay, its hilt glittering with gemstones. 'Bah! You could not peel an apple with that thing.' She kicked the cloak to one side and stood, hands on hips, belligerently regarding Theo, and Elinor, who was trying to push past him.

'You English are mad. I come here to deliver that thing to you for the count. He says you deserve something from the treasure—and I have something for you, too, only I did not expect you to be up here.' She scowled at Elinor, who sat down with a thud on Theo's chair.

He picked up the dagger, turning it over in his hands, then studying the hilt closely. 'Just for show, see, the blade is dull.' He ran his thumb down it. 'It must have been brandished during their rituals. If the stones are genuine, it is worth a great deal of money.' Ana had sauntered over to the dresser and was pouring herself a glass of wine from the decanter that stood there. 'I suppose it was too much to hope you might have given it to me during the hours of daylight?'

'I did not want anyone to see.' She tossed back the wine. 'How do I know if you can trust your cousins?'

'Then thank you for bringing it. What did he send Elinor?'

'A platter, a small one, but good work. You can have it tomorrow.'

'I would not want anything from that place.' Elinor shuddered, thinking about the scenes those glittering objects must have been used in.

'Sell it, then.' Ana shrugged and put down the glass. 'The man is full of guilt for what has happened. That, and perhaps he wants to ensure you hold your tongues. The Chalice has vanished into its hiding place again—the count wants to pretend nothing has happened, that his lies about his mother's collapse are the truth.

'Now I go to my bed and leave you to your strange courtship.' She leaned close to Elinor as she passed. 'It is easier to make love, my respectable English miss, if you are both on the same side of the door.'

'What the hell did she mean by that?' Theo, hands on hips, glared at Elinor. He was still partly dressed, coat and neckcloth gone, his shirt open at the neck, his shoes discarded by the bed.

'Don't glower at me,' Elinor retorted. 'How should I know what she means?' She wanted to go to him and finish unbuttoning his shirt, push it back over his shoulders so she could savour the skin beneath, touch it with her lips and fingertips…

'Why were you following her?'

'I wasn't,' she denied, then realised just where that statement left her.

'You were here already?'

'I couldn't sleep, I needed some air. Eva had shown me the stairs to the battlements.' His expression was sceptical; she couldn't blame him. 'Look at me, for goodness' sake. Do I appear to have dressed up for a seduction? I was sitting outside in one of those niches, that's all.'

Theo took one long step and caught her hands in his. 'For how long? Your hands are cold.'

'I'm not certain, I must have nodded off.'

'Why couldn't you sleep?'

Why couldn't he? she wondered. There was no book beside the chair, no papers. He must have simply been sitting there. 'I was thinking about what I am going to do next.'

'You are going to Aunt Louisa in Avignon.' If he had added *good riddance*, his tone could not have been any colder, even while his hands warmed hers.

'No, I am not. I have been thinking. I want to travel. I have my own money, enough to be independent, very independent. I wonder at myself for never seeing it before. I shall find myself a congenial companion and see Italy, Greece, more of France. But while I am making up my mind who to travel with, I will be staying here. They need an archivist and I am suitably qualified.'

'Travel be damned.' Theo let go of her hands and took an angry pace away. 'Eva is matchmaking. She'll have you married off to that milksop librarian in a month, wait and see.'

'Phillip is not a milksop,' Elinor retorted. Even as she spoke she wondered if he was correct. Was Eva matchmaking? 'He is a pleasant and very intellectual young man. There is no need to sneer at him because he does not go racketing about the country, almost getting himself and everyone else killed in the process.'

'So you blame me for that after all, do you? I cannot recall inviting you to explore dungeons with me or rush up to my bedchamber brandishing a pistol you cannot use.'

'You were grateful at the time, damn you. And if I hadn't been with you in that dungeon, you might be dead now.' She was too angry with him for tears, although she could feel them hot and furious, stinging her eyes.

Theo looked to be in a towering, inexplicable, rage and suddenly she saw why. 'Theo—are you *jealous*?' He turned away, giving her his back, and reached for the decanter.

'Why the hell should I be jealous of that youth?'

'I do not know, that is what is puzzling me,' Elinor confessed, her own anger ebbing away as she stared at the uncommunicative set of his shoulders. 'If you are pouring wine, I will have a glass.'

He set it down with a snap and walked away from her. When he turned, she saw that strange darkness was in his eyes again and his voice was flat. 'I do not understand why, if you want to travel, you will not do it with me, but need to find a stranger. Why, if you need a man, you do not take me. Is he so much more intelligent, is that it? Am I not up to your lofty intellectual heights?'

He was making no sense at all. Elinor stared, then took a deep swallow of wine and sat down. 'I do not want Phillip Finchingfield. He is a nice young man, with the emphasis on *young*. Eva is not matchmaking, she is amusing herself.' She had to work this out as she went along, and her own emotions were so tangled they were not helping one whit.

'How can I travel with you without marrying you? And I have told you why I will not do that. I cannot marry a man who does not love me.'

Theo was staring at her from across the room. Then, very slowly, he sat down on the edge of the bed as though standing was no longer an option. 'You would marry me if I loved you?'

'Yes, of course.' Too late she saw where this had led her: virtually into a confession of her true feelings for him.

'But I told you I did. I told you I loved you that morning after we made love all night. But you hushed me, misunderstood me to mean that I loved you as a friend and made it very clear you did not love me.'

'You meant you *really* want to marry me?' This couldn't be true, surely? Something this wonderful simply could not be happening.

'I do. I want to marry you even if you don't love me. Elinor…' Somehow he was on his knees beside her chair, her hands in his. 'Nell, I love you and I want you and I will do everything in my power to make you happy. I know you like our lovemaking, that we have fun together. That's a start, isn't it—if I can convince you I love you, you will marry me?'

'I believe you.' And she did. That shadow had gone from his eyes—this was Theo looking deep into her soul, Theo, his pulse thudding hard against her fingers. 'And I love you.'

He sat back on his heels and closed his eyes. 'For two intelligent people, we very nearly got this completely wrong, didn't we?'

'It isn't a language I am used to,' she confessed, freeing one hand so she could reach forwards and touch his face. 'I have no understanding of the grammar, or the vocabulary. We must learn it together.' He turned his cheek into her palm and smiled, opening his eyes so his lashes tickled the sensitive skin.

'What, the language of emotions? I think something almost got lost in translation. Let me try in English. Nell, I love you. I don't know how long I loved you, because I've never been in love and I didn't realise why I felt like I did, but I realised when we were on that hilltop overlooking the chateau. When I said I would never marry, it was because I believed I could not have you, not because of any other woman. I want to marry you and live with you and have children with you.'

'And we will travel together?' It was very difficult to speak with her heart so full, but somehow she managed it, her hand stroking the strong lines of the face she had once thought was only passably handsome. 'I am not being left at home, children or no children.'

'Nell, I thought I couldn't have you, that I'd lost you—how could I contemplate ever leaving you behind? I will place the orders for our caravan of carriages at once—I was drawing it, too, so I have both sets.'

'So that is where my sketches went. Theo, I have been looking everywhere for those. I was the woman in all of the pictures, you see.'

'Oh, Nell.' He gathered her in against his heart and rocked her gently. His body felt hard and safe and yet so gentle. 'When can we get married?'

'I don't…' She managed to twist round so she could look up into his face. 'Will your family want a big wedding? Uncle Augustus will want to marry us, won't he? In the cathedral.' Her heart sank. It would all take months.

'That will take too much time, I want to get started on that family immediately.' Theo stood up, bringing her up with him. 'Sit on the bed, Nell, I can't think while I'm holding you.' He paced across the room, then flipped open a map and stared down at it. 'I've got to take that damn Chalice back to England. I'll leave tomorrow. You get Eva to send you down to Avignon with a maid and some outriders. Break the news to Aunt Louisa and interview the English vicar down there—there's sure to be an Anglican church. I'll come right back. In a month we'll be wed, no longer, I promise you.' He paused, frowning. 'You know, I can't help but wonder if she meant this to happen. She's been mighty careless about throwing us together.'

'Theo.'

'Yes, my love?' He looked up at her, his hands flat either side of the map.

'Am I dreaming?'

'Not unless I'm having the same dream, too. Nell, I've never had anyone to share emotions with. Ideas, yes, fun, yes. But not feelings, not the deep ones. And I don't think you have either. We nearly got this wrong because we tried to protect ourselves against being hurt, took what the other said literally, without listening to the truth underneath. I'm going to try very hard not to do that any more.'

'Mmm. I think we should say what we think and what we feel, honestly. Don't you?' He nodded. 'Good, I am glad you agree, because what I want most of all, now, is to go to bed with you and for you not to have to be careful, just to make me yours.'

Theo just looked at her, his eyes hooded, as though his own desires were banked down behind the heavy lids. 'Are you certain? You don't want to wait until our wedding night?'

'No, but if you do—'

Suddenly Theo grinned, the first broad smile she had seen for what seemed like days. 'Nell, we can sit here all night being carefully polite over this or I can do what I have been wanting to do ever since I knelt on that river bank, plaiting your hair.'

'Really? Oh, I knew I felt something, sensed something, even then.' He came and caught her in his arms and it felt right, here in their lonely eyrie, high on the battlements of the great castle.

'In my fantasies I didn't dream I'd be undoing this frightful garment,' Theo observed. 'There go the buttons, never mind, you won't be needing it again.' The old gown slid from his hands and he stopped talking, his mouth curving into an incredulous smile. 'Nell Ravenhurst, you bad girl—not a stitch on under your gown!'

It was impossible to feel shy in the face of his obvious delight. 'I was in a hurry, I wanted to be near you,' she murmured, reaching for his shirt. 'And now I want to be nearer still.'

She had thought she knew what to expect and the thrill of his caresses and the fire in his kisses was the same, yet deeper, more intense. But her heart was pounding and something inside her made her breath come fast as she clung to his shoulders while his mouth roamed over her hot skin.

'Are you frightened?' He looked up and she wondered what he had seen in her expression.

'Yes. A little,' she admitted. 'I know it will hurt, it isn't that, it is just…'

'Just such a big step? I know, my love, I'll be as slow as I can.'

'No,' Elinor protested, 'not slow. Theo, love me now.'

His weight as he came over her was wonderful, powerful, yet he took such care to lift it from her. She ran her hands over his biceps, feeling the muscles taut as they took his weight on his elbows. Her legs parted to cradle him and she sighed at how perfectly they seemed to fit together, how open her body was to him as he moved against her, slowly nudging while her untutored body began to open for him, his eyes holding hers, a smile in them that promised so much, promised his love.

It did not seem possible that he really could fit, she thought hazily, trying to think of nothing but those eyes, that love, while her body struggled against itself to tense up and deny him. 'Theo, I don't think—'

'Exactly,' he murmured. 'For once in your life, don't think, Nell, just trust me, let me in.' He shifted his position slightly, his hand slipping between them to touch the aching core of her and she sobbed, arched to meet the sweetly familiar torment and he surged strongly into her, carrying away the sudden stab of pain with the intensity of it.

'I love you,' she managed to gasp before all she could do was to surrender to the rhythm he was setting, carrying her with him, making her cry out, over and over as he moved within her, filling her perfectly, perfectly at one with her.

'Now, Nell,' he gasped and she opened her eyes on to his intent face, on to the eyes that held her soul. 'Come with me, Nell.' And she was. The twisting, surging pleasure he had taught her was there, all wrapped up in something bigger, more intense, something that was the essence of the two of them, together.

'Theo!' She thought she screamed his name, heard his shout, and then there were colours and pleasure she could never have imagined and finally soft, sweet blackness and the feel of his arms holding her safe, bringing her back into harbour after the storm.

'I love you so much,' Theo murmured into her hair.

Unable to speak, she burrowed up against his chest until she could take his face in her hands and see the brightness of tears in his eyes and press her lips against the strong line of his jaw. 'Always,' she managed. 'Always.'

'*Madame.*' Eva's dresser came back from answering the tap on the door. '*Madame,* that was Annette. She says Mademoiselle Ravenhurst's bed has not been slept in.'

The Grand Duchess fastened one perfect diamond eardrop and turned her head to check her reflection in the mirror before answering. 'Well, thank heavens for that,' she said with a touch of complacency. 'Please ensure that Monsieur Ravenhurst is not disturbed before dinner time.'

Afterword

Neglected throughout the eighteenth-century, the basilica at Vezelay slipped into near dereliction during the Revolution. By the time Theo and Elinor visited it was very dilapidated, and in 1819 the principle bell tower was consumed by fire. In 1834 Prosper Mérimée, French Inspector of Historic Monuments, saw it and was appalled. But he could find no one willing to take on such a colossal work. Finally, an unknown architect, 26-year-old Eugène Viollet-le-Duc, accepted the commission and in less than twenty years rescued this wonderful building. In 1979 the church where St Bernard preached the First Crusade was declared a UNESCO World Heritage site.

The verse from Petrach is from Sonnet 28, *To Laura in Life,* translated in 1795 by an unknown poet.

Dear Reader,

In the course of their courtship Ashe Reynard informed Belinda Felsham (The Outrageous Lady Felsham) that she should stop matchmaking for her bluestocking cousin Elinor because what Elinor needed was an intellectual, someone who could match her intelligence.

The problem was, where could Elinor, firmly on the shelf, find such a man? One who would see past the drab gowns and meek studiousness to the warm, loving, adventurous woman inside? Especially when she was convinced she did not want a man at all.

And then there was Theo Ravenhurst, in disgrace and, so his mother kept insisting, off on the Grand Tour. Only I had my suspicions that Theo was not pursuing a blameless course around the cultural sights of Europe but was up to something altogether less conventional. What would happen if these two cousins met, I wondered?

I hope you enjoy finding out and, if you have read the first three Ravenhurst novels, meeting again Eva and Sebastian, young Freddie and the indomitable Lady James.

Coming next will be The Notorious Mr Hurst. Lady Maude Templeton, having escaped marriage to Ravenhurst cousin Gareth Morant (The Shocking Lord Standon) has already fallen for the entirely inappropriate attractions of theatre owner Eden Hurst. She knows what she wants, and is not used to being thwarted, but this time it looks as though everyone, from Society to the gentleman himself, is set on her not getting her heart's desire.

D(R)